MW00333750

The Reclamation

The Reclamation

Marianne Modica

RESOURCE *Publications* · Eugene, Oregon

THE RECLAMATION

Copyright © 2023 Marianne Modica. All rights reserved. Except for brief quotations in critical publications or reviews, no part of this book may be reproduced in any manner without prior written permission from the publisher. Write: Permissions, Wipf and Stock Publishers, 199 W. 8th Ave., Suite 3, Eugene, OR 97401.

Resource Publications
An Imprint of Wipf and Stock Publishers
199 W. 8th Ave., Suite 3
Eugene, OR 97401

www.wipfandstock.com

PAPERBACK ISBN: 978-1-6667-7137-4
HARDCOVER ISBN: 978-1-6667-7138-1
EBOOK ISBN: 978-1-6667-7139-8

05/12/23

Scriptures taken from the Holy Bible, New International Version®, NIV®. Copyright © 1973, 1978, 1984, 2011 by Biblica, Inc.™ Used by permission of Zondervan. All rights reserved worldwide. www.zondervan.com The "NIV" and "New International Version" are trademarks registered in the United States Patent and Trademark Office by Biblica, Inc.™

To KT, who came with me on the journey.

You are a God who performs miracles;
You display your power among the peoples.

Psalm 77:14

Contents

PART I
The College

1

I t had been a typically quiet, dull day until the ChurchState zombies showed up in their fancy hydrocar and proceeded to chase Wylie through the old, deserted campus. Not that they were real zombies (Wylie knew) and not that zombies were real (she also knew), but the mindless way these cadets carried out the ChurchState's bidding reminded Wylie of the undead hoards she'd watched in a bootleg holo that had kept her and Darwin riveted for hours. The only difference was that these zombies wore smug smiles and had access to the ChurchState's finest rides.

Wylie had woken up that morning thinking about her own ride—the broken down mower waiting for her in the shed. She'd obeyed its call and now here she was, bumping along the commons of what was once Cranbury Christian College. Although there were quicker, more efficient ways to mow a lawn, Wylie preferred feeling the earth beneath her to hovering over it, and besides, hover mowers were expensive, and this old tractor was all they had. She scrunched her shoulders and pulled her black knit cap lower until it met the collar of her new wool jacket—yesterday's find from the dumpster behind the com-lux apartments was new to her, anyway. The weather had turned on a dime overnight and now it felt more like winter than fall. She trembled with cold and impatience as she passed the forlorn, shedding maple, the few brown spotted leaves it'd produced that year fluttering to the ground. She just wanted to get done and get some breakfast. This was her mother's job, not hers, but since Delores had stopped leaving their apartment, Wylie did what she had to do to survive. The groundskeeper position gave them a place to live and put food on the table and they couldn't afford to lose it.

As she bumped along the uneven ground, the mower's rattling engine almost drowned out the soft purr of a boxy, tan hydrocar that stopped dead on the road along the commons. Five kids jumped out, all with the same sickening smirk on their faces. Here we go again, Wylie thought.

Why did they keep harassing her? They lined up at the edge of the grass like clones in pressed khaki pants and sleek red polos, shouting jeers that Wylie couldn't hear above the din of the mower. One of them picked up a jagged rock and threw it hard, but it missed her by a foot. Wylie chose to ignore them and mowed on. Although she wasn't close enough to read the gold embroidery on their shirts, she knew what it said. Penn ChurchState University—where else would they be from? Only ChurchState kids would be arrogant enough to think they could intimidate her on foot while she was behind the wheel of a bladed vehicle, decrepit as it was. She continued her straight row, figuring they'd get tired soon enough and find someone else to harass. After a minute of standing around, gaping at her as if they'd never seen an Uncommitted before, they got back into the car, and Wylie thought that was the end of it, just another morning in paradise. But instead of driving away, the car bumped over the curb and made tracks across the lawn toward her. Suddenly Wylie was a sitting duck in a green grassy pond. The two cadets in the front were cackling like demented chickens, heads bobbing and big teeth protruding from wide open mouths. They headed straight for her, and just when Wylie thought they were going to hit her right there in broad daylight, they swerved, ripped past, and circled around to face her again from the other direction.

Wylie did what Delores had always told her to do when faced with a difficult situation. She ran. Or rather, she rode. She gripped the steering wheel, gunned the gas, and took off through the trees and around the buildings, narrowly missing rows of hedges here and rusty old metal trash bins there. She kept to the small spaces that the hydrocar couldn't navigate as quickly until she reached the back entrance of the nearly deserted dorm that housed the apartment she shared with her mom. Not wanting to give herself away, she passed the building and drove into an empty shed, where she cut the tractor's engine and jumped off. She'd never seen this particular group before and she was hoping they didn't know exactly which of the run-down, abandoned buildings she and Delores called home. As fast as she could, Wylie sprinted back to the dorm, managing to scan Del's ID and fall through the entrance just before the ChurchState kids drove by slowly, clearly on the hunt. Wylie pressed herself against the door and waited, hoping they hadn't seen her. Not that they could get in through the barred windows, but she wasn't in the mood to sweep up glass if they decided to test their aim with one of the lose bricks at the base of the building.

Wylie inched toward the window in the hallway and peeked out. It appeared they were gone, for now. She let out the breath she'd been holding and slipped through the dark hall to their apartment, debating whether or not to finish the mowing later. When she opened the door, she was greeted by eighty pounds of pit bull-boxer mix named Monty.

"Back so soon?" Delores called from the bedroom over the sound of the old-style TV that had come with the apartment.

"I was rudely interrupted by a carload of ChurchState morons."

"The missionaries, again?" Delores said. "You should have taken that dog with you."

Wylie took off her hat and smoothed down her thick brown hair. She left her jacket on. "That would have made things worse," she answered, kneeling down to let Monty lick her face. "Easier to get away on my own." She refilled Monty's water bowl and watched her big, floppy beast lap it up. Then she shook the last dregs of toasted oats into her bowl and tossed the box into the trash. Out of cereal again. She could swear she'd just bought that box a few days ago. Delores must have gotten to it during the night. Plenty of milk left, though, since Del never touched the stuff. Wylie took a whiff and dumped it down the sink.

"They were just punks," she said, sitting at the edge of Del's disheveled bed.

"Punks with power," Delores responded. Dressed in the sweats and T-shirt she'd worn for a week, she reclined in the middle of her queen-sized bed, propped up with pillows and covered with a thick red quilt. Her short brown hair stood up on her head like a brush. Mother and daughter were both pale, but Del's complexion was even more sallow than usual today and the dark circles under her eyes reached to the middle of her face. On the end table next to the bed were last night's dishes.

Delores pointed at the screen. "See what I mean?" Her voice was shrill with anger.

The news was covering a live gathering of ChurchState students and faculty. Oozing with excitement and pride, a female broadcaster announced, "Today, under the supervision of the Appointees, students at Penn ChurchState University join with Committed across the country to celebrate the Reclamation with a call for evangelism. Let's listen in." A tall male student stepped out from behind a large banner that read, "Reclamation Celebration" and approached a sea of cheering red polo shirts that parted before him. Not one of them wore a jacket or sweater. Too arrogant to feel the cold, Wylie guessed, or too arrogant to admit it. She shivered and crawled under her mom's quilt.

On the screen, the cheers of the crowd settled into a chant as the cadet took the platform, joined by a man and woman dressed in gold Appointee robes.

"Reclamation power!

All the world is ours!

All the world to reach,

Go forth and preach!"

The chant went on for several minutes until the young man motioned for quiet.

"My fellow Committed here and across the country," he began, "today we celebrate the fortieth anniversary of the Great Reclamation, which began on the wonderful day that the Lost Document was found. Written by our greatest Founding Father, Thomas Jefferson, it recanted the calamitous separation of church and state, a doctrine that, as we well know, never appeared in the Constitution. The enemy tried to repress Jefferson's writing, but you can't hide from the Lord! Then, just forty years ago today, our great nation reclaimed its roots and restored Christianity as our national religion. We thank God for the Great Reclamation! Reclamation power!"

Again, the chant of "Reclamation power!" rose from the crowd of fist-pumping students while the Appointees smiled serenely. Delores aimed the remote at the TV and the screen went dark.

"I can't listen to this," she said. "Those gullible kids are bad enough, but it's the Appointees I can't stomach. That's what I think of their precious Reclamation." She waved at the poster that hung above her bed like a tapestry. The words "Reclamation = Ruination" were superimposed over images of angry protestors waving signs. At the bottom of the poster was written, "End the Domination. Restore the separation of church and state now."

"You should take that down," Wylie said, "before someone sees it and we lose this job."

"No one comes in here except me, you, and the dog. I know the dog can keep a secret, and I won't tell if you won't."

Wylie sighed and asked the same question she'd been asking since she could remember. "What was it like, do you think, before the Reclamation? When you could follow whatever religion you wanted, or not follow any at all?"

"Technically, you still can. You know that," Delores answered. "That's the genius behind the Domination. On paper, freedom of religion exists. You just can't get a decent job, education, housing, medical care, or anything else you need unless you declare yourself Committed and sign their blasted Statement. Which I refuse to do."

Delores hadn't answered her question, but Wylie hadn't expected her to. After all, her mom had only been three when all this started and had no memory of anything before the Reclamation had turned the world upside down. And Wylie knew full well how Del felt about the Statement of Commitment. Her mother would not have any religion forced down her throat, especially one that defined her very existence as an abomination.

Wylie sighed. It was Del's refusal to sign that had kept them in near poverty all these years and had kept Wylie out of the best school system in the world. It was a small miracle they'd landed this job with its cold, broken-down apartment and meager salary. And soon even that would be gone, once the sale went through and the new owners imploded the old campus buildings to replace them with yet another ChurchState corporate center. Wylie didn't know what they'd do then, but soon she'd be eighteen, old enough to sign the Statement herself and apply to college if she wanted. She couldn't see herself in a bright red polo, chanting with the crowd, but maybe it was better than life as an Uncommitted.

"But why does it have to be this way?" Wylie said, more to herself than to her mom.

"Why, why, why. Always asking why. That's why I named you Wylie. Who knows why? There is no why. There's only what."

Monty jumped up from his spot at the foot of the bed and ran to the door just as Wylie heard a knock.

"You expecting someone?" Delores asked.

"It's probably just Dar." Wylie looked through the peephole and, sure enough, there was Darwin's brown face staring back at her. She could actually see his dark eyes under his curly bangs today. He must have given himself a haircut, Wylie thought. Maybe he'd cut hers when they got back. For now, she twisted her unkempt mop into a knot and shoved it under her cap.

"Going to the library," she called. She and Darwin both had papers to write for their virtual history course, and since Wylie didn't have access to the state-a-base, the musty, abandoned campus library was the best alternative. There, they could take the books they wanted and return them when they wanted, or not return them at all.

"You and your boyfriend be careful," Delores said.

"He's not my boyfriend," Wylie responded automatically.

"Well, whatever he is, be careful. Don't uncover any dead bodies."

Just like Delores to put an ominous spin on everything. In Del's world, evil lurked behind every door, and hiding out in their cramped apartment was the only way to avoid it. But Wylie had always thought differently. Even after all they'd been through, Wylie hoped, maybe believed, there was something better waiting for her, if only she could get to it. She grabbed Del's ID and stepped out into the daylight, letting the door slam behind her.

* * *

"I had another visit from the missionaries," Wylie said as they walked through the steel door that protected the library from unwanted visitors. She entered the deserted lobby and looked around. Everything was how she'd left it. Although in the eyes of the property owners she was the unwanted visitor, this place felt more hers than theirs, at least for now.

She stopped and gazed at the framed document hanging over the old circulation desk. She could have recited it by heart, but that didn't stop her from reading the Statement of Commitment for the umpteenth time. Something about the document, crafted decades ago, sucked Wylie in like a mini black hole.

Statement of Commitment to the United ChurchState of America

In these, the last days, God has revealed himself through the Chosen and Anointed United ChurchState of America, whose Appointees do fully and unreservedly declare AmeriChristianity as the one true religion; all other supposed faiths, religions, denominations, and sects are false, including and especially those who claim to follow the tenets of the Holy ChurchState Bible. All who refuse to commit to the Primary Doctrines and Practices of the United ChurchState of America will be declared heretics and Uncommitted; all such individuals have placed themselves outside of the ChurchState's ark of protection.

I, the undersigned, commit myself fully to the Primary Doctrines and Practices of AmeriChristianity as prescribed by the Founders after the Great Reclamation. In so doing I will receive the full economic, personal, and social benefits of the United Church-State of America.

Wylie tried to picture the group of people who would write such a thing. She knew their names of course—every kid memorized them in school—but what were they like, behind closed doors? Did they smile, and laugh, and cry, and fail? Did they love, and were they loved? Were they ever disappointed, or worried, or afraid? Or were they, like Del believed, a bunch of human robots whose only focus was power and control?

"I hate those guys," Darwin said, dragging Wylie back to reality.

"Hmm? What guys?"

"The missionaries. Isn't that who we were just talking about? Did they try to stare you down, as usual?"

"Oh. Sorry." Wylie shook off the hypnotizing effect the Statement always seemed to have on her. "They're getting bolder. They actually chased me in their fancy hydrocar."

"What! Did they hurt you?"

"Nah, I was on the mower. I think they were just trying to scare me. Idiots." Her pronouncement signaled the end of the conversation. They made their way through the abandoned aisles to the history section, Monty stopping to sniff under the metal shelving.

"What do you think they'll do with all these books, once the buildings are gone?" Wylie asked.

"Probably stage another big book burning," said Darwin.

"Or more likely they'll implode with the buildings." Wylie browsed along the shelves as she spoke. "At least you can get on the state-a-base if you want. All you have to do is log in with your grandfather's account."

"Yeah, I could, if I were interested in their censored, purified version of history."

Wylie reached for a book and read the title: *Jefferson's Recant: The Beginnings of the Great Reclamation, 2020–2030*. She dusted off the cover and flipped through the pages. "This will work."

Darwin gave her a sideways look. "Why would you want to write about the Reclamation? Don't you get enough of that from the mindless tools on the broadcasts?"

"Just gathering all the facts before I decide."

"Decide what?"

Wylie sighed. She'd been trying to avoid having this conversation, but Darwin deserved to know what she was thinking.

"You know what. I need to decide whether or not to sign the Statement of Commitment next summer. I probably won't, but I haven't decided for sure yet." Darwin didn't respond, but Wylie sensed disapproval coming in her direction. Well, too bad, she thought. It was her decision to make and no one else's. Still, she was not in the mood for a fight.

"I'm not saying I'll sign, just that I'm still thinking about it. It's a big decision, that's all." Darwin gave the slightest nod.

They flipped through books in silence. The stale air in the abandoned building was oppressive, and Wylie tried to lighten the grim mood she felt descending. "What if I did sign the stupid Statement? It would just be to get the benefits. Would you still be friends with me?" she asked, knowing full well how ridiculous that sounded. Darwin wasn't just her best friend; he was her only friend, and she, his. They'd been constant companions since they were six, when Darwin's mother had died and his father had revoked his signing and declared himself Uncommitted. They'd found each other while rummaging through the trash bins of the ChurchState supermarket, where perfectly good food was thrown out every day. Like two abandoned lion cubs, they'd quickly learned the benefits of group foraging, but what began as a means of survival had quickly developed into a friendship that sustained Wylie more deeply than the food they shared. Lately, though, Wylie had been sensing that Darwin wanted more. His lingering looks hid a quiet yearning that might trigger another conversation Wylie was trying her best to avoid.

"Sure, friend Darwin, that's me," he said with only the slightest hint of sarcasm. "Anyway, if you sign, you'll have plenty of friends. You'll have a whole new life and you won't need me."

"Don't be stupid," Wylie answered. "If I wanted stupid, I'd definitely sign. Then I'd be surrounded by stupid, twenty-four seven."

Darwin grunted and roamed to the end of the aisle. "Here we go—histories of the sixties. Nineteen sixties, that is. Now that was a time."

"I guess," Wylie said absently, studying one of the photos in the book she'd chosen. "Did you know that before the Reclamation, the symbol for the Committed was the cross?"

"Still is," Darwin said. "And they weren't called the Committed back then."

"I mean a plain cross, without the flag draped over it. Just a plain, wooden cross, at least for the Protties back then, before AmeriChristianity became the state religion. The DoxiRoms used a crucifix, with a body attached. The flag didn't become part of the symbolism until around 2040 or so."

"And your point is . . . ?"

"It's just that they make it sound like things have been this way forever. But really, they haven't." Wylie flipped through pages of photographs showing the progression of crosses from plain wood to the symbol she knew well—the ornate golden cross draped in an American flag that was plastered on every approved ChurchState run institution. The DoxiRoms still used the crucifix, but when their US branch filed affiliation papers with the ChurchState, they covered their dying figure with the flag. Wylie breathed in the stagnant air and coughed as she exhaled.

Interesting stuff for my paper, she thought, but she still needed more sources. She kept browsing until something small and fast scampered by and Monty bounded after it. He wedged his body between a metal bookshelf and the wall, digging at the floor furiously. Before Wylie could get to him, the bookcase toppled over and five full shelves of books thundered down, creating a mini-dust storm as they hit the musty carpet.

"Monty!" Wylie yelled, waving away the dust. "Bad dog!" She picked up one of the fallen books and glanced at the title before tossing it aside— *Miracles of the Bible.* As Wylie reached down to lift the shelf, Darwin rushed over to help, nearly tripping over the pile of books on his way. Together they stood the bookshelf upright, but Monty continued to claw away at the spot where the shelf had been as if a lifetime supply of doggie bones were buried under the carpet.

"Out of the way!" Wylie commanded, trying to brush Monty aside with her leg. But the dog's attention was riveted and he would not budge. The carpet was nearly in shreds.

"Set it back down," Darwin said. Carefully, they laid the shelf back over the pile of fallen books, and Wylie grabbed her dog by the collar. Not happy about the interruption, Monty barked and pulled toward the spot where the mouse had disappeared.

"All this fuss over a mouse," said Wylie. She inspected the floor more closely. Through the tattered carpet she spied something unusual. She let go of Monty and ripped up what was left of the carpet, revealing a panel with hinges on one side and a small, metal handle on the other.

"Check this out. Looks like some kind of trap door."

"Wow," Darwin said. "What do you think is under that?"

Wylie lifted the panel, grunting at its weight, and let it fall open with a bang.

"I'd heard there were tunnels under these buildings, but I wasn't sure I believed it," she said, peering down a steep wooden staircase. "It's probably gross down there." As she hesitated, Monty flew past her and took the stairs in two leaps. There was nothing to do but follow him down into a large open area filled with old furniture and equipment, all encrusted in a thick layer of dust and cobwebs. To Wylie's surprise, the fluorescent lights in the ceiling still worked.

"Looks like this was a basement they used for storage," she said.

"What's through there?" Darwin asked, pointing to an open doorway. They walked through the clutter, choosing their steps carefully, into a long narrow passageway. Wylie felt along the wall and found another light switch.

"This must be a hallway leading to another basement," she said. "Del told me there was once a maze of connected buildings on the campus, back when this was an army hospital. The college took most of the old buildings down, but I guess the basements are still here."

"Wow," Darwin said. "Forgotten treasures."

"Or trash, depending on your point of view." They wandered down the hallway to another large room filled with junk. "This is an asthma attack waiting to happen. Let's get out of here."

"Wait! Let's at least take a look around." Darwin pointed to stacks of cardboard boxes scattered about. "There might be some interesting archives here." He opened the nearest box with the excitement of a kid on Christmas morning, or at least how Wylie imagined Christmas morning once was, based on Sharmila's vague recollections of the time before the ChurchState purged the holiday of its pagan elements. She knew there was no use objecting when Darwin got like this. He could be as focused as Monty, but, unlike Monty, Wylie couldn't grab him by the collar and drag him away. With a look of resignation, she ambled over to the corner where a strange machine sat under a thick plastic cover.

"What's this?" she asked, letting the cover drop to the floor. She tried to figure out what a box with a lamp jutting over it might do. Maybe it was some kind of old-fashioned X-ray machine the army hospital had left behind.

"That was called an overhead projector," Darwin said, barely looking up. "Teachers used them before 3D desk portals were invented."

"Like when they had blackboards?"

"After blackboards, before holograms, they used different kinds of projection systems in classrooms. The overhead was one of them," Darwin explained.

"Of course you would know that." Out of curiosity, Wylie flipped the switch on the side, but nothing happened. She realized it wasn't plugged in and searched the wall for an outlet. A few feet away she found one, already in use by a cord that led to a boxy TV sitting on a cart. This is even older than our ancient TV, she thought—way older. She blew some dust off the top and wiped down the screen with her sleeve. Next to the TV sat a small remote covered with grime. She wiped it on her jeans, pressed the power button, and stared in fascination when the screen flickered on. A tall, thin man in a dark jacket and tie appeared, standing in a classroom behind a wooden podium.

"Okay," he began, clearing his throat, "this is the first time I've recorded a lecture, so hopefully I won't crack the camera lens." The class, not in view, tittered, and the man smiled. His mostly bald head and light eyebrows gave him an egg-like appearance.

"Where is this broadcast coming from?" Wylie asked.

Darwin joined her as the man behind the podium continued.

"What's that?" the man asked, looking up. "Okay." He straightened his tie. "I'm being reminded to introduce myself. I'm Dr. Michaels and this is Theo 433, *Signs and Wonders*. Special welcome to our distance education viewers." He smiled again, this time into the camera.

"What the heck?" Wylie said.

"Watch," Darwin answered. He got down on one knee and pushed a button on the console below the screen. The picture went fuzzy and a flat, plastic, rectangular box popped out. "See? It's a tape. That's how they used to play recordings." He looked over at a partially opened cardboard box next to the machine. "Looks like there's a whole box of them here."

"Wow," Wylie said. "Look at all these." She sorted through three rows of tapes two layers deep.

"This is an amazing archive," Darwin said. "It might give us some insight about the history of the college—why it closed and all."

"We know why it closed. Once the state schools went Committed, there was no more use for these little religious colleges, and they ran out of money. Delores is always pointing out the irony—they pushed for the Reclamation, and it wound up shutting them down. Be careful what you wish for, she says."

Darwin nodded. "Still, I bet there's a lot to learn about how people thought back then. These recordings have to be over fifty years old. It's a miracle they still work." He slid the tape back in the slot, scrutinized the console for a second, then pushed another button. Once again, the man appeared on the screen.

"Today we're going to examine the Bible passage found in Acts chapter five, the story of a husband and wife team, Ananias and Sapphira." Dr. Michaels glanced at his watch, which he had laid on the podium. "In the interest of time, and since this is a senior level class, I'll assume you've read the passage." The audience snickered and Dr. Michaels smiled broadly.

"What's so funny?" Wylie asked.

"No idea," said Darwin.

"Would someone like to summarize the basic events of the first ten verses? Yes, Steve, go ahead."

A deep disembodied voice began, "Basically, Ananias and Sapphira sold some land to give the money to the church, but they held back part of the cost for themselves. So, God struck them dead."

"Is that what the scripture says?"

Wylie heard pages flipping as Dr. Michaels waited patiently.

"They're still using books," she commented. "I guess there was no state-a-base yet."

"The old internet system was taking off," Darwin answered, "but they weren't bringing computers to class yet."

Another male voice spoke up. "Not really. It says they died; it doesn't say God struck them dead."

"Okay, so we're not really sure of the exact cause of death, but we do know that husband and wife died suddenly. Now, using our working definition of a 'sign' as an event requiring supernatural intervention, what is the sign in this passage? Is it the death of this couple?"

"It could be," the first voice insisted. "I think it's unlikely they both had sudden heart attacks. God struck them dead as punishment for lying, and as a sign to the church. Like a warning. Liars earn God's spurn."

Students shifted in their seats and Dr. Michaels leaned forward a bit.

"Don't answer this, but, has anyone here ever told a lie?"

The class laughed nervously.

"Just as I thought," said Dr. Michaels, smiling. "And yet here we are. So, simplistic answers won't suffice." Nice work putting this self-important creep in his place, Wylie thought.

"It's not just that they lied, but why they lied," said another male voice. "To make themselves seem important."

"Okay," said Dr. Michaels, "now we're getting somewhere. Let me ask again, what is the sign in this passage?"

He pointed toward the back of the class. "Yes, Abby?"

A female voice spoke for the first time. "Well, how did Peter know they were lying? Wouldn't that be classified as a sign?"

"People dropping dead is the most obvious sign," Steve called out, provoking laughter from his classmates.

"I've seen enough," Wylie said, shaking her head. She pushed the power button on the remote and turned away from the screen, all the while thinking of Delores. No wonder she was too sad to get out of bed. "All this talk about God striking people dead is depressing. That guy Steve could be the grandfather of the missionaries from this morning."

Darwin frowned as he popped the tape out and tossed it back into the box.

"What?" Wylie asked.

"Nothing. The professor seems cool, though," he said.

"Maybe." She'd suddenly had enough of the library. "I gotta go pick up Del's meds."

"Okay, but to be continued," said Darwin.

"Huh?"

"Come on, you can't tell me you're not curious about what's on the rest of these tapes."

"You're the one who made me feel like a traitor when I mentioned going Committed next summer. Now you want to listen to their bull. Monty, let's go." She navigated through more of Darwin's "treasures" on her way out and climbed the stairs to face the fallen shelf and scattered books. Together, Wylie and Darwin closed the trap door and repositioned the rug over it as best they could. But Darwin insisted they set the shelf up on the opposite wall, in case they wanted to get down to the basement again. Wylie couldn't imagine a world in which that would be true, but she let him have his way.

2

Keeping her mom's meds up to date was one of the many tasks Wylie had taken on when, years ago, their roles had begun a slow but unstoppable reversal. Although a trip to the meds dispensary was a pain, it was far less of a pain than dealing with Delores off her meds. Darwin offered to drive, but Wylie refused, preferring to shake off the lingering memory of the basement tape with a walk. She checked in with Del (who was still in bed), grabbed a couple of sugar wafers, and took off walking with Monty, hoping that this time there'd be no problems. Access to medical care for Uncommitted was sketchy at best. Wylie never understood why the poorer they got, the harder it was to get medication for Del's many real and imagined conditions. Most people had their medical needs covered by the ChurchState, but, of course, they didn't qualify. The Uncommitted were left to the (unmerciful) mercies of the clinics, where they received the full social outcast treatment. To make things worse, their fino-stats were downgraded again last month, which positioned them even lower on the list of uninsured. Maybe (as Delores liked to remind her) they hadn't yet hit the bottom of the Uncommitted barrel, but they were falling fast. So here she was, forced to enter the fray of the noncom pharm (again), not for her own sake, but for Del's, whose stubbornness had gotten them into this mess.

As she walked, Wylie's thoughts drifted back to that morning in the library. What a weird recording. Something about the students chilled her, especially that one guy, Steve. He was so confident, discussing God, life, death, miracles—topics she knew nothing about, but that had somehow determined her destiny—with a certainty that bordered on arrogance. Darwin was right, though, the professor seemed kind of nice. Not for the first time she wished she'd gone to a real school with real teachers instead of submitting one boring assignment after another to the automated self-schooling program she accessed through the outdated portals at the noncom marts.

Feeling suddenly warm, Wylie pulled off her hat and shoved it into her pocket. She dragged Monty past a row of quaint shops and picturesque boutiques. Wylie had never set foot in any of them, even though they were less than a mile from campus. She imagined the proprietors would not appreciate a deposit from Monty under their artsy window displays, so she hurried him along. A block later she passed the entrance to the new housing development where construction was almost complete. Workers struggled to hang an ornate signboard that declared in bright, bold lettering, *Welcome to Faith Acres, Luxury Townhomes for the Committed*. As they passed, a woman in a red business suit looked up from her data stream to eye them suspiciously, but Wylie knew better than to make eye contact. Best not to appear to challenge the authority of a ChurchState employee who might question Wylie's presence in Committed territory. The less attention she garnered from the powers that be, the better. She shortened Monty's leash, kept her head down, and picked up her pace until she got to the intersection that signaled the beginning of the noncom section. Suddenly, the pristine, grass-lined walkway was replaced by a broken, crumbling sidewalk that eventually disappeared altogether. They walked along the side of the road, past a string of decaying brick row houses and rotting wood storefronts. The more the neighborhood declined, the more comfortable Wylie felt, knowing that the Comcops rarely crossed the border. Sure, she'd have to watch her back for occasional muggers, but Monty served as an effective deterrent to those with nefarious intent. Although the dog was a card-carrying wimp, his wide jaw and broad body gave the impression of power. With Monty at her side, most people approached with care. Wylie liked it that way.

Unfortunately, one group that did not avoid noncom territory was the missionaries. They seemed to be omnipresent, always ready to add new members to their ranks. Wylie had heard they received a commission for every Uncommitted they signed. As she joined the two-block queue outside the meds dispensary, a canary yellow hydrocar pulled up alongside them. Here they were again, twice in one day. Wylie suspected the missionaries were targeting her, specifically. She had no way to prove it, but she'd noticed an uptake in her run-ins with them as she approached signing age. She wanted to tell them that the more they harassed her, the less likely she was to sign, but she'd learned the hard way that any engagement only encouraged them. Instead, she added some slack to Monty's leash and let him approach the car. Monty took one sniff and lifted his leg.

"My sentiments exactly," Wylie said under her breath. A little girl standing in front of her giggled, but so far the missionaries weren't paying attention. Through their tinted windows, Wylie counted four figures.

"What do you think they're doing in there?" the little girl asked. She looked up at Wylie with round, dark eyes filled with apprehension. Wylie had never seen her before, but she'd been on the inside of that look more times than she could remember.

"No idea," Wylie answered. "But don't worry. They can say whatever they want, but they're not allowed to touch you." At least Wylie hoped that was still true. Her altercation that morning made her wonder, but no use scaring this kid any more than she was already scared. She smiled confidently, and the girl, relieved, smiled back.

They'd been on this line for ten minutes and had barely moved. What was the holdup?

"I like your dog," the girl said. "Can I pet him?"

"Better not. He's friendly, but we don't want them to know that." Wylie motioned toward the car and right on cue, the doors flew open. Four ChurchState cadets jumped out, dressed in their familiar red polos and grinning like fools. The little girl moved behind Wylie, blocking the missionaries' view of her. The driver walked toward Monty slowly, holding out her hand for him to sniff.

"Careful," Wylie warned. "He's not good with strangers."

The driver got down on one knee and scratched Monty behind the ear. Monty licked her face and leaned in for more.

"He seems friendly enough to me," the missionary said.

"And totally useless," said Wylie, pulling Monty back. "You want something?"

"We just want to chat."

A rusted brown pick-up sped by, dragging its muffler across the cracked asphalt. The taste of exhaust in the air made Wylie's stomach churn.

"No thanks," she said, knowing a polite rebuff would not do the trick and bracing herself for an argument. Once the missionaries got started, only a soundproof door slammed in the face would stop them. The other people waiting in line had turned away, and Wylie couldn't blame them. Only the little girl with the frightened, dark eyes peeked out to face the missionaries with Wylie. And Monty, of course, who was sitting up as if waiting to be served his afternoon tea.

From out of nowhere another hydrocar came to a screeching halt before them. Three more missionaries jumped out, dressed in green polos instead of red. Great, Wylie thought, reinforcements. But these three wore scowls instead of the typical missionary smirk. The two groups faced off with nothing but animosity between them.

"This is our territory!" a tall, skinny, green-shirted guy shouted. "No Trebs allowed!"

Although she was a good six inches shorter, the red-shirted driver stood her ground. "Says who?" She looked up into her opponent's face with quiet fury. "Our group leader said this is contested terrain now. Your Bass claim doesn't hold up any more, and we were here first. So get lost!"

"Your information is as faulty as your praise music, if you can call it that. This has been Bass territory for a decade!" green shirt protested. "Find your recruits somewhere else!"

They went back and forth, getting louder and louder as the crowd of Uncommitted pretended not to listen. Slowly, the line moved forward. When the missionaries got tired of arguing, they jumped into their cars and sped away, each group vowing to take the territorial dispute up with their leaders and threatening censure to the other group.

"What was that about?" the little girl asked Wylie.

"No idea. I'm not really up on the finer points of missionary life."

A slightly built man with a crown of thin, gray hair laughed. He'd kept his distance from the missionaries, but now that they were gone he moved closer. His eyes were deeply set in his lined face but they twinkled as he spoke in a soft, refined voice.

"They were arguing about their music," he explained, still chuckling. "My dad used to teach at the college, back before it closed. Seems like a hundred years ago now." The man's smile turned wistful. "Even back then, there were rumblings over musical style. The red shirts were Trebs. They believe that the treble pitch should dominate their church music. The greens were Basses, who require a heavy bass beat in their worship music."

Wylie didn't know anything about music, and before now she'd thought all missionaries were the same. "I don't get it," she said. "That sounds pretty stupid, even for missionaries. What does it matter if they use treble or, whatever it is, bass?"

"It doesn't matter, or it shouldn't. But the Appointees will do anything to scrape up a bit of power. Someone, somewhere, sometime decided that treble pitch in church music signified grace while bass symbolized good works, and the idea caught on. And so they took up an age-old theological debate under the guise of musical style and before you knew it, you had the Trebs versus the Basses. I doubt any of those kids remember what the fight was about or even the meaning of the word 'grace.'"

Wylie knew less about theology than she did about music, but she nodded.

The old man sighed. "That's the reason my dad never signed the Statement," he said. "Just couldn't get over the way they ruined something meant to be beautiful. And here I am." He coughed and Wylie remembered why she was in standing in a line of downtrodden, demoralized strangers.

"Well, at least their stupid argument made them forget about me," she said. "For now."

Just then another car pulled up, as different from the shiny Church-State hydrocars as night from day. A bedraggled Uncommitted jumped out of an old one-seat transport with a jagged hole in the roof and empty spaces where the windows had been. He looked around warily, and when he appeared sure of no ChurchState presence, he dug into his tattered coat pocket and pulled out a fistful of jewelry. Great, a noncom peddler, Wylie thought. They were almost as bad as the missionaries with their hardcore tactics. It wasn't unusual for them to hit up a meds line, looking for trades. For most Uncommitted, legal prescriptions were hard to come by, so meds were always a hot commodity on the underground market.

"Gold for meds," he called. Most of the people on line looked away, but the little girl stepped closer, mesmerized by the sparkly items the man waved in front of her.

"Here's one I think you'll like," he said, holding a gold cross on a chain at the girl's eye level. Her eyes grew wide with desire and she reached for the cross.

"No touching before the trade," the man said. "Let's see your prescription."

The girl looked up at Wylie who shook her head in a silent "no."

"Mind your business," the peddler barked. "She's old enough to make up her own mind, aren't you, kid?" His lips contorted into what was meant as a smile but more closely resembled a sneer. The little girl stepped back behind Wylie.

"She's not interested," Wylie said. "And is that a cross you're peddling?" Being caught with stolen jewelry was bad enough, but wearing a cross was one of the privileges reserved for the Committed. It was the ChurchState's way of physically marking its members, although there was talk in the broadcasts of tattooing Uncommitted as a clearer designation between the two groups. Although (for now) no such law had been passed, Uncommitted wearing or owning a cross was a violation of the blasphemy laws and the ChurchState took so-called blasphemy very, very seriously.

"You trying to get us all arrested?" Wylie asked. "What if the Comcops drive by?"

At the mention of Comcops the peddler looked around nervously and shoved the contraband back into his pockets.

"I'll see you again," he said to Wylie, punctuating his threat with a wad of chew at her feet before hurrying back into his battered transport and sputtering away.

The old man smiled approvingly at Wylie but she looked away so as not to invite any further conversation. She just wanted to get Del's meds and be done with it. They inched forward so slowly that Wylie began to worry it would soon be closing time, but finally the line began to move, and they entered the dispensary. The little girl had waited silently, but the closer they got to the med-rep's window, the more fidgety she became, pulling at her tight dark curls. When her turn came she reached up to the counter on her tiptoes and shoved the prescription through the small opening in the thick plastic barrier. The ChurchPharm med-rep, a tall, thin, expressionless woman, took a quick look, scooped some pills into a vial, and practically tossed it back through the opening.

"Next," she called, looking over the girl's head to Wylie.

"Um, wait," the girl whispered.

"Next," the woman said again. "I don't have all day."

The little girl held the vial up to what light there was in the dingy room.

"Excuse me," she said, "I don't think this is right. My grandpa said there should be thirty pills."

The med-rep continued to ignore her. "If you don't have a prescription, move out of the way," she snapped at Wylie.

Ignoring the absurdity of that comment (why would she have waited in that interminable line without a prescription?), Wylie wondered if this day could get worse. First the missionaries, then the peddler, now this—it wouldn't be the first time a med-rep had skimmed some pills off the top to sell on the side. Just like them to prey on a kid, she thought. But she'd stuck her neck out enough for one day; the last thing she needed was to get involved in someone else's problems. What with Delores in bed and the missionaries on her tail, she had enough problems of her own.

The little girl and Monty both looked up at Wylie as if she were some kind of miracle worker. She sighed and took the vial of pills.

"Can I see this kid's prescription?"

"What? No, you can't. That's confidential information."

"Fine." Wylie looked to the child.

"Can I see my prescription?" the girl asked promptly. Smart kid.

"No, you cannot. Your turn is over. Now move along before I call security."

"Go ahead, call security," said Wylie. "They might be interested to know why you won't let her see her own prescription." Wylie knew she was taking a chance. If security was in on the scam, the med-rep would call her bluff.

The woman responded with an icy stare. Wylie stared right back, hoping the med-rep's greed did not allow for co-conspirators. "Oh, I see a mistake has been made," she said, glancing at the prescription. "I thought that three was a two."

"Better use that fancy Committed healthcare to get her eyes checked," someone whispered from the line. Others snickered and murmured agreement, but when the woman looked up they were silent. The med-rep added the missing pills to the vial and handed it to the girl, who took off without even a thank you. Wylie didn't blame her.

"Just so you know, mine says thirty pills, too," Wylie said.

"I'd watch my tone if I were you," answered the woman.

That was the second time Wylie had been threatened that day, but this time she knew enough to take it seriously. She bit her tongue and adopted the noncom submissive posture, but when she pushed the prescription through the slot, her hand brushed the med-rep's and a quick static shock passed between them. Suddenly, Wylie felt exhausted. As if the shock had drained her of energy, her shoulders sagged and her head felt like it weighed a hundred pounds. She shoved Del's pills in her pocket and stumbled to the door, wondering what was wrong with her and how she would make it home.

"You're welcome," the med-rep called. "Typical Uncommitted rudeness . . . oh!"

Wylie heard a thud.

"She fainted!" someone cried out as the crowd dashed toward the counter. Holding on to the doorknob for support, Wylie turned to see people trying to get to the fallen med-rep but unable to reach past the bulletproof boundary that had protected her from the supposedly dangerous Uncommitted hoards.

Cries of "Help!" "Call an ambulance!" "I think she's dead!" continued, but Wylie couldn't stay another second. If she didn't get some fresh air soon, she'd hit the floor, too. She barely managed to hold on to Monty's leash, dragging him through the crush of people rushing in to see what was wrong. As she stumbled along the road toward home, she spotted the peddler who'd been hawking jewelry rushing toward her, and she knew she wouldn't have the energy to face him. Luckily for her, two Comcop cars and an ambulance blared past in the other direction, and their sirens sent the peddler running. Wylie plowed on toward home, feeling like she might black out any moment. When she made it through the intersection that signaled the end of noncom territory, she sank to the curb and put her head between her knees. Monty at her side, they sat there a long time until, slowly, Wylie felt her strength returning.

What was that? she wondered. She'd never fainted before, but she hadn't eaten much that day, thanks to the meager food rations left from this month's allotment. However, while hunger might explain her sudden loss of energy, Wylie doubted the med-rep had collapsed for the same reason. Committed didn't go hungry, and ChurchState employees were especially well-supplied with life's comforts. No, that med-rep had fallen as if she'd been struck from above. Funny coincidence, Wylie thought—if only it worked that way. If only people actually got what they deserved.

"Better get going," she said to Monty, rising to her feet. "Del will be wanting her meds, and we need to scrounge something for dinner."

3

The next morning Wylie woke at the first thunder peal. The sky was still dark but the clock said 7:00 a.m., so she slid out of bed and dressed quickly. Delores never got up this early, and Monty was hiding under the table, terrified of the thunder. With notebook in hand, Wylie ran across the campus to the shed. Many times, Del had yelled at her for spending thunderstorms in a metal shed, but Wylie figured the benefit outweighed the risk and she would take her chances. She slammed the rusty doors behind her and climbed up on the tractor, hoping it would rain good and hard. Wylie loved the sound of pounding water on the metal roof; nothing could calm her inner tempest like a real storm. She wished it would never stop. She searched her pockets for a pencil stub and flipped her notebook open to the last entry, written the last time she'd hidden from the world in a storm:

> It's the rain that makes me say
> I'll be better off someday.
> When the rain stops I'll be left with all my blues.
> For the sun can offer me no more excuse.

When the dull smack of rain against the roof changed pitch, Wylie knew the hail had begun. Decade's old warnings from the now defunct weather service had predicted frequent, intense hail storms—warnings that had been ridiculed by ChurchState officials. Wylie could never figure out why environmental regulations offended their religious sensibilities— she guessed she'd add that to the growing list of unanswerable *whys*. She didn't mind the hail, though. Listening to it bounce off the roof reminded her that even the ChurchState couldn't control nature, at least not completely. When the clamor of ice on metal filled her until there was no room for anything else, she wrote:

Oh, the water coming down
Makes me feel like running 'round.
For when everything outside is dark and dreary,
And everyone inside is feeling weary,
Then my soul can finally rest
And my heart can leave its quest
To settle down and listen to the rain
Outside my window.

Wylie studied the page, surprised by her own words. Quest? Where did that come from? Her life was filled with the drudgery of taking care of Delores and Monty, and her only quest was getting food on the table every day. She laughed a little at her uncharacteristic flair for the dramatic and would have torn out the page if the rising clatter hadn't diverted her attention to the roof, which was buckling like it might succumb to the beating of hail across its surface.

Wylie jumped off the tractor just as Darwin burst through the door.

"Are you crazy?" he yelled over the pounding. "Come on! I've got Grandpa's weather shield."

They ran outside and jumped into a small, motorized ball designed to withstand the severest storms. As they sped away Wylie heard the crash of the roof collapsing behind them.

"There goes the mower," she said, looking over her shoulder.

Darwin was not finished with his reprimand. "What were you thinking? Del called me, sick with worry. You could have been killed in there! Good thing I got here in time."

"And good thing your grandfather's rich," Wylie answered flippantly.

"Not funny."

"Okay, okay. I owe you one."

"And don't think I'll forget it." Darwin's frown relaxed. As usual, he couldn't stay mad for long.

They waited a few minutes outside Wylie's apartment, watching hail the size of baseballs bounce off the weather shield and crush the shrubs beside the walkway. Wylie saw her mother's relieved face peeking out from behind the curtain, but by the time the storm subsided, Delores was back in bed.

"You're going to be the death of me," she called from her room.

"Sorry," Wylie said in between licks from Monty. She sat on the floor so they could reach each other more easily. "Are you okay now, you big coward? I know, you're waiting for breakfast." She filled Monty's dish and took two cereal bowls from the cabinet.

"Want some breakfast?" she asked Darwin, who had draped himself across the ratty green living room sofa that doubled as Wylie's bed.

"Sure."

Unfortunately, the food pantry was empty. Wylie put the cereal bowls back.

"I forgot, we ran out," she said, slumping into the living room. The brief surge of energy she'd drawn from the storm had passed. She pushed Darwin's legs to the floor to make room for herself on the sofa, where she sunk in, put her head back, and closed her eyes.

"You need to get some food when the storm ends," Delores yelled. "I think we have enough money for rice, if you can find any."

Wylie nodded, eyes still closed. She felt something soft land in her lap and opened her eyes to a protein bar. Darwin was eating one, too.

"These are the good ones," she said, reading the wrapper. "From Grandpa?"

"Yep. He made me take them."

"You're lucky to have him."

"And you're lucky to have me. And you do have me. You know that, right?" There was that yearning look in Darwin's eyes again.

Wylie looked away. How could she tell the person she loved best in the world that a romantic relationship was not on her to-do list because such a relationship, even with him, seemed pointless and unsustainable? Dating, romance, love—they were all supposed to lead to something, to some future happily ever after that was not part of their daily Uncommitted scrape for survival. An although Wylie knew none of that mattered to preternaturally optimistic Darwin, it mattered to her. But Darwin deserved better than the "It's not you, it's me" treatment, and so Wylie kept her feelings to herself.

"Your silence speaks volumes, Wy. Okay, I get it. I'm making you uncomfortable," Darwin said. "But we can't avoid this subject forever. I need to tell you how I feel."

"Dar, look," Wylie began. She took a deep breath and promptly aspirated a piece of protein bar. She bolted upright and coughed into her hand until her airway cleared a full thirty seconds later. Darwin sat up and watched, ready to spring into action if necessary. Finally, when the coughing subsided, Wylie waved him away.

Darwin sighed. "That's one way to kill the moment. Okay, Wy, you win, for now. Come on, I'll take you to get food, but then you have to do something for me."

Wylie looked at him warily.

"Don't worry, it doesn't involve my unrequited state of being."

And that was how, the next day, Wylie wound up under the trap door in the forgotten archives of the library once again.

4

" We need to make this quick," Wylie said as they sifted through the dusty underground archives. "Sharmila called. She's having some kind of plumbing problem, and Del wants us to take a look."

"And by 'us' you mean me."

"Yes."

"How is it that every time you owe me a favor, I end up doing you two?"

"I'm just special that way," Wylie answered. "Besides, you like Sharmila."

"Mmm. Everybody likes Sharmila." Darwin brushed the dust off a paperback volume. The cover was torn and the first page was gray with mildew. "*Slaves, Women, and Homosexuals,*" he read. "*A Hermeneutic for the 21st Century.* This is exactly what I need." He sat on a box, immersed in the text, and Wiley knew it would be several minutes before he came up for air. She hoped she'd be able to drag him away before Sharmila called Del again, or there would be hell to pay.

Wylie poked around as she waited, letting her thoughts flow freely. What Darwin said was true, everybody did like Sharmila. Sharmila inhabited Wylie's earliest memories like an oasis in the desert of her childhood; her calm, steady presence had given Wylie the sustenance of hope. The day Sharmila moved out was the day that hope had begun to evaporate. Sharmila always seemed to know what Wylie needed, and what she couldn't supply materially, she more than made up for in hugs, understanding, and wisdom. "Clouds that thunder seldom rain," Sharmila would reassure Wylie after a heated altercation with Delores. And while Del had never exactly been a ray of sunshine, with Sharmila around she'd at least gotten out of bed every day. In the years since Sharmila left, Wylie didn't think her mother had smiled once. Sharmila's parting gift to Wylie had been Monty, all paws and ears and puppy kisses, and as angry as Del had been, she'd let the puppy stay.

Wylie picked her way through the junk and saw the TV remote lying in the open box of videos, exactly where she'd left it. She hesitated. Watching the video of the long-gone classroom had stirred feelings in her she'd rather avoid. Did these students understand how lucky they were? If she'd been alive during that time she could have gone to college without having to pledge allegiance to a corrupt authority and risk losing the only meager family she had left. Listening to their discussion of the religion that had ruined Wylie's life would only bring anger, and what was the point of that? Better to avoid these phantoms and get on with life as it was; dwelling on the past would not help her face a hopeless future. The only way to get through the day was to stay in the present. No more videos, Wylie told herself.

But Wylie had never been an especially good listener, even to herself. The remote seemed to be beckoning, and she couldn't resist its invitation to hold it in her hands. When she picked it up, the small device seemed denser than it should, as if it held the weight of Wylie's uncertainty within its plastic casing. Cursing her lack of self-control, Wylie pushed the power button and the set came to life in fuzzy gray static. Randomly, she chose a tape from the box and pushed it into the slot. Dr. Michaels appeared with a questioning look, and Wylie realized the recording had picked up mid-class. Apparently, someone had not followed the directions on the label to "Be kind, rewind."

"Here we have two separate accounts where Moses brought forth water from a rock," said Dr. Michaels. "Some argue these are two tellings of the same story, while others believe they are two separate incidents. We'll get to that later. For now, let's get the basics down. What makes these two accounts different?"

Steve's deep voice answered, and Wylie felt she could imagine what he looked like without ever seeing him. He'd be tall, broad, and totally relaxed, as if he owned the classroom. "Because the second time, God told Moses to speak to the rock, not to strike it," he said. "God was angry that Moses disobeyed. Rebellion earns God's spurn."

Wylie had never heard of water coming from a rock, and she'd never read the Bible. But an angry God, she could picture. If God was anything like the Committed, he was angry all the time. She let the tape play.

"Okay, true," said Dr. Michaels. "And you do like your little rhymes, huh Steve?" The class laughed. "In the first account, recorded in Exodus, God tells Moses to strike the rock. Moses obeys, and water pours forth from the rock. In the second passage, in Numbers, God tells Moses to speak to the rock, but Moses strikes the rock instead. Because of that, Moses doesn't get to enter the Promised Land."

"A little harsh, I'd say," said a male voice that wasn't Steve's.

"Perhaps," answered Dr. Michaels, "and we'll get to that. But here's what I don't want you to lose sight of. What do the passages in Exodus and Numbers have in common?"

Dr. Michaels' face remained inquisitive while several voices overlapped.

"They both involved Moses."

"They took place in the wilderness."

"Water came out of a rock both times."

"They were both miracles."

Dr. Michaels smiled. "You're getting closer. Yes, both times we see a miracle take place. For what purpose?"

"To show God's power," Steve said.

"Is that all? Why choose water from a rock? Wouldn't an earthquake have been a more effective display of power?"

After a few seconds of silence, Dr. Michaels pointed toward the back of the lecture hall. "Yes, Abby?"

"Both times," Abby said, "God was providing water for a group of thirsty people. He was meeting their needs."

"Okay, good. So what does that tell us about God's character?"

"That he cares about his people?" Abby answered tentatively. "That he doesn't want them to go without?"

"Yes, exactly," said Dr. Michaels. "So, yes, we'll talk about God's anger and his punishment of Moses, but let's keep that in the context of a God who cares about his people, his children."

Wylie turned the set off.

An angry God. A God who cares. Which was it, then?

"Let's go. Sharmila's waiting, and I want to get out of her neighborhood before dark."

* * *

They drove to Sharmila's apartment, passing miles of new construction projects before they reached Uncommitted territory.

"It's shrinking," Wylie said.

"What?"

"The Uncommitted zone. It's shrinking. Look at all these new developments they're building."

"Don't you listen to the victory broadcasts?" Darwin asked. "It's because more and more people are signing the Statement and moving to better neighborhoods. At least, that's the ChurchState's story."

"That's not Del's story. She says people in the outer ring are being displaced, driven further to the center of the zone to make room for bigger and better Committed construction."

They drove a few minutes more until they reached the border, where a billboard showed a family of four standing in front of a large house, smiling as if they'd just won the lottery. "Commit your way to the Lord, and He will prosper you," it said in foot-high lettering. Crawling along at the bottom of the sign like ants were the words, "The surest way out of poverty is to sign the Statement of Commitment."

"Not very subtle," Wylie said.

"Subtlety is not their way, you know that. So where do all these displaced folks go?"

"Good question." The downtown area of the Uncommitted zone looked more desolate than ever. "I guess they're moving to other cities, maybe out west. Maybe they're falling off the grid, camping out in the deserted national parks. Del says folks are disappearing altogether, but you know how paranoid she can be. I can't believe that even the ChurchState is capable of wiping out families wholesale."

They travelled another few minutes, until Wylie spotted Sharmila's building.

"That's it," she said, pointing to a tall brick apartment block that seemed to go on forever. Since cars were hard to come by for most Uncommitted, parking was not a problem. They exited the car, Wylie cursing under her breath as she tripped on the broken sidewalk leading to the entrance. The buzzer system had been ripped from the wall, but it didn't matter since the lock on the heavy metal door was damaged, too. They pushed through to the lobby where, as if to complete the cycle of brokenness, an "out of order" sign was taped on the elevator door.

"Of course," Wylie said. They continued down the unlit hallway, catching a quick glimpse of a dark figure slipping through the stairwell door. Instinctively, they slowed their pace and approached the stairwell with caution.

"What's this?" Darwin asked, pointing to a clump of bloody feathers glued to the door in the shape of an X.

"Gross," Wylie said.

Under the gory mess were three lines, scrawled in red.

Walker take heed.

Up you may go.

Down you may bleed.

"God, I hate to think of Sharmila living here," Wylie said.

"Well, lucky we're going up. Come on."

Six floors later an out of breath Wylie knocked on Sharmila's door. After a minute it opened slowly to reveal an unsmiling adolescent on the other side.

"Er, hi," Wylie said. "Is Sharmila here?"

"Sam, I told you not to open the door!" A small woman with a swollen belly rushed over and let them in. "Sharmila, they're here," she called.

"Come in, come in," came a muffled shout from the kitchen, where Sharmila knelt, half submerged in the cabinet under the sink. Two more kids stood behind a pile of old cleaning supplies, rags, dirty sponges, and the rest of the junk that had been displaced when Sharmila went to work on the pipes.

"I don't understand what's wrong." Sharmila ducked out from the cabinet and stood. "Everyone else in the building has water," she said, reaching up to envelop Wylie in a hug. "Good to see you."

Wylie hugged back, letting herself, for a second, feel like a kid again. Only Sharmila could make her feel that way.

"These are my guests," Sharmila said. "Wylie, Darwin, meet Mara and her kids, Sam, Shawn, and Sadie. They're staying with me until they find a place of their own." The kids, all in winter jackets that looked two sizes too small, smiled shyly without making eye contact. Wylie recognized the hollowed look of kids who'd gotten used to going to bed hungry. Darwin grunted hello from under the sink where he'd already gone to work.

So that's where the newly displaced were going, Wylie thought, to Sharmila's small apartment. Well, at least these few, anyway. It was just like Sharmila to take in strangers.

"You look thin," Wylie said, wishing she'd brought some food.

"Nonsense, I'm fine, except for the lack of water. What do you think, Darwin?"

"Everything looks okay under here. What about the bathroom?"

"No water there either."

"Did you call the landlord?"

Sharmila laughed. "A hundred times over the past week. They don't pick up."

"You've been without water for a week?" Wylie asked. "Why didn't you call us sooner?"

"I didn't want to bother you. And I don't want Delores to worry. But the neighbors are getting tired of seeing me at their door and these kids need baths."

"We all do," Mara said.

"Where's your utility room?" Darwin asked.

Sharmila led them to a small closet outside the bathroom.

"Okay, here's your main spigot," said Darwin. He turned it to the right and then left again. "Seems like everything is on. There must be something blocking the pipe. Probably something crawled up in there and died. I need access to the basement to shut off the water from there."

Wylie remembered the poetic warning in the stairwell. "Do you think that's a good idea?"

"It is decidedly not a good idea," Sharmila said. "The basement is Avian territory, and they don't appreciate intruders. We'll make do."

"Avian, here?" Wylie asked. That explained the clump of bloody feathers, but it was unusual for the group to claim space this close to other people. "I thought they had their own buildings."

"They did, until the Comcops kicked them out and demolished their nests. Now they land wherever they can. They mostly leave us alone, but they're very protective of their young and they strike first, ask questions later. Thanks for trying, Darwin, but you can't go down there."

"And we can't leave you here with no water," Wylie said, shaking her head. The kids looked up at her hopefully, and Wylie wondered how many others like them lived in the same conditions, or worse. As bad as things got, at least she and Del had always had their own place. So far—if she remained Uncommitted when the campus sale went through, they, too, might be dependent on the kindness of strangers, and there weren't enough strangers like Sharmila to go around. Even scavengers like the Avian wouldn't want them. All the birds in their nests were required to earn their keep, and Delores had stopped earning hers when Sharmila left.

"There's gotta be a way," Wylie said, knowing Sharmila had long ago rejected the only way out of poverty. She stooped down and hit the pipe with the side of her fist, expecting to feel the pain of hard metal on her soft flesh. Instead, an electric shock jolted her backwards just as the lights went off. One of the kids began to cry.

"What the heck?" said Darwin.

"It's probably a circuit. Hold on," Sharmila said. She felt around in the closet, pulled open a metal panel, and flipped some switches back and forth.

"I guess these buildings were never updated to digital," Darwin said.

"Nope. Strictly twentieth century here," answered Sharmila as the lights came on. "There. See? It's okay," she said, patting the crying Sadie on the shoulder. "Everything's okay."

But Wylie was not okay. The shock had drained her energy and she knew if she didn't sit down, she'd fall down. "I don't feel so good," she said, but the others were distracted by a sound coming from the kitchen.

"Is that . . . ?" Mara asked.

"I believe it is!" Sharmila said, running toward the water gushing from the kitchen faucet. "Wylie, I don't know what you did, but you're a miracle worker!"

But Wylie didn't hear. She slumped against Darwin and before he could catch her, her face hit the carpet.

5

W hen Wylie woke up on Sharmila's couch she had no idea what time it was, but strips of light filtered through the broken blinds into the quiet apartment. Sharmila, who was nodding in a chair next to her, opened her eyes at Wylie's stirring.

"What happened?" Wylie asked. "Where's Darwin?"

"You fainted. Darwin left, but we thought it best you stay the night."

"Del . . ."

"We called her. She knows you're safe."

"Monty . . ."

"Darwin's taking care of him. Now, forget Delores, forget Monty, and tell me about Wylie. What happened last night?"

"I don't know. Like you said, I fainted."

"I know that, but why? And has it ever happened before?" Sharmila tucked the blanket around Wylie and then smoothed the hair out of her face. The motion, more reflex than anything, stirred a memory in Wylie. She hadn't felt taken care of in a very long time.

"Why did you have to leave?" she whispered, letting herself sink into her pillow.

Sharmila raised an eyebrow. "Are you trying to change the subject?"

"No. It's just, being here with you reminds me of how things used to be, before you left. Everything changed after that. I never really understood why you had to leave." Wylie knew she wasn't exactly being truthful. Technically, she knew why Sharmila had packed her bags and walked away from their home. Of course she knew. The Reclamation had brought a change in social mores that did not favor folks like Delores and Sharmila. So, rather than risk Wylie's well-being, Sharmila moved out. Although Wylie knew why, she still didn't know *why*. "Why does it have to be this way?" she asked, sounding and feeling very much like the ten-year-old that had stood at the door watching Sharmila drag her suitcase down the road.

35

"That's my Why-Why-Wylie," Sharmila said, smiling. "Now answer my question. Has this happened before?"

"Not really. Well, maybe once, the other day. At the meds dispensary. I touched the med-rep's hand and I got a shock." Wylie sat up and brushed the cover away. "Just like last night—I touched the pipe and got a shock then, too. After that, I just kind of faded out, like I could hardly stand. Maybe I have some kind of electrical problem."

"I've never heard of anything like that. It's more likely you're anemic. How's your period?"

"Same as always."

"Are you eating okay?"

"Same as always."

Sharmila was not convinced. "Well, keep an eye on it. I wish I could make you breakfast, but I haven't been to the store lately."

Now it was Sharmila who wasn't being truthful, Wylie knew. Most likely she'd let the kids eat up the little food she had, and now they'd all go hungry until Sharmila figured out a way to get more. If housing for the Uncommitted was scarce, jobs were even scarcer. No job, no money, no food.

While Sharmila went to coax some tea out of a worn-out tea bag, Wylie hatched a plan. She drank the weak tea and hugged Sharmila goodbye, assuring her that Darwin was waiting downstairs. But when she reached the first floor there was no Darwin, because Wylie hadn't called him. She stood in the stairwell and took a deep breath, testing her stamina after last night's fainting spell. Although she hadn't eaten, she'd slept well, and she felt strong enough to face the ominous message from the Avian. *Up you may go, down you may bleed.* Bleeding was exactly what Wylie had in mind.

* * *

Wylie had never been in an Avian enclave before, but she entered the basement with all the false confidence she could muster. She'd heard of the group that had adopted a bird persona, but she'd never been this close and she didn't know what to expect. On the cement floor of the large open basement she saw people perched on blankets, old clothing, and other bits of material woven together into what very much resembled nests. Each nest was large enough to accommodate several adults and kids. Their voices echoed off the low ceiling. Some were reading aloud, others were playing card games, and a few of the youngest were sleeping soundly on the layers of soft cloth. The kids looked well-fed, but more than that, Wylie noticed something different about their expressions. Missing were the diverted eyes and haunted expressions of the Uncommitted. These kids were safe, and their visage said they knew it. If it weren't for the feather wreaths and painted faces, this could have been a scene at a Committed family reunion or a ChurchState picnic.

Wylie stood at the doorway, unnoticed, reflecting on the normalcy of it all. Just parents and their kids. But when the heavy metal door slammed behind her, the room that had been almost festive was all at once shrouded in silence. Every eye turned toward Wylie. A tall, thin man wearing a feather cloak stepped out of the shadows, and with him any appearance of normalcy vanished. His beady black eyes were rimmed in yellow and in place of his nose, a hard, pointy beak had been surgically implanted. He walked an uneven path through the nests toward Wylie, bobbing his head and flapping his arms. The adults in the nests stood and broke the silence, screeching, clucking, and flapping their arms. One of the kids closest to Wylie took a swig from a plastic bottle and spit an orange, oily substance at Wylie's feet. Wylie looked down at the thick liquid mess that had missed her shoe by an inch. It looked gross, but it smelled like orange soda.

"Wait!" she shouted, raising her arms in surrender. "I just want to talk!"

The screeching and clacking bounced off the cement walls and drowned out Wylie's voice until the leader, now just a few feet away, raised his wings above his head. The flock immediately fell silent.

"You were warned to stay away," he said in a high-pitched, monotone voice that had a strange tinny quality. At first Wylie thought he had a bad cold, but then she realized it was the beak, which, up close, looked sharp enough to do damage. He took hold of her wrist and lifted his head to strike.

"I came to trade!" Wylie said.

"You have nothing."

"I have blood." Blood, like meds, was scarce and would fetch top dollar on the underground market. The grip on her wrist loosened.

"You carry nothing with you," said the leader.

"Surely you have the means," Wylie answered.

The leader sneered. "Perhaps we do." He nodded and four adults stepped out of their nests to surround Wylie.

"This way," the leader said.

Wylie planted her feet. "Not so fast. I said trade, not give. I want something in return."

"Despite clear warnings, you entered an Avian nest, uninvited. What is to stop us from taking what we want?"

Wylie looked from bird-like face to face. She saw apprehension and determination, but she didn't sense brutality. These folks might pretend to be birds, but under the feathers were humans trying to survive.

"Bird honor?" she said weakly.

A moment of indecision crossed the leader's face and then he convulsed into a series of raspy chokes. Wylie realized he was laughing.

"Yes, there is honor among birds after all," he said, and the others laughed too, seemingly overtaken by an inside joke that Wylie didn't understand, not that she minded. Laughing was better than threatening. Although she knew she was not out of danger, she let herself relax a little.

"Okay, little sparrow, we will trade for your blood."

"One pint of my blood. No more."

The leader raised an eyebrow. "And what do you ask in return for this very small offering?"

"I have a friend who lives in apartment 613. She takes care of people, people she hardly knows. Can you watch out for her? Send a little food her way a few times a week?"

"You wish us to extend our nest to an outsider?"

"Yeah, sort of like a bird adoption. It happens all the time, right?"

Again, the leader squeaked a laugh. "It happens. It also happens that birds smash each other's eggs and drive away unwanted chicks. You ask a lot for a small amount of blood."

"A small amount that's worth much on the underground. If you spend a fraction of that on food for 613, you'll have a ton left for your own chicks."

The leader didn't seem convinced. "How so?"

"I'm Rh-null." Although Delores had warned Wylie never to disclose her rare blood type, she was willing to take the risk for Sharmila.

The leader's yellow and black eyes opened wide, and the Avian to Wylie's left gasped.

"Ah, not a sparrow, but a golden finch. You have a deal. We will watch over your friend for six months. After that, another deposit will be needed to cover the cost."

"Deal," Wylie said. Six months was almost an eternity in the world of the Uncommitted and more than she'd hoped for. A woman who'd been watching from the sidelines joined them as they wove through the nests to a small adjacent room. When Wylie caught a glimpse of a mother bird spitting chewed up food into the mouth of a toddler, she almost gagged, but she needed to stay strong for what she was about to do.

"One more thing," Wylie said, hopping onto a narrow cot. "The occupants of 613 can't know about this arrangement."

"That will not be a problem. We find communication with outsiders highly distasteful. They will simply find a box of food at the door periodically." The leader stood close enough for Wylie to see the stitches that held his beak in place. Repulsion washed over her, but she didn't look away.

The woman spoke for the first time. "Enough, Talon. I have work to do." Talon nodded and bobbed away.

"He must trust you," Wylie said.

"He has no reason not to." The woman donned plastic gloves and busied herself, sterilizing equipment as she spoke. "Besides, Avian do not appoint permanent leaders. He leads today, but others will replace him as the need arises." She moved with swift, sure confidence, finding Wylie's vein and inserting a thin needle. Wylie watched blood flow from her body through plastic tubing to a small bag that hung from the side of the cot. For a second, she let her imagination run wild. What if they didn't stop at a pint? What if they tied her down and exsanguinated her, leaving her lifeless shell to rot under the foundation of a decaying building in the Uncommitted zone? Her blood could make them rich and they knew it.

"What's your name?" the woman asked.

"Wylie."

"Hello, Wylie. I'm Nightingale, and I'm a nurse, or I was one for many years. I've done this hundreds of times. You have nothing to fear." Her blue eyes smiled under feathers of soft brown and white.

"I'm not afraid," Wylie answered.

"No? Okay, good. You looked a little panicked for a minute, that's all."

Nightingale monitored the blood flow. "You're doing fine. Just relax for a few minutes."

Wylie nodded and closed her eyes. She'd need to call Darwin as soon as she was done, but she would never tell him about her little detour into Avian territory.

"Rh-null, huh?" Nightingale said. "You do understand how rare that is?"

"So they tell me."

"You probably don't believe in miracles, but you're a kind of walking miracle, you know."

"Yeah," Wylie murmured, "there's a lot of that going around lately."

A knock on the door beckoned Nightingale, who went to attend a sick child. Wylie took in her surroundings more closely. The small room, probably once used for storage, was now a well-stocked mini-clinic. Fortunately, Wylie had rarely been sick as a kid, because the noncom clinic was pitiful in comparison to this makeshift Avian treatment center. Master dealers in contraband, the Avian knew how to get what they needed. Wylie sighed. At least their kids were getting good care.

She let her mind drift back to the few times she'd needed medical attention. A nearly decayed memory fought its way to the surface.

* * *

Wylie and Darwin stood at the back of a Committed housing development, gaping at an overflowing dumpster twice their height.

"We can't reach it," Darwin said. "Let's forget it and go home."

"No," insisted Wylie. "It's your birthday. You deserve something nice."

"I got something nice. Grandpa sent over that mountain bike, right there. Did you forget how we got here?"

Wylie recalled how it felt to sit behind Darwin as he peddled with all his might. Wind in her hair, she'd closed her eyes and pretended she was soaring through the clouds, flying high where there was no border between Committed and noncom territory. She was used to life as an Uncommitted; she'd never known anything else. But the one thing she resented, the one thing she wished for, was the ability to take flight like the Committed did in their in shiny new vehicles. Anyway, that didn't matter today. It was Darwin's birthday and this day was about him.

"I mean something nice from me," she said. "Boost me up."

Darwin stooped down and Wylie jumped on him, piggy-back style.

"Still too low," she said. "Let me try your shoulders."

Reluctantly, Darwin knelt on the rough pavement and steadied himself as Wylie sat on his shoulders.

"Okay, stand up," she said.

Holding Wylie's legs, Darwin stood, no small feat since they were almost the same weight. He took a few shaky steps toward the dumpster.

"I can almost reach," Wylie said. "Stand still."

"I'm trying."

"Ugh. Just a couple more inches and I'll be able to reach inside. I need to stand. Let go of my legs."

"Are you crazy? You'll fall."

"I won't. Let go."

Holding on to Darwin's head, Wylie carefully moved to a standing position. Darwin gripped her ankles as best he could.

"There's a ton of stuff in here. I can't believe what these people throw out."

Wylie grabbed a blanket from the top of the pile. "I could use this," she said. But when she turned to toss it to the ground she lost her balance and tumbled down, scraping her arm on the side of the metal bin and hitting the pavement hard. Darwin landed next to her, with the rescued blanket between them.

"I told you," he said. "Are you okay?"

"My arm is bleeding. Del's gonna kill me."

Darwin's eyes got big when he saw the jagged gash just below Wylie's elbow. They jumped on the bike and peddled home, Wylie grasping her arm to stop the bleeding and Darwin trying not to make any sudden turns for fear Wylie would fall again. When they reached Wylie's apartment she ran inside without saying goodbye. She needed to get to the first aid kit without being seen by her mom.

Just Wylie's luck, Delores happened to be standing in the entryway, gazing out at the world beyond their small apartment. She did that often—just stood motionless and stared, as if trying to make sense of the world or maybe daring it to come for her, head on, and get the brewing battle over with. At the sight of her daughter's bleeding arm she turned red and dragged Wylie into the bathroom.

"What did you do?" she yelled, grabbing the nearest towel. "I told you to be careful! We can't go to the hospital, ever!" She pressed the towel to Wylie's arm.

"The noncom clinic is free," Wylie answered.

"Stupid girl, this isn't about money!" Delores gripped Wylie with her free hand and shook her. "I told you, your blood is precious! If you ever need a transfusion, you're out of luck. Or worse, do you want to become a permanent blood donor for those pigs? They'll stick you with needles and drain you dry."

Wylie wasn't sure what a transfusion was, but she knew better than to ask. All she could picture was the pig she'd seen once roasting on a spit outside a Committed restaurant. Is that what they would do to her if she went to the hospital? She started to cry but Del only tightened her grip.

"Stop moving! I need to get a bandage."

"Why don't you let me take care of this?" Sharmila asked softly from the doorway.

"Fine. Maybe you can talk some sense into this kid." Delores threw the bloody towel into the sink and stormed away.

"Let's take a look. It's not so bad." Humming softly, Sharmila washed and bandaged the wound and dried Wylie's eyes.

"Sharmila, what does 'precious' mean?" Wylie asked.

"It means very, very special."

"Then why did Del say my blood was precious? I saw Darwin's blood once. It looked the same as mine."

"Delores told you this before, remember? You have a very rare blood type. You're a match for everyone else in the world. So if they needed blood, you could be a donor."

"But that's good, right? I could give some blood to someone who needs it. I could save someone."

"Delores is worried that if the ChurchState finds out, they'll take your blood without asking. And it's not your job to save anyone. If you got hurt and needed blood, who would save you?"

"Oh. Is that why she's mad at me all the time?" Wylie asked.

"She's not really angry at you. She's angry at the world. She tries to fight it, but some days are better than others. Today was a bad day, but tomorrow will be better."

* * *

"How are you doing in here?"

Wylie sat up with a start at the sound of Nightingale's voice. She hadn't been dreaming, exactly, but she'd been lost enough in the memory to almost forget where she was.

"Hold on, let me unhook you before you take off," Nightingale said, smiling. "Your friend must mean a lot to you, to go through all this for her."

Wylie nodded. Her throat was dry and she didn't feel like talking.

"Well, don't worry about her. I'll see she's taken care of."

"Thanks," Wylie whispered, thinking, Sharmila had been wrong. Tomorrow wasn't better.

6

Wylie managed to hide what she'd done from Delores and Darwin without much trouble. Her long sleeves concealed the tiny needle puncture and, besides, she doubted Del would notice if she'd come home with a gaping knife wound to the chest. Her days of hiding scrapes and bruises from her mom were long gone because Delores was too preoccupied with her own losses to see past the walls of her self-imposed prison.

As Wylie went about her daily activities, every now and then she thought of the strangeness of the Avian. What kind of world drove people to emulate birds flocked together in a cold, dank basement? "Why does it have to be this way?" she whispered to Monty, scratching behind his pointy ears. Monty gave his usual answer—a big, wet lick to the face.

Wylie recovered from the loss of blood quickly, being sure to drink lots of water. Within a few days she'd put the incident behind her, feigning ignorance when Sharmila reported that boxes of food had shown up at her door.

"I don't know who it's from, but we'll take it!" Sharmila had said. "I'm not one to turn down a miracle!"

Maybe it was all the talk of miracles that led Wylie back to the library archives one dreary Sunday afternoon, or maybe she was just bored out of her mind. Darwin was with his grandpa, Del was yelling at the broadcasts, and Monty needed a walk. So out they went, tromping across the deserted campus where even the missionaries had given up the chase. As much as she'd meant to stay away, Wylie felt the library's tug, and like a puppet on a string, she surrendered to its pull. Once inside, she flipped through books and tossed them aside. Nothing grabbed her attention until she found herself trotting down the stairs toward the box of videos, the very place she'd resolved to avoid.

"It's no use, Monty," she said. "I'm hooked. Let's check out the miracle of the day."

She searched around the videos until she came across one with a label almost too smudged to read. Only two words were legible: *woman* and *blood*. Blood. The one secret asset Wylie possessed. Funny that she'd randomly chosen this tape after her visit with the Avian. She pushed the video into the console and Dr. Michaels appeared, wearing a tweed jacket and brown tie today. Not exactly a snappy dresser, but he had a quality that Wylie liked; maybe it was his smile, or the way he spoke to the students. He was confident, but kind. He seemed open in a way that Wylie had never seen in the Committed leaders of her time. She wondered what had happened to turn modest self-assurance into the smug arrogance she'd witnessed her whole life. "Maybe you know why," she whispered to Dr. Michaels.

"Today we're going to explore a miracle that is recorded in all three synoptic gospels, commonly referred to as 'the woman with the issue of blood,'" Dr. Michaels announced to the class. Wylie realized what the label on the tape had once said. She had her own issues with blood. Would she have anything in common with this woman?

"So, according to the text, we have a woman who has been bleeding for twelve years who touches Jesus and is instantly healed. Even Luke, the doctor, doesn't give us details about the woman's condition. What can we assume is going on medically?"

An awkward silence followed, until Steve, sitting in the front row again, called out, "Is this what's called a pregnant pause?" A few students guffawed, but Dr. Michaels' face remained placid.

Wylie snorted. There was the Committed she knew so well.

"Where is the bleeding coming from?" asked Dr. Michaels. "This is important if we are to understand the significance of the miracle. Yes, Andrew?"

A small voice from the middle of the room spoke. "From . . . down there?" This time most of the class laughed, and even Dr. Michaels smiled.

"Can we be a bit more specific?"

Abby's voice rang out from the back. "It was menstrual bleeding. Basically, she had her period for twelve years."

"And that is significant because . . . ?"

"It made her unclean," Abby answered. "She wouldn't have been allowed in the temple."

"Good," Dr. Michaels said. "Keep going, Abby."

"And anyone she touched would have been declared unclean, too, which means touching Jesus, like the woman did, would be taboo because it would have made him unclean. But not only did Jesus heal her, he didn't rebuke her. It was his way of saying, no one is unclean. Anyone can come to me." Anyone willing to sign the Statement of Commitment, Wylie thought. She'd never actually been called *unclean*, but *Uncommitted* felt close enough.

"Yes. So, we need to keep in mind the cultural significance of this miracle. This may explain the woman's fear of admitting she'd touched Jesus' garment. What else do you find important in the passage?"

Steve spoke. "Jesus knew power had gone out from him. He sensed it."

"True, although we can't know for sure what Jesus experienced. Perhaps he felt a brief weakening, like a battery being drained." The discussion continued, but Wylie had stopped listening. A drained battery was just what she'd felt like at the med clinic and then again at Sharmila's apartment. What could that mean?

"I thought I'd find you here!" Darwin called from the top of the stairs. "On my way down."

Wylie switched off the TV. "Don't bother. I'm coming up. I have something I need to tell you."

7

"So, you think some kind of power is coming from you, and it's related to those tapes we found in the library?" Darwin took his eyes off the road for a second to search Wylie's face. His curly black hair was combed neatly for once and he wore his grandfather's sports jacket over an uncharacteristic collared shirt.

"I don't know what to think, but it's happened twice now. I watch the tape, then something weird happens that seems related somehow, after which I deflate like a leaking balloon. I can't explain it."

"Well, there'll be plenty of balloons there tonight. Try not to deflate any."

"You don't believe me." Wylie couldn't really blame Darwin for his skepticism. She hardly believed the events of the last few weeks herself.

"I believe some strange stuff happened. But that it all connects back to you and the tapes? That is hard to believe. Anyway, try to stop worrying about it. We have enough to deal with tonight."

"I hate that we have to attend this debacle." Wylie had been dreading the required "informational meeting" for the "future Committed" for months. It was the ChurchState's last big chance to pressure them into signing the Statement in time to attend orientation camp next summer. Of course, one could sign at any time, but the earlier one signed, the higher the status one received, and higher status meant more benefits. Wylie knew that if she signed in time for camp she'd be guaranteed a spot at college, and with a stipend to boot. But sign or not, they had no choice about tonight. If they didn't attend, what little benefits they had could shrivel up. Wylie had heard of firings and evictions for the families of those who snubbed the ChurchState's big party.

"It's nice that you dressed up for the occasion," Darwin said. Wylie was wearing the dirtiest, most worn jeans she could find. Her hair, which she'd purposely not washed for a week, hung down in greasy clumps. To top off her look, Wylie had thrown Del's old, ripped parka over the faded T-shirt she wore when she cleaned the bathroom. "Isn't that the coat Monty sleeps on?" Darwin asked. "I recognize the smell."

"Dress is a form of protest," Wylie answered. "I'm surprised you're all dressed up."

"My grandpa made me. He wants me to give them a chance."

"Will you?"

"No. You?"

"No way." Wylie was surprised at her own resolve.

"Good to hear. A few weeks ago you were weakening."

"Not weakening. Just considering all the options."

"What changed?"

Wylie shrugged and stared out the window. Something had changed, it was true. Even after all that Delores had gone through, Wylie had grown tired of being a bottom dweller. For an instant she'd toyed with the idea that signing was the answer. After all, the Committed couldn't all be true believers. Maybe she could fake it just enough to get by within their ranks. Del would be furious, sure, but she'd get over it on the way to the refrigerator in their new, warm apartment. Maybe. Anyway, it didn't matter now. In the past few weeks her distaste for the ChurchState had grown to near revulsion. Although Wylie couldn't really say why, she knew she'd never sign.

They drove up to the entrance of the Magnolia Hotel, fancy even by Committed standards. Wylie laughed as they passed a few rows of broken-down heaps amid the self-driving hydrocars that had more amenities than Wylie's whole apartment. She even spotted a few aircars and wished she'd seen them land.

"Valet parking," Darwin said. "They really pull out all the stops."

"We might as well enjoy it," Wylie answered, stepping out of the car.

"True. Milady?" Darwin offered his hand and Wylie took it. They promenaded up the steps, through the gilded glass doors and into the lobby of the magnificently adorned building. Wylie stopped and stared, mouth open. The white tile floors reflected the light of the crystal chandeliers hanging from the high ceiling. Marble pillars supported circular balconies scalloped along the edges like flower petals. Vases taller than Wylie mingled with potted palm trees and tables overflowing with fresh flowers. Everything about the space was opulent and inviting.

"Do people really live like this?" asked Wylie.

An attendant in a tight-fitting red tube dress rushed toward them. Her dark hair was so shiny and sleek that Wylie half expected to see her reflection in it.

"Good evening," the attendant said brightly. "Are you here for the ChurchState event?"

"How can you tell?" Wylie asked.

The attendant smiled, the shade of her lipstick matching her dress perfectly. "May I take your coat?"

Wylie pulled the ragged parka close around her. "No thank you, I'll keep it. I wouldn't want to lose such priceless garb."

"I assure you, it will be safe. All our cloakrooms are carefully monitored . . . " The attendant noticed the look on Wylie's face and trailed off.

"Just point us in the right direction," said Darwin.

"Certainly. You want the Constantine Ballroom. Take the hallway to your left, through the double doors. Someone will direct you from there."

"You didn't have to mock her," Darwin said as they walked away.

"Couldn't resist. I hope the food is good. I'm starving."

"It will be. You know their mantra: 'Feed the people, keep the people.'"

"I've never heard that, but it doesn't surprise me. You know a lot more about them than I do. Delores tried to keep me as far from the ChurchState as possible."

"She did you a favor. Believe me, I know more than I want to know, thanks to Gramps."

They walked through the double doors and, as promised, more attendants led them into a glittering ballroom. After Darwin and Wylie pressed their thumbs to a pad and checked twice to make sure their attendance was noted, they were free to wander for a few minutes until the program began.

"What, no balloons?" Darwin said, but Wylie didn't answer. She was overtaken by the aroma of roasted meat. She couldn't remember the last time she'd had a bit of meat—probably months ago, and it was even longer since she'd eaten something green. She tried to make out the other smells coming from the food table. Melted butter and freshly baked bread for sure, and there was something else. Almost overpowered by the platters of juicy meat, fresh vegetables, and warm, crusty bread that would soon be dinner, the delicate aroma of sweet cream and pastry wafted through the air and made her eyes roll back in anticipation. Wylie ignored the shimmering lights and sparkling people dressed in tuxedoes and evening gowns. She hardly noticed the symphony orchestra at the side of the ballroom and the rows of ostentatious gold chairs facing a white marble podium at the front. She headed straight for the food table, ready to dive in.

She was stopped in her tracks by a waiter in a white jacket and red bowtie.

"Sorry, Miss. Dinner will be served after the presentation. Please take a seat. We're about to begin."

Of course. People were more susceptible when they were hungry, and from the look of it, she was not the only hungry person here. Although not normally inclined toward violence, Wylie might have punched the waiter in the face if Darwin hadn't taken her arm. She groaned and let him guide her to her seat as the music began.

"Please rise and join us in the National Anthem," said a smiling master of ceremonies with slicked back hair and perfect posture. Above his head a holo of the stars and stripes appeared in red, white, and blue, superimposed over a 3-D cross. Wylie stood, still looking longingly at the food table. She noticed that an older man to her left remained seated. Two guards appeared out of nowhere and approached the man, speaking quietly. Wylie couldn't hear what they were saying, but she could imagine. Failure to stand during the National Anthem was a high crime against the ChurchState—every school kid knew that, Committed or not. Even Delores, with all her revolutionary venom, had instructed Wylie to stand if she was ever in the vicinity of the Anthem being played. "Stop everything and stand, and put your right hand on your heart," she'd said. "That's one battle we won't win, and it's not worth prison. Remember, you can be sitting on the inside."

Wylie was sitting on the inside as the music got louder, but the man to her left was still sitting on the outside and refused to budge. Wylie knew what was coming. She tried not to look, but the scene was within her peripheral vision, so she found herself an unwilling witness to what happened next. The armed guards pulled the man roughly from his seat, overturning several chairs in the process. As the man shouted, "Separate church and state!" the guards dragged him out of the room, literally kicking and screaming, until one of them zapped him with a stunner and he went limp. All the while the Anthem played on and the people sang along, Committed with gusto, Uncommitted weakly, everyone pretending to ignore the commotion in their midst. Six new guards took the place of those making the arrest—three in each aisle, pacing and peering into the crowd for signs of more trouble. Where do they all come from? Wylie wondered, this steady flow of Comcops and guards who were perfectly willing to take up arms against ordinary people like her. They were the ChurchState's muscle, their real source of authority. Why were they so angry, and did they really buy into the ChurchState's rhetoric, or was it the quest for power that drove them? Why were they so willing to set aside basic human decency to do the ChurchState's bidding? Why, why, why. Maybe Delores was right. There is no why. There's only what.

Finally, the Anthem ended and the orchestra went into a different song that Wylie had never heard before. The melody seemed to echo notes from a distant past. The words flashed on the backdrop of the flag-draped cross, one line at a time:

> Oh for a thousand flags to wave,
> To show our deepest pride,
> In God and Country, bound to save,
> From sin's encroaching tide.

> He breaks the power of untamed mind
> That broken lives create,
> Oh glory! For now, humankind
> May serve our God and State!

> My gracious Country and my God,
> In this, your finest hour,
> Help us to spread the word abroad,
> Of Reclamation power!

The last line was shouted, Committed arms outstretched. The song ended with a loud, long chord that gave people the chance to erupt into applause.

"Amen, amen," the MC said, nodding with eyes closed and hands raised. "We give glory to the creator, who made heaven and earth and our great country." Wylie looked around as the shouts and applause continued, wondering how long this would go on and what to expect next. Twenty-odd frail looking Uncommitted were interspersed within the wildly enthusiastic crowd, assuming the well-practiced position of social invisibility. Head down, no eye contact, arms hanging limply at sides, shoulders slumped. Basically, try to shrink and make yourself as small as possible and hope that no one notices you. Wylie knew it well. Today, though, she didn't feel like shrinking. She stood up straight and surveyed the crowd until her eyes landed on a young girl who looked awfully familiar. She was small and slight enough to fade into her surroundings, but Wylie recognized the kid from the meds dispensary with a woman slouched next to her, probably her mom. Funny to run into her again, Wylie thought. The kid was too young to sign the Statement, but if the mom signed now the kid would be fostered in, and life would take a sharp turn for the better. The girl glanced up at Wylie with a glimmer of recognition and a look in her eyes that put a tiny dent in Wylie's resolve. As much as she hated the coercion of the ChurchState, this kid deserved better.

Wylie hoped the mom would sign. She glanced down and noticed the tear in the knee of her jeans had grown another inch.

When the noise finally died down, the MC motioned for everyone to sit. Then began a steady flow of speaker after toothy speaker, each slicker than the one before, and all with the same message: join the fold and the ChurchState will take care of you as a mother hen cares for her chicks. Wylie thought of the Avian and snickered, but a warning look from Darwin reminded her where she was.

After what seemed like an eternity, finally, finally, finally, the speeches were over.

The MC announced, "Those who have made the blessed choice to sign the Statement of Commitment and join their ChurchState family, please come forward." Almost all of the Uncommitted stood and moved forward, including the little girl and her mom. Wylie smiled and nodded as she passed, and the girl seemed to relax a little. The Committed in the audience also moved to the front, forming a line behind the new recruits and placing their hands on their shoulders and backs as the MC led them in a very long, heartfelt prayer. At the side of the room, waiters were unveiling platters of food in preparation for the meal. Wylie's stomach gave a loud rumble. Her mouth was watering and she didn't know how much longer she could wait. She thought of making a bolt toward the food, but she knew she'd never get past the guards.

"We've been here forever," she whispered to Darwin.

"Just seems like forever."

While the MC prayed, a young woman dressed in a business suit went down the line of the new Committed, scanning their fingerprints.

"They're part of the ChurchState now," Darwin said. "No turning back."

"Your Dad turned back," Wylie said.

"Yeah, and look what happened to him. Six months in prison for breach of contract. If it weren't for my grandpa helping us on the sly, who knows what would have happened."

Wylie couldn't argue with that. Even among the Uncommitted, it helped to know someone.

After another interminable stretch of time, the MC said a loud "Amen!" and announced that dinner was served. The newly Committed were asked to go first to celebrate the wise and anointed choice they had made. The rest of the Committed followed, and finally, Wylie and the other remaining reprobates were ushered to the back of the line. The little girl and her mother, who'd been at the front, had piled their plates high. On the way back to their seats the girl saw Wylie and stopped.

"She died," she said, looking up.

Wylie stooped down to hear. "Huh?"

"The lady died."

Wylie looked up at the mom, who shrugged and shook her head.

"What lady?" Wylie asked.

"The lady at the dispensary, that day when I saw you there. After you left, she died."

"Oh. I'm sorry you had to see that."

"It's okay. Thank you for helping me."

Wylie straightened up and touched the girl's shoulder as the mom moved closer.

"Come on, Robin," she said, "let's sit down before our food gets cold." She led the girl to their seats where they were joined by their new sponsor, a young, female Committed who talked a blue streak. The mother nodded, but neither she nor her daughter took their focus off the food in front of them.

Wylie shifted from one foot to the other, watching the waitstaff appear with full platters of steaming food and then disappear back through a side door that, presumably, led to the kitchen. One of the waiters looked vaguely familiar. He was a bulky sort of guy, and it drove Wylie crazy that she couldn't quite place him. It wasn't his face, exactly, but the way he moved that triggered something in Wylie's memory. He could be one of the missionaries who'd chased her, but Wylie didn't think so. He deposited his platter, spilling a little gravy on the white tablecloth, and skittered away. Just as he reached the door something dropped from under his jacket.

"Is that . . . a feather?" Wylie asked Darwin.

"What? Where?"

"Over there by the door to the kitchen."

"Oh . . . yeah, looks like it. Do you think they're plucking the chickens themselves? Wow, that's commitment."

Normally, Darwin's absurdity got a laugh, but Wylie was concentrating, trying to put two and two together. The bulky waiter, the feather— they added up to something just outside Wylie's grasp. She watched as the waiter burst through the door and flew back into the room, this time not carrying a platter. He threw off his jacket, revealing a feathered vest, and headed straight for Robin.

"Avian," Wylie gasped.

"She's not yours to give!" shrieked the man, grabbing Robin by the arm and pulling her to her feet. The mom jumped up, too, and both plates crashed to the floor. Mother and father began a tug of war with their daughter as the rope.

"Daddy, no!" the little girl cried out in dismay. The Committed sponsor sprang into action, throwing herself at the Avian and breaking his hold on the girl. The guards, who'd been hovering nearby, rushed forward just as the Avian shook off the young woman.

"I mean no harm," he said, putting his hands in the air. "Just let me leave with my daughter. I have legal custody."

"This is your only chance to come quietly," said one of the guards. Wylie was shocked—these guards weren't known for their patience. Stun now, ask questions later (or probably not at all) was their usual modus operandi and it served their purposes with mechanical efficiency. Maybe the palpable fear of the newly Committed child looking on had reminded this guard how to be human.

"Okay," said the Avian, reaching into his vest. "But let me show you my custody order." With birdlike quickness he pulled out a claw shaped knife and lunged for the mother. They both went down, rolling around in spilled filet mignon and cheddar mashed potatoes, with the Avian ending up on top. Only a second later the guards grabbed him, but the damage was done. When they lifted him off the woman it was clear that the blood he was covered in wasn't his own. The knife slipped out of his hand and fell to the floor. The Avian followed, stunned unconscious and swiftly dragged from the room.

"Mommy!" Robin cried, staring at her mother in shock. Blood from the woman's thigh had soaked through her pants and was forming a puddle on the shiny wooden floor. Amazingly, the mother was conscious and trying to lift her head. No one in the room came near to help. Only the little girl knelt at her mother's side.

"Stand back, everyone," the MC commanded through his microphone. "Keep a safe distance. Her blood hasn't been tested yet. Professional help is on the way."

Wylie had seen this before. The Committed didn't fear much, but exposure to the potential diseases of the Uncommitted absolutely terrified them. Their emergency medical teams wore hazmat suits when (and if) they arrived at the scene of an accident in Uncommitted territory. It was as if the Uncommitted were . . . the word "unclean" popped into Wylie's head and she thought of the last tape she'd viewed in the basement of the old campus library.

Robin took her mother's head in her lap and met Wylie's eyes. "Please," she pleaded. "Help her."

The guards and Committed attendants turned their backs to the wounded woman and with arms spread wide, herded the crowd away. Only Wylie and Darwin ignored them and slipped through a gap in the human barrier. Darwin ripped off his grandfather's sports coat and used it to cover the leg wound while Wylie knelt by Robin and took her hand.

"Thank you," the mom whispered. "Please take care of my daughter. I only signed for her sake."

"I know," Wylie said. "Hang on. Help is coming."

Darwin was pressing down on her leg with both hands now, looking grim. "He must have hit an artery." He turned toward the crowd and yelled, "We need help here. Where's the ambulance?"

"On its way," someone answered, but no one came closer to help.

"It won't get here in time," Darwin said, up to his elbows in blood and despair.

"Please," Robin said again. "Help her."

"I'm doing the best I can," Darwin answered.

"No," Robin said to Wylie. "You help her. Like you helped me, before."

Against all rational reasoning, Wylie understood. She slid down next to Darwin and reached toward the wound. "Let me try."

Darwin didn't look up. "It won't help. I'm already pressing as hard as I can. She's bleeding out."

"I know. I might be crazy, but let me try," Wylie said again. The woman groaned and closed her eyes, losing consciousness.

"Please!" Robin begged.

"Ambulance is two minutes out," someone called from the crowd. "Major traffic disturbance, but they just took flight. They'll be here soon."

"Not soon enough," Darwin said, nodding toward the spreading crimson puddle.

Wylie slipped her hands under Darwin's and he relaxed a little, letting her cover the wound. She pressed gently and felt the wet, sticky blood seep into her pores. "Move away," she told Darwin, and as soon as he did Wylie felt the shock, bigger and more intense than before. But this time the jolt didn't propel her backwards; instead, it exploded in a burst of heat that radiated through her fingers to her hands and up her arms, pulling her downward as if she and the woman had entered a bubble of denser gravity. Wylie would not have been able to lift her hands if she'd tried, but she didn't try, because the warmth flowing through her felt tender and soothing. She closed her eyes, allowing whatever this was to do its work. Something she'd never felt before welled up from a place inside herself she'd never been, even for a visit. Not a feeling, exactly, it was more like a presence that was herself and not herself, drawing her in and linking them together. As she knelt, covered with blood and surrounded by panic, the situation desperate, Wylie felt peace. She was at the same time alone and not alone. She opened her eyes, looked past the chaos, and sensed herself encompassed in a sad, knowing smile.

"Wylie, they're here!" Darwin said.

The med team had appeared next to her, although she hadn't heard them come in. As usual, they were dressed from head to toe in full protective gear, complete with face masks and safety goggles.

"Okay, we'll take over," one of them said, reaching toward the wound. "Let's see what we've got here."

Wylie didn't move.

"You can ease up," the medic said more forcefully, but Wylie didn't know if she could. She felt stuck; disengaging herself from the woman now felt like amputating a limb.

"I, I don't think I can," she stammered.

Although Wylie couldn't see the medic's face, she could hear the scorn in his voice.

"This woman is a newly Committed and is under our jurisdiction. Now move out of the way and let us do our jobs, unless you want to be arrested for interfering with official ChurchState business."

The crowd stepped back and waited in anticipation. Three arrests in one night had to be some kind of record. Darwin took Wylie by the shoulders and gently pulled her away.

"Come on, Wy, you've done all you can." As soon as she felt Darwin's touch, Wylie's connection to the woman dissipated. She removed her hands from the laceration and stood, backing away from the scene.

The medic peeled away Darwin's blood-soaked jacket and examined the woman's injury.

"This doesn't look too bad," he said confidently. "Looks like the bleeding has stopped."

"Probably missed the artery," said his partner. "All this fuss for a flesh wound."

"A flesh wound?" Darwin said, incredulous. "How do you explain all this blood?"

The medic ignored Darwin. "Let's get her on the stretcher," he said.

The bleeding woman had come around and held on to Wylie's sleeve as the stretcher passed.

"Thank you," she whispered.

"Come along, we don't have all night," said the medic, but the woman didn't let go.

"What about my daughter?" she asked.

The Committed sponsor who'd been assigned to them earlier rushed forward, placing her arm around Robin's shoulders. "We'll take care of her. She's one of us now." She met Wylie's eyes with a cold, dismissive stare.

Up until that moment Wylie had been feeling strong, as if something beyond herself was filling her with a calm, steady energy. But when the stretcher moved away her tie to the energy was cut like an umbilical cord and she went limp.

"Oh, no you don't!" Darwin said, catching her before she hit the ground. "I had a feeling that would happen. Let's get you home."

Darwin half dragged, half carried Wylie to the door, passing the now empty food tables.

"Wait," Wylie mumbled, only partly aware. "We never did get to eat."

8

The sight of her daughter being carried into the house, semiconscious, was enough to get Delores out of bed for the first time in weeks. She even ventured into the kitchen to heat up a can of tomato soup and brought it to Wylie in a cracked mug with no handle.

"Mom, I'm okay," Wylie said, coughing as the rough, red liquid chafed her throat. With Darwin on one side, Monty on the other, and Delores hovering above, the small living room was getting smaller by the minute. "Give me some space to breathe."

Delores peered into Wylie's face like a pilot reading a map. Wylie sipped her soup and stared back.

"Okay," Delores said finally, and went back to bed.

"So much for motherly concern," said Darwin.

"I really am fine. It was different this time. I mean, it took more out of me, but I'm getting my strength back quicker."

"By 'it' you mean your power to do miracles, I presume?" asked Darwin. Wylie understood perfectly the doubt in his voice.

"Whatever it is. You saw what happened."

Darwin nodded. "I saw something happen. You stopped that woman's bleeding, but I'm not sure how. And you got a funny look, like you were in another world."

"It felt like that. I'm not sure I can describe it. It was like . . . " Wylie thought of the intangible presence she'd felt and let her voice trail off. Even if she could find the words to make Darwin understand, she wasn't sure she wanted to. She wasn't ready to share her experience, at least not yet. It was private, just between her and—who? What? Some kind of spirit or ghost, maybe? She shook off the absurd notion.

"Anyway, I'm fine. You can go."

Reluctantly, Darwin left and Wylie stayed put on the couch, snuggling next to Monty in the deepest, most peaceful night's sleep of her life. She dreamed that it was spring and she was raking up the remains of wet leaves to make way for the tulips poking their heads out all around the campus. A pale-brown cardinal flitted through the warm air, carrying twigs and grass to the low branch of a maple tree while her bright red companion looked on. Wylie was absorbed in a long, vivid conversation during the dream, but when she woke she couldn't remember who she'd been talking with or what they'd been saying. She only remembered how she'd felt, like she'd been with someone who knew and loved her well. For the first time her internal question, the unending *why* that ached faintly at the edge her thoughts, took the embryonic shape of *who*.

"Wake up, Sleeping Beauty," Delores yelled from the bedroom. "Sharmila called. She thinks that woman who's living with her is about to pop. Wants to know if you and Darwin can drive her to the noncom clinic."

Wylie had just been dreaming of Sharmila. Or had she? Her thinking was still fuzzy. She tried to remember the woman who lived with Sharmila. What was her name? Mary, Maria . . . Mara, that was it. Wylie stretched and dragged herself into the kitchen, where Monty was waiting beside his empty bowl.

"I know, you're hungry." She shook the half-empty bag of dry dog food and poured some, wondering if they'd have the money to buy more when it ran out. She made herself a piece of toast and since there was no butter, no jelly, and definitely no honey, she ate it dry in Del's room, remembering the feast she'd missed out on last night.

"You're famous," Delores said, pointing to the screen. Del had the sound off, but Wylie saw herself kneeling at the wounded woman's side. The caption beneath the picture read, *More Uncommitted terror!*

"They've been running this all morning," Delores said. "Luckily they didn't mention your name. Probably didn't want to give an Uncommitted credit. Nice work, by the way," Del added, as if Wylie had refinished a cabinet instead of saving a woman's life.

Wylie moved closer to the screen. There she was, hovering over the injured woman, eyes closed and hands on the bleeding leg. She tried to recall the otherworldly feeling she'd had and the warm energy she'd felt flowing through her, but the feeling had faded as she slept and she couldn't summon it back. Now she was shocked at the image of a ragged, ordinary-looking Uncommitted girl who happened to be in the right place at the right time.

The scene cut back to the reporter and at the bottom of the screen the words *curfew instituted* flashed.

"That's new," Delores said, and turned up the sound.

"The attack was carried out by a terrorist group known as 'the Avian.' Driven by hate for AmeriChristianity, the group is dedicated to disrupting

ChurchState events whenever possible. Terrorism experts believe the stabbing was meant to serve as a warning for anyone thinking of signing the Statement of Commitment."

"Well, they got the group right, anyway," Wylie muttered.

"Avian, Extraterrestrials, Necromancers, and who knows how many more?" said Del. "These crackpot groups are all the same, looking for a way out and too crazy and disorganized to pose any real threat to the ChurchState."

"That may be true of the others," Wylie said, "but the Avian seem pretty organized to me. Their nests are better stocked than most noncom clinics." She realized immediately that she'd said too much and hoped Delores wouldn't notice her sudden expertise on a group she'd supposedly never encountered. But she needn't have worried. As usual, Delores was too preoccupied to really listen to anything her daughter had to say. "Shush, I want to hear about the curfew" she responded gruffly.

Wylie wondered why someone who never left the house would worry about a curfew, but she turned her attention to the broadcast.

"This just in from ChurchState authorities: Due to this latest act of terrorism, effective immediately all Uncommitted must observe a 6:00 p.m. to six a.m. curfew. Any Uncommitted caught on public streets or property between those hours will be arrested and duly processed. No exceptions.'"

Wylie knew what "duly processed" meant. When the Comcops picked up Uncommitted, they might not be heard from for months.

The broadcaster continued, leaning toward the camera with a look of renewed intensity. "And that's not all, folks. We've just received word that the Appointees have called a special session to discuss the citizenship status of Uncommitted. As you know, it's long been debated whether or not those who refuse to align themselves with the ChurchState should enjoy the benefits of citizenship. The Appointees hope for a definitive answer soon."

"Benefits of citizenship? That's a joke!" Delores spit, turning down the sound. For once, she looked fully present and concerned. "You're going to need to be careful, Wylie. I don't see how you and Darwin can get this woman . . . "

"Mara. Her name is Mara."

" . . . *Mara* to the noncom clinic and be back before 6:00 p.m. It's almost noon and the clinic is nearly a three-hour drive."

Noon, already? Wylie hadn't realized she'd slept that long. "If we hurry we can just make it," she said.

"If you stop to eat or even go to the bathroom, you'll break curfew. And if the Appointees act quickly, you could be declared a non-citizen while you're in police custody. That would not be good. This is not your problem, Wylie. You've helped enough. Stay home today."

"It's Sharmila's problem and that makes it my problem. We'll be fine." Wylie reached for the phone to call Darwin.

Delores sighed. "Mother Teresa calls and you answer. Be careful."

Wylie had no idea who Mother Teresa was, but before she left she didn't mention that Darwin couldn't make it. She'd have to get Mara to the clinic on her own.

* * *

Wylie had driven Darwin's car a few times before but never on the highway and never with a pregnant woman moaning in the backseat. On the way out of town Mara had cursed at every Committed hospital and birthing center they'd passed, all five of them. None, of course, would take Mara without ChurchState credentials. Wylie drove as close to the speed limit as she could without breaking it, knowing that Darwin's noncom license plate made her a likely target for the Comcops. She'd brought Monty along, not because he'd be any help, but because at least he'd be company on the drive home. True to form, he slept soundly next to her, the steady pattern of his snores interrupted now and then by Mara's moans and pants.

"How much further?" Mara asked.

Wylie glanced at the geo display. "We're about halfway. You gonna make it?"

Mara frowned. "What if I don't?"

Wylie had asked to be polite. She had no idea what to do if Mara and the baby couldn't wait. "Yeah, sorry."

"It's okay. I should have said something sooner. It's just that my other kids took forever to come and I didn't want to hang around that filthy clinic any longer than necessary. If she weren't breech, I would have had her at home."

"Breech? You mean, feet first?"

"Yes, at least last time I was checked, which was a month ago. She may have turned by now, but I couldn't be sure."

So not only might Wylie need to deliver a baby, but a breech baby at that. Unfortunately, the two-hour mandatory first aid class Wylie took last year did not cover childbirth (or anything else, for that matter, since the teacher never bothered to assign any work). Sharmila would know what to do. Why hadn't Wylie stayed with the kids and let Sharmila do the driving? It was too late now, so Wylie hit the gas harder and with a guilty twinge turned up the music to drown out Mara's groans. The next several minutes were the longest of her life, but at least the traffic wasn't bad going in this direction. Across the median she saw cars and trucks in the noncom lane backed up for miles, but she couldn't worry about that yet. Maybe traffic would clear by the time she headed home.

"Not too much further," she said finally.

"Good. Contractions are two minutes apart," Mara answered. She was down on all fours across the back seat, wagging her tail like Monty begging for a walk.

"Are you okay?" Wylie asked.

"Yoga pose. Helps with the pain. You'll find out when you have kids." Mara closed her eyes and took a long, deep breath.

If Wylie's jaw hadn't ached from clenching throughout this hellish journey, she would have laughed. Having kids was not something in her Uncommitted future, and if she hadn't known that before, she sure knew it now. She glanced back at Mara, who had pressed the top half of her body flat into the stained, torn upholstery and was somewhere between a pant and a yowl. No, Wylie would never do that to herself or to a child. She had Delores to take care of, and that was quite enough.

When, at last, they exited the highway and approached the clinic, Wylie was alarmed at how desolate the entrance appeared. For a brief second, she panicked. What if this clinic had shut down like so many noncom facilities?

"Wait here," she told Mara, and then realized the silliness of her command. Mara, now groaning from a fetal position, was clearly not going anywhere. As Wylie jumped out she heard a gurgle and a splash.

"Hurry," Mara moaned. "My water just broke!" Wylie looked in through the window. The backseat of Darwin's car would never be the same.

As she feared, the clinic was locked. She cupped her hands around her eyes and peered through the glass into the lobby where, thankfully, she saw a female attendant dressed in white sitting behind a cluttered desk. The woman was punching at an outdated tablet and either didn't notice or chose to ignore Wylie.

"I need help!" Wylie screamed, banging on the glass. "I've got a woman about to give birth!"

Barely looking up, the attendant pointed to the side of the doorway, where Wylie noticed an intercom. She hit the button and yelled again, "Help! I need a stretcher, right away! Someone is having a baby in my car!"

The attendant glared at Wylie. "No stretchers available," she said through pursed lips. "You'll have to get her in here yourself."

Wylie felt anger brewing but she knew that arguing would just make matters worse. They were at the mercy of this ChurchState tool who could, and probably would, use any excuse to claim that Wylie was dangerous and deny them entrance. She flew back to the car and hauled Mara out, almost buckling under the weight of the leaking, panting woman.

"Come on, you can make it!" she said, dragging Mara to the door, which was still locked. With her free arm she banged again. "Let us in!" Mara cradled her swollen belly and wailed.

Again, the attendant pointed to the intercom.

"Are you kidding?" Wylie shouted. "Let us in!"

Like an instant replay at a football praise rite, the attendant moved in slow motion. Finally, she pushed the control and the doors slid open. "Just like an Uncommitted," the attendant complained as Wylie dragged Mara in and deposited her into a wheelchair. "They expect us to jump every time they pop one out."

* * *

Once the clinic staff had almost reluctantly wheeled Mara away, Wylie was instructed to leave the premises immediately. But as much as she wanted to get out of there and safely home before curfew, she had to make sure Mara was okay. Otherwise, what would she tell Sharmila? She hung around, using the bathroom and pretending to look for a snack machine, until she heard the cries of Mara's new baby. She peeked her head behind the screen just long enough to catch a glimpse of mother and child gazing into each other's eyes. Wylie was shocked at how Mara's countenance had gone from anger and agony to pure bliss in the span of a few brief moments.

Wylie checked the wall clock—3:15—and ran out of the building to the car, only to find that a security guard, still lurking a few feet away, had plastered yellow warning stickers across the car's side windows.

"What's this?" Wylie asked, careful not to make eye contact.

"No parking zone," the guard replied coolly, pointing to the sign.

"Where were you when we needed help?" Wylie muttered. "You people have no heart." She threw herself into the car and slammed the door behind her, hoping the guard hadn't heard her risky outburst.

"And you're no help, either," she said to Monty, who was trying to lick her face. In all fairness, there was nothing Monty could have done, but Wylie was too irate to care. She brushed him away and drove off. It would be a miracle if she made it home before curfew, but her only choice was to hit the gas and hope for the best.

Traffic in the noncom lane was moving for now, but Wylie knew how quickly that could change. As if she needed reminding, every few minutes she passed a holo that flashed a curfew warning. *Violators will be prosecuted!* it screamed in angry red letters. Guess they forgot the skull and crossbones, Wylie thought, gripping the steering wheel a little tighter.

About twenty minutes in Monty began to whimper and Wylie realized she hadn't let him out to pee. "Sorry, boy," she said. "You're gonna have to hold it." Monty answered with some pitiful scratching at the door, and the thought of returning Darwin's car with a soaked backseat, stickered up windows, and a urine drenched front was just too much.

"Okay, okay, next exit. I should have left you home with Del" she sighed. Just then an aircar took flight next to her and she knew there was trouble up ahead. Regulations only allowed highway takeoffs in extreme circumstances, which, for the Committed, included the inconvenience of a traffic slowdown. Sure enough, the geo told her to expect delays ahead. Wylie tried not to think of what life would be like if she could fly away whenever she needed.

The crawl toward the exit was excruciating, and Wylie realized that at this rate she'd never make it home before curfew. Maybe after their pit stop they'd do better on back roads. Although it was too early for dusk, low clouds had created a dark haze. A storm was coming, and why not? A storm would be a fitting addition to her perfect day. More aircars took flight around them, clearing up the Committed lanes for those still on the ground. How ridiculous that Wylie wasn't allowed to scoot over and pick up some speed, but she knew better than to try, and with the new shoulder alarms in place, stopping on the side of the highway was also out of the question. A distress signal would bring Comcops scurrying like cockroaches to trash, and the result could be far worse than some dog pee in Darwin's car. There was no other choice but to plug along until finally she exited the highway to a narrow country road. The pending storm had darkened the mid-afternoon skies so that it could have been night. Wylie had no idea where the meandering road would take her. She drove through a woodsy area for a few minutes before she came to a safe place to stop. Nothing looked familiar, which wasn't surprising since she'd rarely traveled beyond the noncom zones.

"Pee fast," she said, opening the passenger side door. Monty jumped out and complied, but instead of jumping back into the car he took off in the other direction, into the woods and out of sight.

"Monty, come back here!" Wylie shouted, cursing the dog, the day, and anything else she could think of. When he didn't respond, she ran after him, not even stopping to lock the car doors. She tromped through the trees, following Monty's increasingly distant bark. She hadn't taken Del's phone, but tucked in her pocket was a pink flashlight pen that she'd found on the ground outside a dentist's office. She used the tiny pinprick of light it generated to find her way through the thicket under the ever-darkening sky. The further she moved into the woods, the more she worried that she'd never be able to find her way back, and she'd certainly never make it home before curfew now. Still, abandoning Monty was out of the question. What had gotten into him today? Monty had not left her side of his own volition since he came to her as a tiny puppy. Wylie had the feeling the dog was running to something, although what, she couldn't imagine.

The barking stopped suddenly, and Wylie slowed her pace. She sensed someone or something a few yards ahead. The pen light chose to die at that moment (of course), but before it did she caught a glimpse of a towering silhouette against the dark sky. She stopped dead in her tracks, heart pounding. Should she run? Somehow the idea of being chased through the woods in the dark seemed worse than facing whatever was before her, so she stood her ground and waited. The rustling of a bird taking off through the brush made her jump, but she steadied herself and stared straight ahead, squinting to make out the figure that was approaching. As it got closer a light shone at her feet and Monty came bounding toward her, greeting her as if he hadn't seen her in years.

"There you are!" Wylie exclaimed. Relief flooded through her just as the rain began in torrents. She grabbed Monty's collar and waited for the dark figure to come closer.

"I guess this is your dog," said a gruff voice. "The way he came running, I thought someone was in trouble out here." The man took a spare flashlight from his pocket and handed it to Wylie.

"Thanks." Through the rain Wylie could make out a tall, broad man with short dark hair and a scruffy beard. "Do you mind if I take this back to my car?" Wylie asked, motioning at the flashlight. Just to be safe, she stopped short of admitting she didn't think she'd be able to find her way without it. Never give more information than absolutely necessary, Delores had always said, and never appear weak.

"Sure," said the man, "but you might be better waiting out the storm in my barn."

Wylie took a step back. "That's okay. We'll wait in the car."

The man looked her up and down. "Uncommitted, right?"

Wylie nodded, annoyed at him for being able to read her so easily and annoyed at herself for being so easy to read. "Guess it's obvious."

"Not sure where you're headed, but if you stay on the road the Comcops will surely spot you. How 'bout this—once you get to the car, pull ahead slowly until you see a path on your right that'll take you to the edge of my field. If you came straight through the woods, it can't be more than a few hundred feet further up. No one will bother you there, and as long as you stay on my property the Comcops will leave you alone. Tell them Ed gave you permission to be there. They all know me."

The Comcops knew him by name—was that supposed to make Wylie trust him? That's the Committed, she thought, just one big, happy family. Still, she had to admit Ed's plan sounded better than taking her chances on the highway, where she'd surely be detected and pulled over. Unless, of course, this guy was luring her in to something worse with his promise of safety.

"I'll think about it," Wylie said.

"One more thing." The man reached inside his coat and Wylie thought, here it comes, some unspeakable perversion against a shabby Uncommitted girl was about to unfold, with the Comcops securely tucked into this man's front pocket. But the man retrieved a water bottle, a handful of protein bars, and an apple. "Take these."

It had been a long time since the piece of dry toast that morning, and even longer since she'd eaten before that. She looked at Monty, who was chomping down on a stick.

"I have no money."

"Not asking for any."

"And nothing to trade."

"I know." He held out the food. Reluctantly, Wylie took it.

"Thanks again," she mumbled, unsure if it was adequate. No stranger, especially a Committed, had ever given her something for nothing, and she had no idea how to respond.

"Is there someone I should call to let them know you're okay?"

Delores. Wylie hadn't thought how worried she'd be.

"Here," the man said, handing Wylie his phone. "Plug in the number and I'll call when I get back to the house."

Wylie agreed, keeping one eye on the man and the other on the phone. "Thanks," she said again as she gave it back.

"Better be off now, before the hail starts."

Wylie turned to go but the man had one more thing to say.

"We're not all the same, you know, us Committed. Some of us actually serve the one we're committed to." With that he was gone. Wylie ran back the way she'd come, thankful for the light to guide her way. She slept snuggled with Monty until the faded orange sunrise told her it was time to go home.

9

A pile of mildewed books fell to the floor when Darwin dragged a dusty chalkboard past them. Wylie didn't look up, intent on her search through the box of videos. She was literally looking for a miracle. Her hand fell on a tape labeled "John 11."

Darwin scrounged around for a piece of chalk, opening and closing the drawers of a rusty metal desk until he found what he was looking for.

"Let's go over this one more time," he said, chalk raised, and Wylie pictured him as the teacher he might have been in a different world, or could be in this world, if he signed the Statement of Commitment. With his smarts and charisma, Darwin could choose any career he wanted. All it would take was the flick of a pen and the betrayal of all he believed.

"We'll make a list of what's happened so far." Darwin drew two columns. He labeled the first "Tape."

"First, there was the husband and wife who dropped dead, right?"

"Ananias and Sapphira," Wylie said.

"Yeah, right. Okay." Darwin wrote the names on the board. "I'm not sure how you spell it, but no matter. So, they get struck down because . . . what? They didn't give enough money to the church? If that doesn't sound like ChurchState propaganda, I don't know what does."

Wylie tried to remember what they'd heard on that first recording. It seemed so long ago now. "It wasn't like that," she said. "It wasn't about the money. It was that they lied about it, remember?"

"Okay, whatever. You said that after each tape, something happened to you, right?"

"Not just something. Something weird, like some kind of power came out of me. That first day, when we watched the class about Ananias and Sapphira, I went to the meds dispensary. The med-rep was trying to cheat this kid—"

"The same kid that turned up at the recruitment dinner, right?"

"Yeah, her. So, I spoke up. A minute later I touched the med-rep by accident, and she dropped dead, just like that."

Darwin labeled the second column "Real Life" and under it wrote, "Med-rep drops dead."

Wylie placed the tape she'd found in the console and picked up the remote.

"I told you all this," she said. "What's the point of going over it again?" The remote seemed to grow heavier in her hands.

"A little patience, please. What was the second tape about?"

"About Moses getting water from a rock. And after that we went to Sharmila's and fixed the pipe."

"Except we didn't fix the pipe. It just started flowing again after you touched it." Darwin's voice grew serious. "I was there for that one."

He wrote, "Water from rock" and next to it, "Water from pipe."

Wylie inhaled sharply and dropped the remote. She'd known something extraordinary was happening to her, but until now she hadn't fully grasped the connection between watching the old class recordings and the events that followed. She sat on an unopened box with a thud.

"What's wrong?" Darwin asked.

"This just got real."

"Do you want to stop?"

As if he would—it was obvious that stopping now was the last thing on Darwin's mind. He was poised on the balls of his feet like a rocket about to blast into the open sky. Wylie shook her head. "You know, all my life I wanted things to change. I'd say they're changing now, wouldn't you?"

Darwin nodded. "It's beyond crazy, but I've seen it with my own eyes. What was the next tape about? I can't remember."

"I watched that one alone. It was about this woman who was bleeding for twelve years. She touched Jesus' clothes—his garment, they called it—and the bleeding stopped."

"And right after that we went to the dinner and you stopped that woman's bleeding." The weight of realization brought Darwin back to earth. They were silent for a moment.

"What did it feel like, when it happened?" Darwin asked finally. "I mean, when you were doing it. Before you collapsed into a driveling mess."

"It felt—good, I guess. Warm. I don't think I can describe it." She remembered the feeling that someone else was there, maybe the same someone who showed up in her dream later. But she couldn't tell Darwin that. Or she didn't want to.

"What do you think this means?" Wylie asked. "And what's next?"

"No clue. But let's watch and find out." Darwin picked up the remote and pointed it at the screen.

"Our passage today," said Dr. Michaels, "is, in my opinion, one of the most important in the New Testament. We're going to look at John, chapter 11, the chapter in which Jesus raises Lazarus from the dead."

Wylie stood and took a step back, almost tripping over Monty, who was dead asleep behind her. He yelped and sat up.

Darwin pushed pause.

"What'd you do that for?" Wylie asked. "Keep going."

"You look like you're about to run screaming from the room."

Wylie considered the door and the dog, who was standing now, ears up, eager to accompany her out to the brisk, open spaces of the college. Maybe she should follow Del's longstanding advice and run. But Wylie knew that there was no running from this. Whatever it was, it would run right alongside her.

"Play it."

Dr. Michaels continued. "The gospel writer is careful to emphasize Jesus' relationship with Lazarus and his sisters, Mary and Martha. What is he trying to show us?"

After a few seconds of quiet, Abby spoke up. "Jesus loved them."

"God loves everyone," Steve said in a tone that implied that everyone was equal to no one.

"Yes, even those who interrupt," Dr. Michaels said, earning a laugh at Steve's expense. Wylie liked this guy more and more. "Go ahead, Abby. Unpack that a little more."

"Well . . . I know that God loves everyone, but that's not what I meant. Jesus loved that family like a human loves other people. Like, like I love my family, or my friends."

Dr. Michaels nodded. "Yes, we see a very real, very human love here for the family; John notes that several times. And of course, we see it in Jesus' reaction at the tomb in verse 35, everybody's favorite Bible verse. All together now—"

Dr. Michaels waved his arms like a maestro conducting a symphony as the class recited in unison, "Jesus wept!" and burst out laughing.

Wylie and Darwin exchanged puzzled glances but kept listening.

"So, in this passage, John, who, remember, was 'the apostle that Jesus loved,' works hard to show us both the humanity and deity of Jesus. He was both fully human and fully divine. Hard to wrap our brains around that, right?" Dr. Michaels paused, looking reflective. A few "Amens" were muttered from the group.

Over the years, Wylie had heard lots of ChurchState preachers on the victory broadcasts, but she'd never heard anything like this. Here was none of the usual talk of God's special love for our country. No one had mentioned how the Committed were the Chosen, preordained to reign above all earthly nations. Wylie had heard variations of the same sermon so many times that she could have preached it herself. And no matter how the sermons started, they always ended the same, with a proclamation of greatness and a call to arms to spread AmeriChristianity across the globe. The tone was cold and hard and repellent. But these tapes, this class, were different. Dr. Michaels was the opposite—he seemed warm and kind. There was something in his way, his manner, that was inviting, although Wylie wasn't exactly sure what she was being invited to. She realized her mind was wandering and focused back on the tape.

Dr. Michaels was saying, "So Jesus knows before he arrives at Bethany that Lazarus is dead. He also knows that he plans to raise Lazarus—in verse 15 he tells the disciples, 'for your sake I'm glad I wasn't there, so that you may believe.' Let's think about the exchange between Jesus and Martha. Would someone like to read verses 20 to 26?"

Steve's voice rang out and for an instant Wylie thought of the victory broadcasts again.

> "*When Martha heard that Jesus was coming,*" Steve read, "*she went out to meet him, but Mary stayed at home.*
>
> *'Lord,' Martha said to Jesus, 'if you had been here, my brother would not have died. But I know that even now God will give you whatever you ask.'*
>
> *Jesus said to her, 'Your brother will rise again.'*
>
> *Martha answered, 'I know he will rise again in the resurrection at the last day.'*
>
> *Jesus said to her, 'I am the resurrection and the life. The one who believes in me will live, even though they die; and whoever lives by believing in me will never die. Do you believe this?'*"

The question made Wylie's heart sink. No, she thought, I don't. But I couldn't sign that Statement even if I did.

"So," said Dr. Michaels, "was Jesus giving Martha the run-around? What was he trying to tell her?"

Silence.

"Let me restate that," Dr. Michaels said. "If Jesus knew he was going to raise Lazarus, why didn't he just say so?"

"Maybe," Abby answered slowly, "he was making Martha think. He was saying, 'I'm about to do something great. I'm gonna raise your brother from the dead. But remember, that's not the best thing I do. The best thing I do is give eternal life to everyone who believes.' 'Cause Lazarus was gonna die, eventually, right? We all are. So even though this was a great miracle, this raising from the dead, the bigger miracle, the more important miracle, is the resurrection we all have in Christ."

Dr. Michaels smiled broadly. "Well said, Abby. Let's read on . . ."

"Turn it off," Wylie said. "I can't listen to any more." She left the archives feeling more melancholy than ever before and asking herself why. Darwin knew enough to let her be, and only Monty bounced through the field as if their lives hadn't been shaken from the ground up.

10

Over the next few weeks Wylie tried her best to forget. At first, she'd avoided the outside world completely, worried that the bizarre recording to real-life pattern would continue, and someone would drop dead right in front of her. If that happened she didn't know what she'd do, but the idea of raising someone from the dead was beyond ridiculous, and the more she thought about it, the more outlandish it seemed. She kept to herself, not even allowing Darwin beyond the invisible barrier she'd constructed around her. As the days and nights crawled by, Wylie convinced herself that the events of the last few weeks had been some kind of melodramatic coincidence, amplified by an overactive imagination. She was just Wylie, a plain, Uncommitted girl. There was nothing special about her, and her entire life attested to the fact that there were no such things as miracles.

"Miracles do happen," the announcer of the Sunday victory broadcast said. Wylie lay at the edge of Del's bed with one hand on the old wooden headboard to stop from falling to the floor. Monty, sprawled out on his back and sound asleep, took up almost as much room as Delores, who, for once, was up, pacing back and forth in front of the screen like a leopard in a cage.

"And here to tell us about it is ChurchState correspondent, Andre Jamal. Andre, what do you have for us today?"

"Thanks, Cynthia. Today is a special day, indeed, in Reclamation news. With the passage of CS.H.R. 1011, The Committed Bill of Rights, we hope to see a return to the long-lost family values that the Founding Fathers established at the inception of our great nation."

Delores stopped pacing and stood at rapt attention.

Andre continued, "Also included in the bill is the long awaited 'Designation Clause,' requiring Uncommitted over the age of thirty to mark their status with a tattoo. Researchers believe that once Uncommitted reach thirty, the likelihood of joining the ChurchState is less than five percent while the tendency toward criminal behavior rises exponentially. This bill will protect our families and help to keep us safe."

Delores hit the off icon with the side of her fist so hard that the screen shook before it went blank.

"Careful!" Wylie said. "If you break it, there's no money for a new one."

Delores turned toward Wylie with fury in her eyes. "You're worried about the TV? Don't you get it? We've always been outsiders, but this bill makes it worse. We're going to be marked, physically marked, and we're one step away from losing our citizenship completely. And you know that 'family values' stuff is code. They're on the brink of branding anyone who's different as criminals. Do you understand what that means? Public trials, prison, or worse."

"What could be worse than prison?"

"Plenty. Now get this dog off my bed and leave me in peace." Delores collapsed onto the sagging mattress and gave Monty a shove, but Monty only turned onto his side and forced Wylie to the hard, wooden floor.

"Sorry," Delores mumbled. She downed a handful of pills and buried her head under her pillow, where Wylie knew it would stay until at least the next morning.

"Come on, boy," she said. Monty, suddenly alert, hopped off the bed and followed her into the kitchen.

Wylie opened the refrigerator and closed it again. "I know, you're hungry too." She tried the pantry, but that was empty except for a box of stale crackers.

Monty whimpered.

"I can't go to the store without money, and pay day isn't till tomorrow."

Monty raised an ear.

"I'll check, but I doubt there's any money left." She opened the cabinet and felt for the money envelope on the top shelf. "As I thought, empty."

Monty yawned.

"No, I'm not going to call Darwin. We'll have to make do with what's here."

They ate through the last sleeve of crackers and washed them down with water from the tap. "Ahh," Wylie said, "a meal fit for the gods. How about we top it off with a walk through paradise?"

This, Monty actually did understand. He ran to the door, quivering in expectation. But as Wylie tossed the empty cracker box in the trash, something caught her eye. A crumpled piece of paper sat atop the pile of garbage. Wylie had been looking at that trash for days, trying to get motivated to empty it, and funny as it sounded, she knew her trash better than anyone should. And she knew that paper hadn't been there the last time she'd looked. She retrieved it and smoothed out the wrinkles.

Final notice, it said in big, bold letters. *The former Cranbury Christian College is scheduled for demolition. All occupants must be evacuated by 11/15. Ignore this notice at your own risk.*

The starkness of the warning ran a chill down Wylie's spine. At least the Avian's threat had rhymed.

"Del, what's this?" Wylie shouted. She stormed into the bedroom, waving the notice like a flag. "Why didn't you tell me? November fifteenth is two days away!"

But her mother was out cold. Wylie shook her shoulder, hoping the pills hadn't had time to kick in fully, but it was no use.

She pulled out the stack of boxes she'd been pilfering from behind the supermarket. It was time to pack.

* * *

Wylie thought packing would be easy, seeing as how all their earthly possessions had fit into this one-bedroom apartment, but she'd been surprised at how much junk they'd accumulated over the years. Her clothes still fit in one trash bag, but the kitchen cabinet was full of chipped mugs and vases she'd appropriated, thinking they might have some trade value at the noncom flea market. Since she'd never gotten around to hauling them there, here they sat, a sad collection of thrown-away glassware and pottery that looked as worn out as she felt. Out they went in the trash, along with the tape dispensers, burned-down candles, broken frames, old shoes, and a bunch of other junk that should have been left in the trash to begin with.

"Why are you bothering?" Delores had asked during a rare moment of consciousness. "You know you don't have to leave the place clean for the new tenants, right?"

Wylie ignored her. She needed to pack, and she needed to clean. She needed to remove every trace of herself from this apartment before they leveled it to the ground. As part of her leaving ritual she'd wanted to take a box to the old library, hoping to rescue her favorite books if she'd found a place to store them. Sharmila would have made room, but noncom population control had finally caught up with Sharmila and she was being evicted for breaking the lease by housing unauthorized Uncommitted. A patrol had heard the baby's cries, and that had been that. Darwin had taken so many of his favorite books from the library that Wylie hated to ask him to make room for more. So now the books that had cushioned the incessant crashes of Uncommitted existence would be imploded into nothingness and scraped from the building's footprint in a heap of cinder and dust. In Wylie's current mood, somehow it almost seemed fitting. She and Delores would have ended up in a similar heap on the street if Darwin hadn't agreed to smuggle them into his grandfather's pool cottage while the old man was out of town.

"It's all closed up for the season," Darwin had said. "No one will ever know you're there. By the time he comes back you'll have found a place."

Any place was better than no place, but the pool cottage was temporary and they needed to travel light. Resigned to abandoning the books that had been her refuge over the years, early in the morning on the day of the demolition Wylie went to the library to say her goodbyes. Her feelings seemed trivial compared with impending homelessness, but she'd miss having a quiet place to sneak away from Delores and get lost in shelves full of worlds that didn't exist. At least that's what she told herself, but as she wandered through the aisles, touching the pages and spines of her old friends for the last time, she felt the pull of the basement archives, the real reason she'd come instead of getting Del ready to depart when Darwin arrived. She descended down into the archives one last time for a final look around. She combed through the box of old tapes that had repelled and attracted her in equal measure. At the very bottom she spied a thumb sized holodrive, out of place among the obsolete video recordings like a time traveler trapped in the past. She hid the small device in her pocket and walked away without looking back, hoping to shake off the fog of confusion those recordings had brought. Sad as she felt, maybe it was a good thing this library was going under. When it died the craziness of the last few weeks would die with it, and she could forget about tapes and miracles and other such nonsense.

On her way out of the library Wylie passed workers dressed in gray jumpsuits, dragging equipment through the doors.

"What are you doing in here?" one of them yelled at her. "These buildings are supposed to be empty!"

Wylie ignored the worker and took off running. She needed to get to Delores, still inside and likely still in bed, before the action began. Demolition crews were scattered across the campus, and in front of her apartment was a crowd of spectators that had gathered for the big event. Yellow police tape marked the perimeter of the building and workers were swarming in and out, talking with each other through headsets and carrying metal boxes and electronic gear. What were they doing here so early? Wylie looked around desperately to see who was in charge. A tall woman in a blue wool coat and red high heels was addressing the growing crowd.

"This campus is a testament to the many decades Committed suffered as an oppressed minority. Imagine how they must have struggled without the backing of the Appointees and the God-ordained ChurchState to help them fight the good fight! And now we are only moments away from the big event. May the smoke and ash rise as an offering like the sacrifices of old!"

Only moments away from the implosion? Wylie doubted that even the ChurchState had had a human sacrifice planned as part of the day's festivities. "Excuse me!" Wylie shouted, "My mom is still in there!" To make matters worse, she realized that Monty had stayed back this morning as well, too cozy in bed with Delores to move. "And my dog. My dog is in there, too. You need to delay the implosion until I can get them out."

The woman sent a dismissive glance in Wylie's direction. "Notice was given. The building should have been properly evacuated weeks ago."

"I know, but they said demolition would commence at noon today," Wylie yelled. "It's barely 7:00 a.m.!"

"Yes, well, the owners felt a morning implosion would allow our audience to participate without missing a workday, so here we are!" The woman smiled brightly, completely oblivious to Wylie's escalating panic. "We wanted to give this historic campus a fitting send-off as a thank you for the legacy of faith it represents. Isn't that right?"

The crowd applauded. A little boy in the front raised his hand.

"Why aren't there any wrecking balls?" he asked, standing on his tip-toes as if a thousand-pound ball hanging from a twenty-five-foot steel crane was hiding behind the victory broadcast van. "I thought they'd smash the building to bits."

The crowd tittered and the woman's gaze grew fond. "You're right, buddy, sometimes buildings are demolished with cool machinery like wrecking balls. But because most of the structures on campus were built with poured concrete walls, the new owners decided to implode all of the buildings at once. It will make quite a show! From our viewpoint we'll be able to see two adjacent buildings come down, just seconds apart. But don't worry, we're all perfectly safe from the dust and debris as long as we stay behind the safety perimeter. Now, let's send the old girl off with the Anthem, shall we?"

"My mom is still in there!" Wylie shouted again, but the crowd had burst into song and her voice bounced back in her face. There was no use arguing. She needed to get into the building, and fast. The front entrance was blocked with workers, but years of avoiding the missionaries had taught Wylie every possible way to sneak into the old deserted dorm.

A familiar voice behind her spoke. "I see the blasters are here early," Darwin said. "Come on, are you ready to go? No need to watch this. Where's Del?"

Wylie spun around and gripped Darwin's arm. "Inside! They're still inside, still sleeping! I've gotta get in there and get them out."

As usual, Darwin needed no further explanation. He took a deep breath and set his jaw. "How?"

"There's an old maintenance entrance around back. Let's go."

They ran past workers, news crews, and more crowds of bystanders positioning themselves for the best view of the implosion. The entire area was taped off, but the metal cellar door that sat under a mess of overgrown shrubs and bramble was wide open.

"They must have gone in that way to plant the explosives," Darwin said. The demolition crew stood a safe distance away, backs turned and bent over a holographic image of how the building would collapse. "We can make it. Come on."

Wylie stopped cold. The "we" in that sentence was so Darwin—never a second of hesitation to help when help was needed. But she couldn't let him, not this time. She couldn't risk him getting hurt because of her and her crazy mom.

"Not you," she said. "Go around the front and make them wait. I'll only be a minute."

"I can't let you go in there alone."

"I need you to tell them to wait until we get out. Now go! I'll meet you at the front."

Wylie ducked under the tape and sprinted across the grass to the open cellar door. Heart pounding, she ran into the basement and through the hall, jumping over a configuration of electronics and metal boxes that she guessed housed the explosives. She rushed into the stairwell, took the stairs two at a time, and burst into the first-floor corridor. Monty was barking furiously from inside the apartment—even Delores couldn't sleep through that, Wylie hoped. Sure enough, when Wylie opened the door, there she was, pale and shaking, sitting on the sofa with her coat on and a travel bag at her feet.

"We have to get out of here!" Wylie cried.

"I was waiting for you," Delores answered in a voice that Wylie didn't recognize. "Where did you go? I thought something happened to you."

Wylie forced herself to remain calm. "I'm sorry. They came early, and I couldn't get in the building. Come on, Darwin's waiting."

She helped Delores up and pulled her into the hallway and down to the main entrance, leaving the trash bags and boxes she'd packed behind. Only a few more feet, and they'd be outside. With a little luck and a lot of hustle they'd clear the blast zone before the buildings blew.

Monty ran out first, but when Del reached the door she stopped, squinting into the gray light of the hazy sun. Wylie realized she hadn't been out in the daylight for years—how many, she'd lost track of. Added to that, there were now hundreds of people watching. When they saw Delores in the doorway they gasped and pointed. The workers looked alarmed and waved at them furiously, but some of the crowd laughed at the spectacle they made, standing in the middle of an implosion site like lost tourists in a strange city. Delores groaned.

"I can't do this," she said, turning away from the crowd. "I'm going back inside."

Wylie grabbed the knit cap off her own head and put it on Del, pulling it down over her eyes.

"Come on," she said, "I'll lead you. You don't need to look."

She led Delores down the walkway, across the field, and toward the safety of the yellow caution tape with Monty at her heels.

"Hurry," she thought she heard Darwin yell—or maybe it was her own inner voice echoing around in her head. She dragged Delores as best she could, but Del, paralyzed with fear, was moving at a snail's pace.

"You're doing great," Wylie said. "Keep going." She wished that Darwin would grab Monty, who was running back and forth between them and the safety zone in a game of catch-me-if-you-can.

They were almost out of danger when a series of blasts shattered their ears. Wylie looked over her shoulder and caught a glimpse of the dormitory collapsing, almost in slow motion. Then she and Delores were engulfed in a tsunami of dust and debris. Wylie choked and gasped for air, fighting off the sensation of drowning. She pulled her turtleneck collar over her mouth and nose and tried to rub her burning eyes clear. Through the dust she saw Del on her knees, swaying and holding on to Monty for support. She had to get to them. But just as Wylie stumbled to her feet, another series of blasts began, knocking her over again and propelling more wreckage toward them. Wylie felt, more than saw, a chunk of cement fly past, missing her by inches. Delores cried out in pain, and then, a microsecond later, Wylie heard a yelp from Monty. She crawled toward them on all fours, coughing and squinting. She got close enough to see that the flying debris had hit both Del and Monty. They lay there next to each other as they had through so many long afternoon naps, looking morbidly peaceful in the stillness of their pose.

"Help!" she screamed, tasting soot and choking on dust. Her ears were ringing so loudly she couldn't hear her own voice. All she could do was keep screaming, hoping to get help for her mom before it was too late. In the back of her mind, Wylie knew that Monty was in trouble, too, but she pushed the thought away, too numb to feel her heart breaking for her sweet, silly dog. She could barely keep her eyes open in the dust, but she needed to find someone, anyone to help them. She forced herself to stand and limped toward the safe zone.

"Help! Over here!" she shouted again and again through a cough that doubled her over every few feet. Her throat was raw from soot and screaming, but she continued, hacking and stumbling and begging for help as loudly as she could, until, after what seemed like forever, she heard a voice call to her through the gritty fog.

"Wylie! Wylie, where are you?"

Wylie stood up straight and peered into the safety zone until she saw Darwin and a team of workers rushing toward her. Frantically, she waved them over.

"Darwin, I'm here! Del's been hurt!" She continued to shout, stopping only to spit the soot out of her mouth. A minute later Darwin was at her side, and together they ran toward Delores. But when they got closer Darwin caught Wylie's arm and tried to pull her away.

"Wylie, it's too late," he said, sobbing. "They're both gone."

"No!" Wylie screamed. She escaped his grip and lunged toward Del, but she tripped over Monty and lost her balance, landing next to him with her hand on his side.

As soon as she touched Monty, Wylie felt it. A warm energy welled up in her and rushed down her arm to the dog's lifeless body. She looked up at Darwin in horror.

"It's happening again!" she wailed. She tried to move her arm from Monty to Delores, but she could no more control her movements than command the power exuding from her. She lay there, feeling the atmosphere around her change, as if she and Monty existed somewhere else, somewhere filled with peace and laced with a quiet, overwhelming power that Wylie sensed was connected to the other, the presence she'd felt before. Wylie wanted to give in to that feeling, to let it surround and fill her, but when she thought of her mother lying next to her, forever silenced and alone, an anger welled up inside. What good was it, what good was she, what good was all this power if she couldn't save her own mother? As if it understood, the aura around her changed, growing dense with sorrow. Wylie felt herself crying and felt the power pouring from her mix with tears that she couldn't wipe away. After a minute, it was over. The power left and took with it every bit of energy in Wylie's body. The last thing she felt was Monty's tongue on her face as the world went dark.

PART II
The Butterfly

11

L ife was good and Wylie was happy and nothing bad had happened, at least not in her dream. Delores was there, sitting up, talking, smiling, saying all the things Wylie had always wanted her mom to say.

I love you, honey.

You're the most important thing in my life.

Don't worry, we'll get through this together.

We can face anything, as long as we have each other.

But then, in the twilight moments before she woke, the universe shifted. Delores, in bed, yelling at the broadcasts.

Fascists!

Narrow-minded hypocrites!

She'll sign your Statement of Commitment over my dead body.

Over my big, fat, cold, dead body.

Delores's dead body, lying in the dirt. Eyes open and empty, staring past Wylie at nothing. Only her mouth still alive, words pouring out like bile.

Where were you that morning?

Why did you let me die?

You got what you wanted, right?

You know you wanted this.

I'm gone, the dog is here.

You finally got what you wanted.

Everything came at a cost, even the escape of sleep.

Wylie bolted upright and shook herself awake twenty minutes before the alarm would sound. Twenty more minutes of sleep if she wanted it. But she needed to control what went on in her head, and sleep would not allow that. She jumped out of bed and turned on the lamp just as she heard the heat kick on.

The pool cottage was bigger than she'd imagined. Of course, it would have been a lot smaller if Delores had been there, but for girl and dog the two-room cottage was downright luxurious. After sleeping on the couch for all those years, the soft double bed made Wylie nervous, as if it might vanish out from under her in the middle of the night and leave her sprawled on the cold tile floor.

Del's voice again—*things worked out well for you, didn't they?*

Wylie pushed the harsh voice away. She let Monty out and waited at the door, hoping the icy rush of late winter air would sweep away the remnants of her nightmare. The real Delores would never speak so cruelly to her. Del had embodied the anger of hopelessness, that was true. But in all her mother's brokenness, Wylie had known the truth. *She's not really angry at you,* she heard Sharmila say. She shook herself to clear her head. There were too many voices rattling around in there.

When Monty was done, Wylie headed for the coffee pot. The place was fully digitized and voice responsive, but Wylie was too used to doing things for herself to start talking to a house or a bunch of mini-drones buzzing around her head. She'd save her one-sided conversations for Monty. She'd deprogrammed everything except the heat and the security system, but apparently one lone housekeeping drone hadn't gotten the memo. It buzzed over Wylie's head to the bedroom and swooped low toward the messy covers on the bed.

"No, you don't," Wylie said. "I like my bed just the way it is." She grabbed at the drone, but it avoided her grasp and dove for her pillow, placing it to the side.

"Hey, cut it out! Drone, stop!" Wylie shouted, but the determined little craft kept working, flying from one corner of the mattress to the other, pulling and smoothing the rumpled covers in mechanized efficiency. Wylie waited in absolute stillness until the drone got closer, then she struck like a lioness hunting her prey. In one swift movement she snatched the drone and disconnected its fuel cell.

"Gotcha." She shoved the drone into the nightstand drawer, ignoring the item that sat next to the lamp on top of the nightstand.

"Now, where were we?" Wylie asked Monty, who'd watched the exchange in fascination. "Coffee. Right." She opened the cabinet and surveyed three different bags of coffee beans staring back at her. She'd never heard of any of them, but according to Darwin the one on the right was made with elephant dung, so she steered clear of that. She set up the brewer, fed Monty, and poured herself some cereal while she waited for the coffee. The refrigerator was full, and Wylie could have cooked up anything she wanted for breakfast, but old habits die hard. Even after all these weeks, she still wasn't quite used to not being hungry, and a rich breakfast just didn't appeal.

On most days Wylie needed to be outside with the gardening team by 8:00 a.m. That was the deal she'd struck with Darwin's grandfather, although she'd not actually met the old man yet. Even in winter, there was plenty to do on the expansive estate. In exchange for her work, she got room and board and free time to finish up her school curriculum, boring as it was. Unfortunately, this sweet arrangement was temporary, since the newly passed Committed Bill of Rights made housing an Uncommitted adult on Committed soil overnight a crime, and on her next birthday Wylie would officially reach adult status. But that was months away, and maybe Sharmila would be settled by then and ready to take her in.

Wylie had never realized how much of her time was spent scrounging around or waiting on long lines for basic necessities, all the while avoiding the missionaries. She wanted to enjoy her brief respite from the real world, but the vastness of a Saturday stretched before her like an ocean, and she felt small and insignificant in its presence. She'd watched every old movie that made it through the vid censors, and although she was surrounded by books, the cottage library consisted of ChurchState philosophy and inane testimonies of destitute Uncommitted who'd seen the light. Wylie couldn't believe she'd once considered writing a paper on ChurchState history. Now, plopped in the middle of ChurchState territory and surrounded by its benefits, she clung to her outsider status like a life raft.

She'd tried to start a new journal since the old one had imploded with everything else she owned except the clothes on her back and the lint in her pockets, but the words just weren't flowing any more. The only other item that had survived with her was the one that now lived on the nightstand next to the bed. Wylie had no idea what was on the holodrive she'd rescued from the library the terrible morning of the demolition, and she wasn't sure she cared. It sat there, commemorating where she'd been and where she hadn't been when everything changed. If guilt could be an object, that holodrive was it.

The coffee pot beeped, but before she could get to it, Wylie heard someone outside. She could have asked the security system for an ID, but by the way Monty was carrying on she knew it had to be Darwin. She opened the door and there he was, arms filled with bags of groceries and supplies.

"What, no elephant dung?" he asked, heading straight for the coffee.

"You can tell that from the smell," Wylie said, shaking her head. "You're up early."

"I thought I'd make us a good breakfast."

"I have breakfast," Wylie replied, pointing to the bowl of untouched, soggy cereal she'd left on the counter.

"You're in Grandpaville now, at least for a little while, and his employees eat well." Darwin fed the cereal to the garbage disposal as Wylie swallowed her shock at seeing good food go to waste. She wanted to point out that there was already plenty of food in the fridge, but Darwin was in one of his perky, productive moods, and she knew there was no use arguing. While Darwin scurried around the kitchen, Wylie sat at the small, round table and caught the ghost of her reflection in its glass top. No wonder Darwin had the irresistible urge to feed her. Under her mop of uncombed hair, she looked as pale as the porcelain bust of Thomas Jefferson staring down from the shelf above her.

Within no time, a steaming plate of potatoes, eggs, and toast appeared, and Wylie's appetite returned with a vengeance. She ate without talking, letting the food fill her stomach but knowing the other, deeper void that had been her constant companion would remain. When she was done she set the plate on the floor for Monty.

"Gramps would not like that," Darwin said. "He's a bit of a germaphobe."

"Monty always does the prewash," Wylie replied. Once the plate was licked clean she placed it in the dishwasher while Darwin retrieved a small metal box from his backpack.

"What's that?"

"Just something I thought you might need. It's a holodrive player." Carefully, Darwin carried the box into the living area, where he placed it gently on the floor. "This part is the chrysalis. Here's why." He touched the top lightly and it unfolded into a multilayered system of steps on each side that resembled wings. "See?" Darwin said, beaming as if he'd invented the thing himself. "It looks like a butterfly when it's all opened up. That's why it's called the Butterfly."

Wylie inspected the contraption the way she would any insect, with part curiosity and part revulsion. She'd heard of this technology, but she'd never seen it up close.

"This is one of the ChurchState's shining accomplishments," Darwin continued, pushing expanding panels and opening hidden drawers until the apparatus took up almost the entire room. "And Grandpa had the latest model, just sitting in a drawer. Of course, the holo-tech has been around for decades, but they've updated it to test the resolve of the newly Committed. I guess too many people were faking it to get the benefits. This baby examines their responses to see if they're true believers, and if they aren't when they go in, they will be when they come out."

"So much for the Science Wary movement. I guess there's no problem with science when it serves the ChurchState's purposes," Wylie said. She had to admit she was taken aback by Darwin's unbridled enthusiasm for what amounted to a brain washing device, until she realized for the hundredth time how much he'd given up by refusing to join the Committed. He could be so many things—teacher, scientist, explorer—but he'd never be more than a handyman unless, by some miracle, the world turned right-side-up and undid the last fifty years.

Wylie sighed. "And you brought this technological marvel here because you thought I needed some re-education?"

"What? No, of course not. The ChurchState uses it for indoctrination, but on a lower setting it creates a virtual reality that you can observe as a spectator. It's like watching a video simulation."

"That still doesn't explain why it's in my living room." Except this wasn't her living room. Not for long, anyway. Wylie made a mental note to stomp out the strands of attachment skittering around her ankles.

"You know why. That holodrive you found in the library has been sitting on your nightstand for months. When you're finally ready to see what's on it, just plug it in here," Darwin pointed to a port on the front panel, "and put on the neural simulator cap." He took a neatly folded cap made of cloudy, soft material from a drawer and pulled it down over his eyes and ears.

"You look like you're about to rob a convenience store."

"One more thing," Darwin said, pulling off the cap. "This works by voice command, so no remote needed. It will give you several options and do whatever you say."

Can it bring Delores back? she almost asked.

"Thanks." Wylie tried not to sound dismissive. From the look on Darwin's face she knew she hadn't succeeded.

"Thanks," she said again, "really. Monty needs a walk, and then I have schoolwork. But maybe I'll try it later."

"Okay. I gotta get going too. My car needs a battery and I want to be first in line at the junkyard." Darwin pushed the top panel again, and in a few smooth moves the Butterfly folded back into itself until only the small rectangular box remained. "See you later. And good luck."

"Yeah. Thanks again." Wylie forced a smile. As soon as Darwin was gone she hid the holodrive and the player under a pile of blankets in the bottom dresser drawer, where they stayed for a full twenty minutes while she puttered around and tried to think of something to do. Then, like a puppet with no will of its own, Wylie set up the Butterfly, donned the cap, and entered another world.

12

Wylie stood at the back of an outdoor gathering where hundreds of white folding chairs faced a large wooden platform sandwiched between electronic speakers almost four feet high. The chairs were empty, except for the sweaters, jackets, and purses left behind as people milled around the perimeter of a treelined field. Everywhere, families were smiling and hugging and taking pictures, and some of the girls held flower bouquets. All at once she realized where she was. This was the very same field she'd mowed a hundred times. She was standing on the commons at Cranbury Christian College and, judging by how everyone around her was dressed, it was graduation day.

What year was it? She walked closer to the back row of chairs to get a look at a program, but since she had no feet, or legs, or body, for that matter, her movements were more like zooming in and out than actual walking. She was there but not there in the holoworld, like a ghost who could see but not be seen, like an observer watching a movie from the wrong side of the screen. She focused on the program and read the date—May 3, 2002, a beautiful sunny day at a place that was brimming with life. For the first time Wylie felt sad for the fate of the campus she'd once called home.

She focused in on the students around her, wondering if any had been in Dr. Michael's class. She hadn't seen any faces, but maybe she'd recognize voices. Moving to the left of the platform, she saw older people in fancier robes who, she realized, must be the teachers. Wylie could see that they were talking, but the sound was muffled and she couldn't make out what anyone was saying.

"How do you turn up the volume?" she said.

"Do you wish to enter narration?" a flat, tinny voice asked.

"Explain," she responded with distaste. She'd already had an argument with one machine that morning and she didn't relish talking with another.

"You may remain in spectator mode or you may enter the narration at any time with a voice command."

"Yeah, I got that, but what does it mean to enter narration?"

"There are many ways to experience the holostory. The most common is for the user to take the perspective of its creator."

"You mean I'll *be* the creator?"

"If you wish."

"What if I don't wish?"

"You may take the perspective of any character or create your own."

"Can I just watch, and hear what they're saying?"

"You may," said the Butterfly.

"Okay, do that then. And don't correct my grammar."

"Do you prefer spectator mode with or without creator cognition?"

"What?"

"Do you prefer spectator . . . "

"I heard you. Explain."

"Spectator mode with creator cognition allows you to understand the thinking and motivations of the creator as you witness her story."

"Oh. And who is the creator, anyway?"

"This holostory was created by Abby in December 2051."

"Okay, so twenty years ago. Abby who?"

"No last name is provided."

Was this the same Abby from the videos? If so, she'd created this holostory when she was old, probably in her seventies. What story was so important to tell after all those years?

"Yeah, creator cognition," Wylie said.

"With or without emo-ling?"

"Are you kidding me?" Wylie was dangerously close to pulling the cap off her head and packing the whole thing in. What was she doing, anyway? Why did she care what happened to some girl she didn't know all those years ago? She had enough problems of her own. But as much as Wylie wanted to forget, as much as she'd tried to suppress the memories of the last several months, the sensation of power and presence flowing through her wouldn't die. If this was the same Abby from the videos, maybe her story would help Wylie understand what had happened to her.

"Emo-ling—I assume that means I'd feel the emotions of the creator?"

"Correct."

"Okay. Do it. Full emo-ling. Now shut up and let's get started."

"Would you prefer the voiceless interface? If my voice offends you we could communicate in writing."

"For God's sake just start the thing, before I change my mind!" Wylie said.

Instantly a young girl appeared, dressed in a black graduation robe, her long brown hair flowing loosely under a tasseled cap. A middle aged couple—her parents, Wylie guessed—buzzed around her like bumble bees on a dandelion. A petite woman in a blue striped dress handed Abby a thick bouquet of roses and then enveloped her in a hug, crushing the flowers between them.

"Thanks, Aunt Delores," Abby said, eyes closed and smiling. "I couldn't have done it without you all." Wylie was overtaken by a wave of warmth and gratitude. Suddenly she understood the power and danger of this device and why the ChurchState, no friend of science and downright enemy of the gaming corporations, had worked so hard to develop it. Take folks who had nothing, who lived on fear and hunger and need, and throw a little love their way, even if you have to force it into their brains through a skull cap, and it wouldn't be long before the arrogant smirks of the missionaries would feel like the adoring glances of a devoted mother. Who could resist?

And speaking of mothers, *Aunt Delores*? Was this some kind of coincidence or was the Butterfly messing with her mind?

"Do you wish to pause?" the voice said.

"Huh?"

"Your brain wave patterns indicate inattentiveness. Do you wish to pause the holostory?"

"You can tell that? Can you tell what I'm thinking?"

"Negative. User's thoughts cannot be accessed."

"And do you know who I am?"

"This unit is not connected with any outside database. Your identity remains anonymous."

"Then why is her aunt's name Delores?"

"The names of the characters have been programmed by the creator. Do you wish to continue?"

This was all too weird, but whether because of her own curiosity or the addictive nature of the machine, Wylie couldn't stop now. "Okay," she said. "Continue. And don't interrupt again unless I tell you to."

"Come," said Abby. "I want to introduce you to one of my favorite professors." She led her parents and Aunt Delores to the group of teachers who were starting to disburse. One or two had removed their caps and were headed away from the commons with the posture of escaped convicts. Dr. Michaels stood off to the side, surrounded by students. Among them was Steve—not Abby's favorite person, but it was graduation day and she was feeling especially charitable. She reached up to give him a hug.

Dr. Michaels joined them, all smiles and congratulations. "We're excited for your new position at Great River, Abby. When do you start?"

Abby caught a disgruntled look from Steve and shifted uncomfortably. She'd heard that Steve had interviewed for the position, too. Abby had no idea why she'd gotten the offer, but a full-time youth minister job was not easy to come by, and she'd accepted without question and with gratitude.

"Monday," Abby said. "I'm all packed and ready to go. I'll head out in the morning and spend the weekend settling in to my new apartment."

"Congrats again," Dr. Michaels said. "Make sure you stay in touch. First time positions can have their share of challenges, but remember we're here for you." Abby felt a sudden sense of foreboding—what did Dr. Michaels mean? Were his words a subtle warning? Did he know something about Great River that she didn't know? This didn't seem the right time or place to pursue the conversation, and, in any case, Dr. Michaels turned to greet more students and families with cameras at the ready. The feeling faded and Abby's attention shifted to Steve, who was slipping away, alone. She hated to admit the relief she felt that she wouldn't be seeing him again. "Please help him," she whispered.

Abby spent the night tossing and turning, too nervous and excited to sleep. If she hadn't promised her parents that she'd wait till morning she would have taken off in the middle of the night, just to give herself something to do. Besides, she'd arranged to meet with the pastor that afternoon, and she didn't want to make a bad impression by showing up at the church four hours early. When, finally, the sun came up, she hit the road and drove in silence, stopping only once along the way for a quick bathroom break.

"Pause," Wylie said. The picture froze as Abby approached the front door of a large, modern looking church. "How do I know all this? It's not like I've been watching her try to sleep all night or sitting next to her in a car while she drove six hours."

"The simulation is functioning in compression mode," the Butterfly answered. "Do you wish to switch to real time?"

"Explain compression mode."

"Time in compression mode advances in a series of instantaneous impressions, not in seconds and minutes."

"So, I feel like time is passing, but it isn't. Not in the real world."

"Correct."

"Like in a dream."

"The brain in dream state is not fully understood, but it is believed that the same posterior zone . . . "

"Yes or no?" Wylie interrupted. This thing was as wordy as the preachers on the victory broadcasts.

"Yes."

"Okay. Continue."

"It is believed that the same posterior zone used in dreaming . . . "

Again, Wylie had the urge to pull off the cap and throw the whole stupid machine against the wall, but she couldn't deny her fascination with this pre-reclamation world. "No, I mean continue the simulation," she ordered.

Abby was being led by a middle-aged woman through the spacious church lobby past the sanctuary and down the hall to the offices. Wylie had never been inside a church before, and she was surprised at how warm and friendly it felt. Then she realized she was seeing and feeling her surroundings through Abby's eyes, not through Del's dark memories of a rising authoritarian state. Del would hate that she was in this place, even virtually. For a split second she felt herself on a tightrope, balancing between Abby's optimistic excitement and Del's deep disapproval. But Delores was gone, and the truth was that Wylie wanted, somehow needed, to see what happened next.

A young man with a buzz cut greeted Abby and showed her into his office. He took a seat behind an expansive, shiny mahogany desk, while Abby perched at the edge of a straight-backed chair. The desk was empty except for a silver engraved nameplate that read "Pastor Rick" in fancy lettering. They exchanged small talk about graduation (Pastor Rick was an alumnus but couldn't make it that year) and Abby's drive to Great River. After a minute or two they ran out of things to say, and an awkward silence fell. Abby waited patiently while Pastor Rick took a baseball out of the bottom drawer and tossed it from one hand to the other. At that moment he looked more like a high school kid waiting to take the field than the senior pastor of a midsized church that was growing in district influence.

"Well, um, did you get my email?" Abby said finally.

"Ah, yes, right—I meant to respond, but then the time got away from me. Can you remind me what it said?"

"Oh, well, mostly I was wondering about the youth service this week. Who'll be introducing me, formally, I mean? When will I have time to connect with the lay leaders and the worship team? I've been preparing a talk . . ."

Pastor Rick's face went blank. "I'm sorry, I thought they got in touch with you."

"They?"

"Yes, the youth group leaders. They decided to give you some time to ease into the position. They'll run the youth group through the summer and you can just sort of watch, like an intern. Then, if all goes well, you can take over in September, when school starts."

Abby was speechless. This was not what she'd expected. She'd come wholly prepared to jump into her position as full-time minister of youth. That was what she'd planned and prepared for all those years at school. She tried to choose her words carefully.

"Okay, it's just that I've already done an internship. My understanding was that this was a full-time position."

"Yes, true, and we are still committed to that, assuming all goes well. But Layla and Bill thought this would be a better transition for the kids. And it will give you time to get settled, like I said."

Layla and Bill. Abby remembered meeting them briefly. They were a married couple, probably in their forties, who'd been running the youth group on their own for several years. They'd seemed friendly enough and Abby had admired their commitment to the church. Suddenly their dedication took on a more ominous tone.

"Now," Pastor Rick continued with a smile, "it just happens that the childcare center is looking for a teacher for the three-year-old room. We thought that would be a good way to help them out and give you a salary, as well. You'll start there Monday."

"But . . . I have no experience with young kids. That's not why I was hired. I have the invitation letter from the Board, right here . . . " She fumbled through her purse, searching for proof that she was right, but knowing it would make no difference.

Pastor Rick's face turned to stone. "You don't like little kids?"

"Well, uh, of course I do. They're cute and all. It's just that I've never worked with them before."

"I wouldn't worry about that. It's more like babysitting, anyway. You'll love it."

Again, Abby was too stunned to speak. Before she knew what was happening she was being led back out to the lobby with a packet of new employee forms under her arm. She walked to her car in a fog. When she was sure no one was watching she put her head on the steering wheel and cried. "Help me figure this out," she pleaded. "I don't know what to do."

"Hold on," Wylie almost yelled, wiping her eyes. "Pause." The simulation faded to gray. "I get that I'm reading her thoughts . . . "

"Not exactly," the Butterfly answered. "Shall I explain how creator cognition works?"

"No, don't bother. What I want to know is, who is she talking to?"

"The last scene consisted of a conversation between the creator and the lead pastor of Great River Christian Center, a church in north central Ohio."

"That not what I mean. Who is she talking to in her head? It's like she's having a side conversation with someone who isn't there." Wylie suspected the answer, but she wanted to be sure.

The Butterfly cranked and hummed for a few seconds. "The creator is speaking to a religious entity," it answered. "She calls it *praying*."

"That's what I thought. Can you delete that part?"

"Do you wish to exit creator cognition mode?"

"No. Can you just delete the praying parts?"

"The thoughts of the creator cannot be segmented."

Great, so it was all or nothing. What was next? Maybe Abby would go out and stop someone's bleeding or raise someone from the dead. Why was this happening, and why couldn't Wylie escape the noxious trappings of a religion she'd been taught to hate? She pulled off the cap, grabbed Monty, and ran from the house without a coat, not caring that she was still wearing the sweats she'd slept in and letting the cold numb her thoughts. As she ran she heard Del's voice keeping time with her steps: *Why-Why-Wylie, always asking why.*

13

"I 'm not even sure why I'm wasting my time on it," Wylie said, pulling her rake through the ivy that ran alongside the cottage. She and Darwin had been working on spring clean-up for the last hour, and for most of that time Wylie had been arguing with herself while Darwin listened quietly. "I mean, why should I care what happened to some religious fanatic decades ago?"

Monty spotted a squirrel and sprinted after it, giving up the chase when the squirrel scurried up a nearby oak.

"Okay, maybe that's harsh," Wylie continued. "Abby's not really a fanatic, I guess, although she's religious, that's for sure. I can only imagine what Del would say about her. Del would hate that I'm even using the Butterfly, and I wouldn't blame her. That contraption is so weird. It gets into your head until you feel like you really know the person, you know what I mean? I feel like I know Abby, like I am Abby, in a way. But that's not really it, either. I don't know—maybe she's the friend I never had."

Darwin looked up from the pile of clippings he'd been scooping into the trash, a fleeting flicker of hurt in his eyes.

"The female friend, I mean," Wylie said, instantly regretting her words. "Of course, I always had you."

"Yeah, of course. So, you're going to finish her story?" Darwin brushed off Wylie's unintended slight, but Wylie felt the sting on his behalf. I'm so stupid, she thought, I'm always saying the wrong thing. She hesitated, not sure of how to continue, when Darwin spoke again.

"Well? Are you going to finish the story or not?"

"I guess. You know me. I don't like unfinished business."

"Which is why you always finish a book before I do and then make sure to spoil the ending for me."

At that Wylie smiled, thinking of the many small abuses Darwin had suffered at her hands over the years. Why did he put up with her? But, of course, she knew why.

"Yeah, I hate a story without an ending," she said. "Not that I really care, but I might as well see what happens. It's not like I have anything better to do."

"You go ahead and tell yourself that if you want," Darwin replied.

Wylie stopped raking. "What?" She turned toward Darwin and tightened her grip on the rake.

"Look, Wy, let's face it, you are connected to that holostory in some very weird way, just like you were connected to the tapes at the library. Haven't you wondered why the strange happenings stopped?"

"What do you mean?"

"This power, or whatever it was, that you felt after every tape—it hasn't happened again, right? Not since the implosion."

Darwin had a point. To Wylie's relief, no further miracles had interrupted her dull, everyday existence. She'd gone back to being just a commonplace Uncommitted who, for the moment, was safe under the protection of a Committed with money and influence. "I figured when the library ended, the happenings ended with it."

"That much is obvious," Darwin said. "But why? What was the connection? Was there something about that room? Did the building house some kind of power that transferred to you somehow? And it can't be a coincidence that Abby was on the tapes, and now you're watching her story. Maybe she's stuck in some kind of vortex and she's trying to communicate."

Wylie frowned. "You've watched too many bootleg sci-fi movies."

"Maybe, but there has to be some explanation. I think you need to finish the story to find out, so you can stop wondering and move on with your life."

Wylie snorted. "What life?" she muttered and went back to work. Her life held very few prospects, but she didn't need to tell Darwin that. What did any of this matter? Nothing would change her pariah status. Still, aside from the crazy talk about power and vortexes, Darwin had a point. Ignoring what had happened only took her so far and even her newly developed superhuman ability to repress couldn't completely erase the still, small *why* nagging at the peripheral of her thoughts. All these months she'd been looking over her shoulder, waiting for the next bizarre event to overtake her. She needed answers. Maybe those answers could be found in Abby's story, or maybe not. But there was only one way to find out.

* * *

Pastor Rick had been right about one thing—Abby did love the kids in her class. How could she not? They were sweet and stubborn and funny and mean all at the same time, and they treated her like a goddess. She loved sitting on the floor, reading stories and building with blocks, and she loved chasing them around the playground in a game where she was the bee collector and they were the bees. And even though she knew she didn't belong there, Abby loved the thought that one day these little kids would be youth—maybe, hopefully, her youth, and she'd know them more deeply, more intimately, because she'd been their preschool teacher for a little while. That realization saved her from drowning in humiliation every time Pastor Rick walked by and flashed her his vacuous grin.

Sometimes, when she was pushing a kid on a swing or patting someone to sleep, she would quietly sing:

Wash me, wash me,

Wash me in your love.

Wash away my tears,

You bought them with your blood.

Wash me, wash me,

Wash away my pain,

Replace it with your self

And give me joy again.

One day Abby and her twelve kids were out on the playground when a gentle, unexpected rain began. Rather than run inside, she let the warm drops run over her face. Arms raised, she began to sing the little song she couldn't get out of her head. The kids thought standing out in the rain was the best idea in the world, and before Abby knew it they were in a circle, singing together like a sweet, angelic choir. The sight of their chubby little arms raised toward heaven and the sound of their off-key voices melted Abby into a sense of joy she hadn't felt since she'd arrived.

As they finished the chorus for the second time the rain began to come harder, and Abby knew it was time to get inside. She herded the kids through the parking lot and had almost reached the school entrance when Pastor Rick came rushing toward them holding a huge striped umbrella.

"Don't you have any common sense?" he yelled once they got inside. The kids, who'd been jumping up and down and laughing, stopped dead in their tracks and looked up at him with big, round eyes. "One of them could have been struck by lightning!"

Callie, the youngest of the bunch, wrapped her arms around Abby's leg, whimpering softly. The others took the cue, and Abby knew if she didn't get them out of there quickly they would have a storm of a different kind to deal with. "You're scaring them," she said softly.

"*I'm* scaring them? You're the one who kept them out in a thunderstorm!"

"There was no thunder," Abby said under her breath. "Okay, friends, time to go back to our classroom," she told the kids. "I brought my favorite story to read today. Who can guess the name of it?" She led the children away from Pastor Rick, who was still steaming. As Abby turned the corner she noticed someone lurking in the doorway of the church office.

Steve.

Abby hadn't seen or thought of Steve since graduation. What was he doing here? Did his presence signal the end of her hopes to move into the youth pastor position? She felt her anxiety widen from a trickle to a stream. She took her break during naptime, as usual, and since it was still raining she headed to the sanctuary for some quiet. She needed time alone to process and to pray. But quiet was not to be found—there was Steve, ripping up carpet and pulling up nails with Jason and Jon, two guys from the youth group. Abby thought about ducking away, but Steve had seen her and she didn't want to be rude. Maybe this was her opportunity to build bridges.

"Hey!" she said, trying to sound cheerful. "How are you?"

Steve stopped working and stood to give Abby a small, awkward hug. He shuffled his feet and looked away. "I forgot that you were at this church."

Abby doubted that was true, but she let it go. "Yeah, I came right after graduation. What's ya been up to? I'm surprised to see you here."

"Still looking, applying to churches all over the place. I thought it might be good to get away, you know, see other parts of the country." He yawned and rubbed his hand over his beard stubble. "Anyway, I thought I'd come and help out at my cousin's church for the summer while I figure out what to do."

"Cool. Who's your cousin?"

"Rick. Pastor Rick. Didn't you know that?"

Abby's anxiety rose to near flood stage, but she kept her voice even. "Oh. I guess I didn't. Well that's fun. So, you're staying with him? For how long?"

"Till something opens up, I guess. Probably through the summer. Yeah, he wanted to hire me, but a couple of Board members wouldn't go for it. Some stupid thing about nepotism and the appearance of evil. There's always some that will give you a hard time. Rick's hoping they'll step down soon."

Abby had heard there was trouble brewing between Pastor Rick and the church Board of Trustees, but she stayed as far away from church politics as she could. She nodded, planning her exit move, but Steve was not done yet.

"Yeah, when the Board wouldn't consider me, Rick decided to bring someone in who was less threatening, uh, more neutral, I mean. That way if things don't work out, you know, he's covered, you know, with the district. But no offense. I'm sure you'll do great." As he spoke the rain outside intensified and a dark shadow fell across the sanctuary.

"Hey Steve, can you give us a hand with this, man?" called Jason, who, Abby remembered, happened to be Layla's nephew. Just one big happy family, she thought.

"I'll let you go," she muttered, turning away.

"You coming tonight?" Steve called after her.

"Tonight?"

"Yeah, youth group. Tonight, at seven, right? You coming?"

Was *she* coming to youth group? *She* was supposed to be the youth pastor, as Steve knew very well. "Uh, yeah. Are you?"

"Yeah, Layla invited me and Rick thought it was a good idea. You know, give the guys an extra role model and all. See you later." For the first time Steve smiled a wide, toothy grin and Abby understood just how completely she'd been set up to fail.

* * *

Delores had never been one to sing her daughter to sleep; in fact, once Sharmila left, Wylie's bedtime routine degenerated into nothingness. She'd stop and flop on the couch or a chair and stay there until morning. But as Wylie drifted off that night, Monty snuggled close, she heard Abby's voice so clearly she could have been there in the room. She was singing *Wash Me, Wash Me,* and Wylie dreamed of tears and blood and the Avian and rain so hard it made the roof cave in. And even though the stuff of nightmares floated through her head, Wylie did not feel afraid.

14

If Pastor Rick has planned to replace Abby with "Cousin Steve," for now those plans seemed to be on hold. When summer ended Abby was hired as full-time youth pastor while Steve took a retail job in the area. Fall retreat was the first official event Abby would lead and she'd been looking forward to it for weeks. When her stint at the childcare center had finally ended she was surprised at how hard it was to say goodbye to her kids, but she consoled herself with the fact that her old classroom was right down the hall and she could pop in whenever she needed a boost of self-esteem. She'd kneel in the doorway as a pack of joyful three-year-olds ran at her from all directions, practically toppling her over with hugs.

If only her relationships with the youth at the church were so straightforward. Bill and Layla continued to attend every meeting and event, steadily spinning the web of influence that kept the teens close to them and far from Abby. Steve never seemed to have anything else to do, either; he circled the room like a wasp ready to strike. Even when he was silent, Abby knew he was judging every word she said and probably stewing over how much better he would have said it, and that was on the good days. On the bad days Steve, Layla, or Bill would interrupt Abby's talks to correct her theology or give examples that contradicted her point. The guys in the group especially seemed to enjoy these attempts to humiliate Abby. They gathered around Steve behind an impenetrable barrier of sports talk and macho one-uppers as the girls clustered nearby, hoping to get their attention.

Only two of the girls, Cora and Jane, seemed friendly and open to developing a relationship with Abby. As newcomers, they were among the few who hadn't been attending the church since before they were born. On the way to the retreat center Abby squeezed in the back of the van with them, for once more than happy to let Steve do the driving. The two girls pointed out the window and giggled over a series of private jokes until Abby struck up a conversation.

"So how long have you two known each other?" she asked.

"Since fifth grade," Jane responded, brushing her long red hair behind her ear.

"I was the only black kid in the class," Cora said, "and Jane was the only one who would talk to me."

"For a while, anyway. Once everybody got to know you they were okay."

"Yeah, but they followed your lead. Admit it, you were the fifth grade goodwill race ambassador." Cora laughed and though she was several inches taller, she put her head on Jane's shoulder.

Jane smiled and patted Cora's knee. "Just doing my part for humankind."

"So how did you end up at Great River?" Abby asked. "I mean, we're really happy to have you here, but just wondering."

"My mom found the church. She brought me and I brought Cora," Jane said.

"Just like Andrew and Simon in the Bible," Abby replied with a smile.

The girls exchanged confused looks, and Abby realized they had no idea what she was talking about. "Anyway, I'm glad you're here."

Cora frowned as she nodded toward the front of the van. "I don't think everyone's glad we're here."

Now it was Abby's turn to be confused. "You mean Steve?"

"Yeah," Cora said. "I don't think he's so open to diversity, if you know what I mean."

Abby thought back to the four years she'd known Steve at school. Although the college was mostly white, there had been several black, Hispanic, and Asian American kids around, and Steve had been friendly with all of them. For all his faults, Abby had never known Steve to travel the path of racial prejudice.

"He may come across kind of, well . . . " Abby could think of plenty of ways to describe Steve, but the words, *do to others as you would have them do to you* popped into her head and she let her sentence trail off.

Jane jumped into the lull. "Conceited?"

"Arrogant?" said Cora.

"Spiteful?" Jane added.

"Okay, okay, I know he's not perfect," said Abby in a lowered voice. "But I really don't think he has a problem with race."

Cora sighed. "Maybe not more than most white folks, but that's not exactly what I meant." She looked to Jane who shook her head almost imperceptibly.

"He sure is mean to you," Cora said. "Why is that?"

Abby noticed the deflection maneuver but she focused on trying to come up with an answer to a direct but difficult question. She could defend the indefensible or claim ignorance, but Abby wasn't in the habit of lying.

"I leave that up to the Lord," she said simply. "I can't control other people. I can only control myself. Most of the time, anyway," she added, smiling.

"But doesn't it hurt?" Jane asked. "When they treat you so bad? Why do you put up with it?" Abby could hear the pain in Jane's question—this girl was speaking from experience. She thought for a minute.

"Yeah, it hurts. I guess it's especially hard because this has never happened to me before. I mean, always before, in school, I've gotten along with everybody. I've kind of been the peacemaker in the group, the one that people go to when they need a shoulder to lean on. But I guess the real world isn't like that. There are going to be people who just don't like you, no matter what you do. I can't change them. I can only forgive them."

"Tell me about it," Cora said.

Abby tried not to look surprised. She suddenly felt very naïve. "Has that happened to you a lot?"

"Not a lot, but enough. You sort of learn to cope. But it hurts every time."

Jane patted Cora's hand.

"Anyway, my parents prepared me for it. That's just the way things are," Cora said. "They always tell me, 'Don't let other people's ignorance get you down.'"

"That doesn't make it okay," said Jane.

"No, it doesn't," Abby agreed. "Look, I'm not comparing my experience to yours. But I'm not giving up on Steve." She swallowed hard and prayed her words were true. "And it helps to know I'm where I'm supposed to be. I'm not here to please people, I'm here because Jesus wants me here. When he tells me to go, I'll go. I just have to remember that it's not about me."

Cora looked wistful, but Jane's face shut down. "That's easy for you to say," she muttered.

"What do you mean?" Abby asked, but Jane only stared out the window with her arms crossed and for the rest of the trip Abby wondered what was up with her. She made a mental note to check in with Jane later.

The retreat center at the southeastern part of the state had a hilltop view that was as breathtaking as any Abby had seen. It was finally jacket weather, and the red, orange, and yellow foliage against the clear blue sky was the perfect backdrop for pumpkin carving, hot chocolate, and touch football. The only unpleasant moment came when Steve carted the pumpkins out of the van and Abby gave out the carving utensils. Layla, who'd been watching from the sidelines, approached Abby with a concerned look.

"You're sure it's wise to give them such sharp objects?" she asked. For a minute Abby thought she was serious, but then Layla's face broke out in a wicked grin. "I mean, you're not the most popular person around. You never know what could happen."

"True, you never know," Abby responded, smiling sweetly and raising the six-inch long carving knife in her hand.

"Watch you don't trip and fall on that," Layla said, matching Abby's sweet smile. "That blade could go right through your heart, and then all our problems would be solved."

Abby should have known better than to trade sarcastic quips with the devil. She shook her head and moved away, making sure to watch her step.

On the last evening of the retreat, after dinner, Abby asked the group to gather around the fireplace in the main lounge. Steve relaxed on the sofa, surrounded by his usual pack of guys, while the girls sat in armchairs scattered around the rustic, wood-beamed room. Cora and Jane had squeezed into a large cushy armchair together.

Abby stood in front of the fireplace, facing the group. Layla and Bill, meanwhile, set up two folding chairs on either side of her.

"Er, it's a little crowded up here," Abby said politely.

"We're fine," Bill replied with a stony look. "Let's get your spiel over with. Try not to be too boring tonight."

Abby had spent the good part of a day preparing this devotion, but now her confidence wobbled. She stepped to the middle of the circle so that her back was to Bill and Layla, determined to ignore their presence. Then she took a deep breath and reached out to a different presence. She smiled and kept breathing, in and out, in and out. Breath in, *you're mine,* she thought. *Wash me, fill me, use me.* Breath out, *I'm yours. Every part of me belongs to you.* A sense of peace and purpose filled Abby. She was ready to begin.

"Let's pray," she said.

* * *

"Wait. Pause!" Wylie shouted. Immediately the scene dissipated. There it was again, as Abby spoke—the change in atmosphere, the sense that something or someone unseen was there with them, with Abby in some strange way. Wylie felt the edges of it, but couldn't get hold of the middle. "What was that? That feeling she had? What was it?"

"In emo-ling mode you experience the emotions of the creator," the Butterfly answered patiently.

"But that was more than an emotion," Wylie insisted. "I've felt it before." Images of kneeling over a bleeding woman and running toward Delores in slow-motion flooded in, and with them came the memory of the thing, the aura, the knowing. Wylie pushed the cap away from her eyes and looked around the room as if she expected to see someone there, but there was only Monty, snoring on the sofa. "What is that?" she asked again, knowing it was ridiculous to plead with a machine, but not caring.

"In emo-ling mode the user experiences the emotions of the creator," the Butterfly said again. "Do you wish to discontinue emo-ling?"

The feeling that had been so real a second ago was fading. "No," she said. "Keep going. But skip the prayer part."

"You guys did a great job carving pumpkins today," Abby began. "And we didn't even need any of these." She pulled a variety of different sized bandages and a tube of first aid cream from her pocket and laid them out on the small end table next to the sofa. "Not one injury! Good job, guys."

"Maybe they weren't trying hard enough," Bill said, and not quietly. Steve and his entourage laughed.

Abby ignored them. "Of course, since we don't live in a bubble, sometimes in life, injury is unavoidable. When we were kids we all got bumps and bruises and skinned knees."

"Would you kiss my boo-boo and make it better?" Jason called out.

Abby frowned, but she knew that responding would make it worse. She kept her gaze outward and tried to maintain her focus. It wasn't easy, but she breathed a wordless prayer and kept going.

"If, God forbid, you happened to get badly hurt– like, say you were in a car accident, or . . . " Abby turned toward Jason, deadpan, " . . . say your youth pastor accidently dropped a pumpkin on your head." Some of the girls laughed but Jason rolled his eyes. "Thankfully, there would be medical treatment available. And if you were hurt really badly you might need a blood transfusion, and the blood you received would have to match yours or else it could be deadly."

"I faint at the sight of blood," said Becca from the girl's side of the room. Abby noticed that her complexion did look a little greenish.

"Way to go, genius," Layla muttered.

"That might sound scary," Abby continued, giving Becca a sympathetic smile, "but if you're like most people you have a common blood type, and you wouldn't have a problem. But did you know that there is one blood type that's so rare that only about forty people in the whole world have it? It's called Rh-null blood, and it's so special because it doesn't have any of this stuff called antigens that all the other blood types have."

"This isn't med school," Bill said.

"So, a person with Rh-null blood could donate blood to anyone, even people with other rare blood types. That's what makes it so valuable."

"Get to the point," said Layla, and Abby pictured herself sticking gauze pads over Bill and Layla's mouths. She took a deep breath and continued.

"Now, I can't guarantee it, but hopefully no one here will ever get hurt badly enough to need a blood transfusion. But there's a different kind of hurt, an inside kind, and those wounds aren't so easy to avoid. Some wounds come from other people, even from our friends or our families. Sometimes we might seem happy on the outside, but on the inside we're wounded. We feel sad, or lonely, or guilty, or like we're not good enough. And the truth is we aren't good enough, none of us are. We all make mistakes and blow it. The Bible calls that sin, and it says we all do it. We all sin, and because of that sin we hurt ourselves and other people every day, whether we mean to or not."

The invisible bandages seemed to take hold because for once Bill and Layla were silent. The mood in the room grew somber, and Abby noticed that Cora and Jane looked stricken.

"That kind of hurt can't be fixed by Rh-null blood," she said, "no matter how rare and special it is. Fortunately for us, the Bible tells us about another kind of blood, an even more special kind of blood, that can fix our hurts and take away the guilt and pain, and that's the blood of Jesus. Colossians 1:20 says that God made peace with everything in heaven and on earth when Jesus died on the cross. That is a really big deal. And here's the kicker—remember I said we all sin? That's not exactly true, because Jesus is the one person in the history of the universe who never, ever sinned. Jesus didn't deserve to die, but he gave his life for us on that cross. If we come to him and ask his forgiveness, through the blood of Jesus we can have peace with God."

Tears leaked down Cora's cheeks. "What if you can't be forgiven?" As she spoke the spotlight of teenage gaze shifted toward her and she covered her eyes to avoid the glare. "What if what you've done is so bad you can never be forgiven?" she asked quietly.

"There's nothing that can separate you from the love of God," Abby said. "No matter what you've done, Jesus will forgive you."

"What if you can't stop doing it?" She turned her eyes toward Jane, but Jane looked away blankly.

A coarse whisper came from Steve's direction. "They're homos. I knew it."

Abby snapped toward the guys on the couch, but it was too late to tell who'd said it. She turned back to the girls, opened her mouth, and closed it again, at a loss for words. She tried to smile but she couldn't quite get her lips to move in that direction.

"I'm not sure what to say, but let's talk about this later," she said quietly.

Bill jumped up with his Bible open. "You may not know what to say, but the word is clear. 'As for those who persist in sin, rebuke them in the presence of all, so that the rest may stand in fear.' First Timothy 5:20. Yes, Jesus loves sinners, but those who persist in sin go to hell."

A wave of protective fury rose in Abby. She closed her eyes, knowing that Bill's smugness might carry her to the point of no return and partly welcoming the journey. "That's enough," she said, surprising herself with the force of her own words.

* * *

"Yes, that's definitely enough," Wylie said. "Stop the program." Finally, she understood Del's full and complete revulsion of anything related to the Committed. If these girls could be treated so badly decades before the Reclamation, what must Delores have gone through once its tendrils had wrapped themselves around every aspect of daily life? No wonder her mother had stopped leaving the house.

But something else about this episode was bothering Wylie even more than the pain on Cora's face.

"Can you go back?" she asked the Butterfly.

"Please specify where in the simulation you would like to begin."

"Go back to the stuff about blood types."

Wylie listened again to Abby's description of Rh-null blood. How could Abby know about something so rare? She wanted to believe it was a coincidence, but how could it be?

"Skip to the next day," Wylie said, but then Darwin was at the door and Monty needed a walk. The next day would have to wait until the next day.

15

C ora and Jane didn't show for breakfast the next morning. At the end of the evening session they'd quietly slipped away and refused to leave the girl's dorm that night. Abby had begged them to come out for a walk on the beautiful, crisp fall evening, but while the other kids played Capture the Flag with glowsticks, Cora and Jane stayed in, both with noses buried in books and not even talking to each other.

Finally, after breakfast, when everyone was packed and ready to return home, the girls dragged their belongings outside and waited by the van. They chose the backseat again but piled their bags next to them, leaving no room for Abby to sit. Clearly, they wanted no further contact. Abby's heart was sinking, but she wasn't about to give up so easily. She'd wait for the first rest stop and when the van was empty she'd throw the bags in the back so that she could sit with the girls and try to get them to talk, even if it was just to set up a time to meet away from the listening ears surrounding them today.

When the van stopped and the kids piled out, Abby set her plan in action. Layla, of course, was watching.

"What are you doing?" she asked.

"Just shuffling things around to make some room," Abby replied lightly.

Layla nodded and jiggled the van keys in her hands. Then, with a smile of deep malevolence, she headed for the plaza, leaving Abby to wonder what was next. That morning she'd found a dead bird in her jacket pocket and her private, personal journal had gone missing. She'd been too worried about Cora and Jane to mention it, and besides, she knew direct confrontation would backfire. She'd have to find another way. As Layla disappeared through the glass doors, Abby stood still for a moment, looking up at the feathery clouds that decorated the sky like lace on a bright blue blanket. She breathed one quiet word—a name—closed her eyes, and waited. When she felt ready, she walked to the plaza and joined a long queue outside the women's restroom, where, apparently, most of the stalls were out of order. As she waited, she noticed the youth group girls were already heading back to the van with enough coffee to keep them buzzing for days. This will be a fun trip home, Abby thought. She looked around for Cora and Jane, but they were nowhere to be seen. This line was taking forever. Abby considered abandoning the whole idea, but she didn't think she'd make it home without a bathroom break, and she knew Bill would never stop again for her. In fact, if Bill and Layla found out she needed another rest stop they'd use the information to torture her on the way home and probably for the rest of the year. No, she'd better wait to use the bathroom while she had the chance.

Just when Abby was finally getting closer to an empty stall, a maintenance worker entered the restroom with a puzzled look on her face. "What's all this?" she asked, pointing to the "out of order" signs scribbled on sticky notes and stuck to several stalls. She jiggled the door closest to her, but it was locked.

"We thought they were out of order," said the woman in front of Abby.

The worker shook her head. "These aren't our signs. Somebody's idea of a bad joke, I guess." She ripped off the sticky notes and opened the locked stall doors with a key. "There you go. Nothing wrong with these toilets," she said. "Cleaned them myself not an hour ago."

Odd, Abby thought. Must be national prank day. She finished as quickly as she could and hurried through the plaza, knowing she'd never hear the end of it if she kept Bill and Layla waiting. She rushed through the doors into the parking lot, where understanding hit her like a blast of frigid air. She was too late. The van was gone and in its place was a sticky note stuck to a lamppost. In the now familiar scrawl, it read, "Too slow, loser. Have fun getting home."

Now what? Abby flipped open her phone and speed dialed the church office.

"Great River Christian Center," announced the bright and perky receptionist on the other end. "How may I help you?"

"Margaret, it's me, Abby. I'm at the turnpike rest stop. They left me here."

"What?" Margaret's voice went from perky to pestered. "Who left you where?"

"We were coming home from the youth retreat and Bill drove off without me. They left me here, on purpose."

"Oh, I'm sure that can't be true. It must have been an accident. Why didn't you stay with the group?"

Margaret had unknowingly stated the opposition's defense. They would simply claim they hadn't noticed Abby was missing, and the blame would fall on her.

"But they left a note," Abby said weakly.

"There must be some mistake. I've known Bill and Layla for fifteen years. They're the best."

Right—the best something, but Abby didn't want to say what, and it wouldn't have mattered if she did. It seemed like a force beyond Abby's control had blinded Margaret and everyone else from the truth. She crumbled the sticky note into a tiny ball and threw it away.

"I need a ride back," she said.

"Well, I'm sorry, but there's no one to get you. Can you call a friend?"

The sad truth was that Abby had no friends at Great River. Not one. Her nearest friend was back at the college, over four hundred miles away.

"No."

"Well, I don't know what to tell you." Margaret's fingers clicked at the keyboard as she spoke. Abby might need to walk fifty miles along the side of a highway to get home, but at least the church bulletin would be ready on time.

"Uh, could I be of help?" A mild male voice spoke in the background. "If someone needs a ride, I'd be glad to go."

Margaret's voice warmed. "Oh, we couldn't trouble you like that."

"It's no trouble at all. I'm free as a bird until the Missions Committee dinner tonight. I'd be happy to help."

"Well, okay then, if you're sure." Her voice dropped in temperature when she addressed Abby again. "Seems it's your lucky day. Our missionary guest, Pastor Reynolds, is willing to come get you. Do you think you can manage to tell him where you're at?"

Abby was too relieved to feel offended. She described her whereabouts to the gentle voice at the other end of the line, and within an hour she was seated next to a slightly built, middle-aged man with a balding head and wire rim glasses, headed back to the church where she hoped her overnight bag would be waiting.

"I can't thank you enough, Pastor Reynolds," Abby said.

"No problem, and please call me Cam. These things happen. We once left our youngest son behind at church. I thought my wife had him; she thought I had him. Just like Jesus at the temple, huh?" He smiled and glanced at Abby, who was doing her best to hold back tears.

"What's up?" Cam asked. "Everything else okay?"

Should she or shouldn't she confide the truth to this stranger? Who knew what relationships Cam had with the ingrown membership of Great

River? For all she knew, Cam's wife could be Layla's best friend. Maybe they were bridesmaids at each other's weddings. It had been a long time since Abby had met someone she could trust, and she wasn't sure she should start now. Still, Cam had been willing to come get her, no questions asked, and that had to say something about his character. Abby decided to err on the side of trust. Slowly, deliberately, and with as little emotion as possible, she relayed to Cam her experiences since she'd arrived last spring. She included every detail, even the fact that her journal went missing that day and that she fully expected her most private thoughts and personal feelings to turn up as a bulletin insert tomorrow.

"Wow," Cam said when Abby was done. "That sounds pretty unbelievable."

"I know, and I don't blame you if you don't believe me. I don't think I would believe it myself if it wasn't happening to me. Not exactly what I expected ministry to be." Abby took a deep breath and relaxed a tiny bit. Whether Cam believed her or not, she felt better for having told her story.

"Have you told the pastor about all this?" Cam asked.

"Several times. He doesn't want to get involved. His exact words were, 'They were here before you came and they'll be here after you're gone.'"

"How about the district superintendent?"

"Without the pastor to back me up, it would be my word against theirs. And like you said, the whole story is pretty unbelievable. I've been praying and waiting it out, for now."

Cam was silent for a few minutes as they sped along the highway. "You know," he said finally, "the truth is, people can be tough sometimes. And while I've never heard anything quite this drastic, I have known of many hurts in the ministry. If there's anything my family can do to help, let us know."

"Thanks." Abby felt calm enough to change the subject. "So, I heard you've been in Korea for the last four years. How was that?"

"South Korea is wonderful. The churches are flourishing, more than here in the States."

"People say Christianity is really big there, with the mega church and all. Someone I know thinks it might become the state religion." That someone was Steve, but Abby didn't want to ruin the peaceful moment by mentioning his name.

Cam laughed. "Not exactly, although there's no doubt that Christianity has some political influence in South Korea. But the state religion? May it never be! That's the worst thing that could happen to the church, there or anywhere else. There's no quicker path to corruption, as far as I'm concerned."

"But we were founded as a Christian nation, right? People are always saying that we need to reclaim our Christian status." Abby had heard that notion many times at school, and not only from Steve, and she'd never seriously questioned its veracity. "We pledge that we're 'one nation under God,' and our money says, 'In God We Trust.' Isn't that proof enough that we were intended to be a Christian nation?"

"Most people don't realize those phrases weren't added until the 1950s. The Founding Fathers were Christian, in name at least. But they had a variety of beliefs and ways of living or not living out their faith. Most were deists, which means they didn't believe in the personal God that you and I have given our lives to."

"Oh." Abby had heard that, too, but it never seemed important enough to remember.

"Let's face it," Cam continued, "the Founders were inconsistent in lots of ways. Did you ever ask yourself how the person who wrote 'all men are created equal' could have owned slaves?"

"You mean Thomas Jefferson?"

"Yes—a complete study in inconsistency, if you ask me. He worked toward abolishing slavery while owning slaves. He freed a few before he died, but many more were sold off to pay his debts."

"Umm."

"Sorry, I didn't mean to go off on a rant. I just find it amazing that so many people want to live in a theocracy without really understanding what that means. They think of ancient Israel, but they forget to look at modern-day theocratic movements and see what life is like there. The separation of church and state is the greatest gift the Founders could have given us, as far as I'm concerned. No, I wouldn't want our church leaders in charge of the country. I can't even imagine the divisions that would cause."

Abby pictured Steve, Bill, Layla, and Pastor Rick in the White House and almost laughed out loud. "You're right about that. If people can do so much damage in a small-town Ohio church, imagine what they'd do if they had real power."

As they reached the turnpike exit, Abby directed Cam to the church, which was now about twenty minutes away. She knew once they got back Cam would be swallowed up by Pastor Rick and the head of the Missions Committee, who happened to be Layla's sister. This would probably be her last chance to talk with him alone. Abby had not seriously thought about the mission field, but her experience at the church made travelling great distances seem appealing.

"So, what do you guys do in Korea?" Abby asked.

"Officially we're in campus ministry. We also support the discipleship efforts at one of the smaller outreaches. Unofficially, I can't say too much. But God is working in areas that might surprise people."

"Have you ever crossed into the north?" Abby asked.

"I can't really say. But keep us in your prayers. Like I said, God is working."

Abby felt her perspective shift. Compared to risking imprisonment, her problems seemed a little more manageable. She sat back and allowed herself to enjoy the fall foliage. The grass had been covered with frost for the last few mornings, a sure sign that winter was coming soon.

When they got to the church, Abby had no trouble finding her suitcase, since it was lying open with her belongings strewn across the back lawn. Cam offered to help her gather her things, but Abby was too embarrassed to allow it. They parted ways, Abby thanking Cam profusely. She'd needed their conversation more than he would probably ever know.

That evening at the missions dinner Cam and his family sat at the dais with the rest of the church staff and Steve (who had no official position in the church), while Abby sat at the furthest table from the podium with Jason and Becca and some of the other youth. She spent most of the dinner trying to stop them from lighting the paper tablecloth on fire with the candle centerpiece.

Jason, who usually ignored Abby, deigned to look her way as dessert was being served.

"Too bad about this morning," he said with a smirk. "I heard you got a ride home with the missionary."

"Sure did. He's a great guy, and I learned a lot from talking to him. Just like Joseph said, sometimes when someone means evil against you, God means it for good."

Jason's face was the epitome of innocence. "Amen," he said. "We had a good talk in the van while you weren't there, as well."

The table suddenly went quiet and Abby felt a sense of unexplainable dread. "Is that right?" she said. "How so?"

"Well, without you to run interference, Bill and Layla were able to talk openly with those two new girls."

"You mean Cora and Jane?"

"Yeah, the two . . . well, I'm too nice to say it but we all know what they are."

"Go on," Abby said. "Tell me about this conversation."

"Like I said, without you there, Bill and Layla were able to set them straight. You know, tell them what the Bible says about hom—about certain lifestyles. They laid it on the line. You can repent and change your ways, or you can go to hell. That's the simple gospel, right there." With his hands behind his head, Jason leaned back in his chair and Abby felt the sudden urge to tip him over. Maybe a hard hit to the floor would wipe the smugness off his face.

Instead, she grabbed her phone and fled the room, hoping to reach Cora or Jane to see if they were all right. As she dialed Cora's number, she noticed Becca had followed her into the lobby. From Becca's troubled expression Abby knew that she had something to say and that it wouldn't be good news.

"Listen," Becca whispered, although there was no one else around, "I didn't want to get involved, but you should know what happened in the van. It wasn't just Layla and Bill talking. They were really mean to those girls, asking questions and trying to get them to admit stuff. Then Steve started a chant and they kept it up until we got home. It was pretty awful."

"A chant? What kind of chant?"

"They were chanting, 'Homos earn God's spurn,' over and over. I'm not even sure what 'spurn' means, but the girls were crying when they left. I felt terrible but I didn't know what to do. Anyway, I thought you should know."

"Thanks, Becca. I'll try to reach them."

Abby turned back to her phone, but Becca wasn't finished.

"Abby, one question. What Jason said before about repenting or going to hell—that's not really the gospel, is it? I mean, is that what we believe?" Her eyes were wide with expectation, and Abby couldn't resist giving her a hug.

"No, Becca, that's not the gospel. The gospel is so much more than that. Let's talk later, okay?"

Becca nodded and went back to the dinner while Abby tried, unsuccessfully, to reach Cora or Jane. She had a strong suspicion the girls had blocked her number and that she would never see or speak to either of them again.

16

Wylie carried around a mix of emotions like an invisible backpack for days. On the one hand, everything she'd grown up believing about the Committed, every horrendous experience she'd had with them, could be traced back to Abby's time. Why, she asked herself, would anyone want to follow a religion filled with such narrow, hateful people? On the other hand, there was Abby. Petite and unimposing, Abby was someone Wylie might pass on the street without a second glance. But after spending several virtual months in Abby's head, Wylie knew better than to underestimate this quiet young woman from the past. She had sensed firsthand Abby's connection with something greater, even if Wylie shunned the idea of what that something might be. On the outside, Abby was as frail and finite as any other person. She got headaches and colds and was tired to the bone more often than not. Like everyone else, Abby felt happy and sad and worried and discouraged, but just beyond those feelings, or sometimes right in the middle of them, was something more—an essence, an unseen presence that seemed to go on forever. Sometimes Wylie didn't sense the presence at all, but at other times she couldn't tell where Abby ended and the presence began. Abby had a name for the presence—a name that Wylie refused to say.

Cam, too, represented a contradiction that nettled at Wylie like a pebble in her shoe. Wylie had only used the word as a slur, but now she understood that the term "missionary" had meant something different then. For her entire life she'd thought of them as mean, dim-witted automatons dedicated to advancing the ChurchState's cause of uniformity, and much of her time had been devoted to keeping them out of her hair. But Cam, like Abby, was different. His kindness poked holes in Wylie's model of religion, and she wasn't happy about it. Life had never been easy, but until now at least it had been consistent.

Darwin mentioned Wylie's funk one early spring morning as they cut back the shrubs on his grandfather's estate. Under the deadwood, tiny new branches and buds pushed their way into the world, demanding space to grow.

"Things not going too well for Abby?" Darwin asked.

"What makes you say that?"

"Something is bothering you."

Wylie frowned.

Darwin continued. "You're hacking at those branches like you have someone's head in the clippers. Ease up before you kill that poor rosebush."

"Oh. Sorry. I wouldn't want to damage Grandpa's precious roses." Wylie threw the clippers to the ground and plopped down on the limestone garden wall.

"See what I mean? What's up? I thought your present mood might be related to the holostory."

"Sorry," Wylie said again, this time meaning it. "I guess it is. I thought I might find some answers there, but of course I didn't. Just more questions."

"Questions aren't necessarily bad."

"They are if they don't have answers. I just don't understand Abby, and now Cam. They're genuinely good people, surrounded by idiots. Why do they stay? The Uncommitted were free in those days. They could go anywhere, be anything."

"Remember, that was before Committed and Uncommitted existed as political entities. They were part of a religious movement that they chose for themselves."

"I know. But I still don't know why. Maybe it would help if I could find out more about them, outside of Abby's perceptions."

"We could look them up in the state-a-base. Do you have their full names?"

"Cam, yes, but Abby, no. I asked the Butterfly once, but it just said, 'The creator has not released that information.' No idea why."

"Well, we can at least look up this Cam guy and find out what happened to him. He might even still be alive."

"He'd be really old."

"Yeah, but with the Committed health care system at his disposal, who knows? I'll come over after work and we'll check it out."

"Thanks."

"Don't thank me. I'm doing it for the roses."

Wylie went back to work feeling a little bit lighter inside. To show her appreciation, when Darwin arrived that evening she opened an extra can of soup and broke out a brand-new box of crackers, which she presented to Darwin on his grandfather's shiny gold serving tray.

"You know you have access to real food now, right?" he asked.

"This is my comfort food," Wylie answered. "Let's get started."

Darwin felt under the front edge of the small desk in the living area. A holographic display appeared.

"Access state-a-base, code 78383." He pressed his thumb to the corner and the screen came alive.

"How does it recognize you?" Wylie asked. "Uncommitted aren't supposed to have access."

"Grandpa has his ways. Perks of the job, I guess."

Wylie never really knew what position Darwin's grandfather held, but she knew he was high in the Committed food chain. When Darwin's dad revoked his signing, it hit the family hard, but somehow Grandpa had managed to maintain his power. And now, here she was, under his protection. Not for the first time in the last few months, Wylie shuttered to think what her mother would say.

"What was his name again?" Darwin asked.

"Cam, short for Cameron, I guess. Last name Reynolds."

"And you said missionary to South Korea, right? Around what year?"

"Try 2002. That was the year Abby graduated."

Darwin's fingers moved across the screen. "Voice activation would be quicker, but it would be listening for Grandpa's voice. Okay. It's asking for a denomination."

"A what?"

"Before the Reclamation, the Protties were divided into different groups. They called them denominations."

"Oh. I'm not sure. Is that a problem?"

"No, it'll just take longer. Wait a second . . . here he is, right here. Looks like he was an author. Rev. Cameron Reynolds, born 1965, died 2053."

"That's the year we were born," Wylie said.

"Yup." Darwin continued reading. "Served as a pastor, missionary, then pastor again. Four kids, first wife died, married again . . . oh wow, what's this?"

"What?"

"He spent two years in a North Korean labor camp. Officially charged with spying. Wow. Did he seem like a spy to you?"

"Definitely not."

"I didn't think so. He was probably there to proselytize. That's what missionaries do, right? Some things never change."

"Cam was different. He wasn't like the ChurchState missionaries are today. He was smart, and kind, and, I don't know, deep in a way."

"Maybe, but he was still a proselytizer. Here's his book—he wrote about his imprisonment once he got home. Hmm. Interesting."

"Let me see." Wylie pushed her chair in closer and read silently for a minute. Cam had been sentenced to fifteen years hard labor, but had been released after two. He'd toured with his book for a while, but after a few years he'd gone back to pastoring a church in Ohio.

"Oh wow!" Wylie almost shouted. "Great River! That Abby's church! So Cam wound up being the pastor there in 2015. Well, that had to be an improvement." She thought for a moment. "Why isn't Abby listed in the old church records? She was the youth pastor."

Darwin scrolled through the pictures and printed information. "Not sure. Maybe she was there before the church had an official website. Or maybe they never added her to their records. Based on what you've told me, that wouldn't be surprising." He squinted at the display. "Look at this. In 2030 Rev. C. Reynolds was part of a commission to study the Reclamation." Darwin followed along with his finger as he read. "'Reynolds ultimately denied his faith by refusing to sign the Statement of Commitment. As a result, his book describing his experiences in Asia and all other subsequent writings were banned. Reynolds was removed from his position when Great River Christian Center officially affiliated with the ChurchState body in 2033. He died in obscurity.'"

"I hate them," Wylie said quietly.

"I know. But remember, this is the state-a-base version of the story. We don't really know the truth of what happened to him."

"I wonder if she signed—Abby, I mean. I can't picture her doing it. She'd never be a part of all that."

"I guess there's only one way to find out," Darwin said, glancing at the Butterfly, now folded snugly in its chrysalis. "You have to finish the story."

17

When Abby walked into to the youth room, she knew something was off immediately. The room was deadly quiet, and the youth were deeply absorbed in a handout of some sort while Steve looked on like a Jedi master instructing his padawan. Although the youth service was supposed to be Abby's domain, Pastor Rick had insisted Steve be given one night a month to speak, and tonight was one of those nights. Abby always dreaded these sessions, but there was nothing she could do to stop them. She approached Becca, who was concentrating hard on the paper.

"What ya got there?" she asked, trying not to sound concerned.

Becca looked up guiltily, but before she could answer, Steve swooped in.

"Never you mind," he said. "You'll find out soon enough."

Great, Abby thought. They'd already handed out excerpts from her journal and published her student loan debt in the church bulletin (under the guise of "please pray for Abby," of course). What new devilry was this?

The service began with three of the five usual songs, and Abby noticed some of the kids were even more distracted than usual. But instead of playing handheld video games or filing their nails, they were still studying Steve's document. Abby tried to sneak a peek but it was no use; obviously, the kids had been told to keep her in the dark.

When the music was over, Steve stood to speak, holding the same document the kids had been reading. He looked a bit pale and thinner than usual, and his recent haircut, buzzed close to the scalp, added to his cadaverous appearance. He had a slight darkness under his eyes that Abby hadn't noticed before. Even with the rough history between them, Abby felt concern stirring. Until Steve opened his mouth.

"This is an important night," he began. "Maybe the most important night of your lives, because what you do tonight will affect you throughout eternity."

What could Steve possibly be planning? He'd told Abby he was speaking on Hebrews, but as he continued it became clear that he had no plan to open a Bible. In fact, he was concealing something in his right hand that was definitely not a Bible.

"Over the last few months we've noticed a trend in youth group to take the easy way out." The door at the back of the room opened and in walked Bill and Layla. They ignored Abby, but smiled warmly at Steve.

"We talk about all the easy parts of the Bible," Steve continued, "the love and all that. Now that's all well and good, for what it's worth. And of course, God loves us, we know this is true. But if you think God's love is enough, you're wrong. God wants your full commitment. It's all or nothing with God, one hundred percent commitment, twenty-four hours a day, seven days a week. This is a Christian country, and we're God's soldiers. Soldiers can't be weak. We need to be tough and strong and not tolerate infiltration from the enemy." Steve looked straight at Abby. "The enemy would water down the gospel into some kind of mother's milk for babies. No, like Hebrews 5 says, you need solid food so that you can tell the difference between good and evil. Evil has been tolerated in this youth group in the past, but no more. Tonight is the night we commit ourselves fully to the cause of Christ."

Bill and Layla came forward and unrolled a three-foot-long scroll.

"No more messing around, vacillating, and depending on God's love to save you. We are asking each of you to sign this Statement of Commitment tonight. I'd ask you to sign it in blood, if I could; that's how important this is."

As Steve flipped open a pocket knife and poised it over his finger, Abby sat up in alarm. This was going too far. Was he actually going to sign the scroll in blood? She stood and looked around for help, but Pastor Rick, who had slipped in unnoticed, was nodding his approval from the back row.

Steve closed the knife and pointed it toward the group. "Like I said, I wish we could sign this document in blood. There's sin in the camp, and God hates sin. Do you want to go to heaven or not? If not, there's a nice hot spot waiting for you in the fires of hell. You've all read the statement I handed out to you earlier. Now come up and sign. Prove you're one of the committed."

Steve nodded at Simon, a tall, shaggy blond who played keyboard on the worship team. Simon played a series of low chords while Layla turned the lights down low. One by one the members of the youth group rose, walked quietly to the front, and signed Steve's statement, not in blood but in the thick red marker he had provided. Abby still hadn't read the statement, but when she tried to get a closer look, Layla blocked her way.

"Stand aside," she sneered. "This isn't for you."

"I have a right to see what they're signing," Abby said.

"You've done enough damage with your watered-down gospel. We are under Pastor Rick's authority, and he gave his permission."

Before Abby could reply, there was Pastor Rick, hovering over her like a raptor ready to strike. "Let's step outside," he said. Abby had no choice but to follow him into the hallway.

"Is it true you gave permission for this?" she asked as soon as they'd cleared the doorway.

"Yes. Steve came to me last week with his idea, and I thought it was a good one. I can't see why you'd object to encouraging full commitment from the youth."

"Of course I want them to commit themselves to Christ." Abby was about to add that she should have been consulted and she'd like to see this statement, but Rick cut her off.

"Are you sure?" he asked with a patronizing smile. "From what I've heard, you're afraid to give them the whole gospel. You even let those two girls infiltrate the group."

"Do you mean Cora and Jane? We were just getting to know them."

"A little leaven leavens the whole lump. It wouldn't take long for them to corrupt the others, and we have a commitment to these kids and their parents to keep the youth group pure."

"That's not true," Abby said, and as much as she hated to take a defensive position, she couldn't stop herself. "I share the whole gospel every time I speak."

"So you say. But look, this isn't a conversation I want to have with you in the hallway. Why don't you just call it a night? Steve will finish up and I'll make sure the building is locked before I go. And by the way, anytime you don't agree with my decision making, you're free to hand in your resignation."

And there it was. The unsaid words between them were finally spoken. Finally, Pastor Rick's goal was clear.

"Why did you bring me here?" Abby whispered. "Why not just hire Steve to begin with?"

"District politics. Had to avoid the appearance of nepotism and all that. But once you resign, the district will see that I had to appoint Steve for the sake of the youth group. Steve will provide continuity and a smooth transition." He turned his back on Abby and returned to the youth room, letting the door slam in her face.

There was nothing for Abby to do but leave. When she stopped in her office to grab her purse, she noticed a foul odor coming from her desk. She opened the bottom drawer to see a dead racoon staring up at her. Under its front paw was a note: "Enjoy the road kill."

Abby knew when she'd been beaten. She closed the drawer and left. That night she typed her official letter of resignation. She'd give notice to her landlord tomorrow, and, if all went well, she could be back home with her parents by the following week. She tried to pray, but all she could do was whisper a wounded, confused plea for help. As she slept, the same bewildered thoughts circled round and round in her dreams. She'd worked so hard, prayed so much, believed so deeply that she'd been called. How had this happened to her?

When the buzzing sounded, Abby thought at first it was her alarm, but as she woke from a fitful sleep she realized it was her phone. Who could be calling at 2:37 a.m.? She flipped her phone open and squinted at the name on the display—Becca.

"Hello?"

There was silence on the other end, and then an almost soundless gasping for breath that Abby recognized as sobbing.

"Becca? Are you there? What's wrong?"

Becca didn't answer, but the crying grew slightly louder.

"Becca, are you home?" Abby asked. She jumped out of bed and turned on the light. "I'm coming over."

Finally, Becca spoke. "No, don't. Please. I'm not home. My parents are away."

"Where are you?"

"I'm at a friend's house. I'm safe. I just needed to talk to someone."

"What friend?" Abby trusted Becca, but something told her to press the issue.

Becca did not want to be pressed. "It doesn't matter. Go back to sleep. Sorry I bothered you."

"No—wait! Becca, don't hang up. I'm here. What's going on?"

"It's just . . . I told a lie tonight. A really big lie."

Abby almost smiled. "That doesn't sound so bad."

"You don't understand. I signed that statement. We all did. It was a big lie. And Steve said that liars go to the lake of fire, just like murderers and idolaters. He said it's in the Bible. He said don't sign the statement unless you really mean it." Becca's words were swallowed up in quiet sobs.

"Becca, listen to me. God doesn't expect you to be perfect. The Bible also says that we all sin. All of us—even Steve." Especially Steve, Abby thought. "But that's why Jesus came, to die for our sins. Whatever it is, no matter how terrible, God will forgive you."

"It's all my fault," Becca moaned. "My shirts are too low and my dresses are too short. My mom always says that. And the drinking—I know I shouldn't, but I do. We all do and then what happens after that—it's my own fault."

Becca stopped and Abby heard her gulp something down.

"Are you drinking right now?" she asked.

"I can't lie anymore."

The line went dead.

"Becca? Are you there?" Abby dialed her back, but Becca didn't answer. She called Pastor Rick, but he declined her call. She threw a coat over her pajamas and drove to Becca's house, on the off chance that Becca had been home all along, but the house was dark and empty. From the car Abby called every other member of the youth group she could think of. Most didn't answer, but those who did knew nothing of Becca's whereabouts. Finally, out of sheer desperation, she called Steve and told him of her conversation with Becca.

"Relax," Steve said. "I just talked to Becca. She's fine. Layla is on her way to pick her up. She'll spend the rest of the night at their place."

"Oh," Abby said. "That's a relief. I'm really worried about her. She said some strange stuff to me. Someone needs to check it out."

"Well, from what I hear she's not your problem anymore. You've messed up this group enough. We'll handle it from here."

"What? How have I messed anything up?" Suddenly Abby was ready for a fight. Maybe they'd won, but she wasn't about to slink away without telling Steve exactly what she thought of him.

But there would be no fight. Steve hung up and Abby was left with nothing but her overwhelming frustration.

* * *

Abby had overestimated the time it took her to tie up loose ends and go home. Within three days she was sitting in her old bedroom at her parents' house, trying to reflect on what had happened. She decided to take some time to heal before she planned her next move. To keep busy she helped out at her parents' church, folding bulletins, dusting the sanctuary, and volunteering for any other tasks that kept her hands busy and her mind calm. Little by little her prayers were able to take the form of words again. She sought the counsel of trusted friends and a few professors from the college that had known her well. They confirmed what Abby knew, deep down—nothing had been her fault. When Abby was invited to help with the youth group, she agreed, happy to get her feet wet in ministry again, even as a volunteer. To pay her bills she took a job at the local UPS store. Gradually, the bad memories faded, and she began to feel like herself again.

So it was with great trepidation that Abby opened an email from Bill four months later. Her heart sank as she read.

> *Abby,*
>
> *Steve didn't want me to write, but Layla and I feel you need to know the full extent of the damage you caused here. Last month our dear Becca took her own life. We don't know what advice you gave her, but had you alerted us to the seriousness of her problems we feel we could have intervened and this precious life would not have been cut short.*
>
> *Please do not contact Steve, as he has not been well and hearing from you would surely make him worse.*
>
> *We pray you will never be allowed to go near a youth group again.*
>
> *Bill*

Abby turned from her computer and fell to her knees.

Wylie pulled off the cap and found that she, too, was on her knees, sobbing along with a girl she'd never met.

PART III

The Chase

18

Wylie had not logged in to her school account for a good month. She'd been too obsessed with Abby's story to focus on anything else, but that was all over now. It wasn't like Wylie to leave something unfinished, and she knew the Butterfly wasn't quite done, but she just couldn't reconcile how a world could be so much better yet so much worse than her own. At least in her world she knew where she stood. No one pretended she was anything more than a second-class citizen (and maybe not a citizen at all before long, if Del's prediction came true), an apostate bound for hell. Life was hard, but there was a directness to her existence that was almost elegant when compared to the duplicity Abby had faced. Her virtual immersion in Abby's life left Wylie feeling more confused and depleted than ever.

The noncom school website was slow to take her login, which wasn't all that unusual, especially for a weekend when the second-tier wireless was especially slow. Wylie waited patiently, looking up from the outdated console at the noncom grocery store. People were lined up at the only self-checkout station that still worked, probably feeling lucky they'd been able to find any food on the half-empty shelves and keenly aware of the armed guards at the entrance and the camera drones flying above. Wylie thought of the full refrigerator back at the cottage and felt a twinge of guilt. She focused her attention back to the whirling school logo as the website continued to struggle. After a few minutes the screen went dark except for the words *Account deleted for insufficient work* blinking back at her.

"What?" she said aloud. How could that be? She was only a month away from completion. She tried to log in again and again, but it was no use. The same unforgiving pronouncement appeared each time. Just like that, she was no longer a student. Not that a high school education would do much for her, but still, the abrupt ending to her inauspicious scholarly pursuits left her feeling like a half-eaten ketchup sandwich.

Now that her school life was over, Wylie figured she might as well devote her energies to her prestigious career in weed removal. She walked back to the estate, planning to engage in some highly skilled dandelion elimination, but she arrived to find a man with a hydro-seeding truck blocking the road in front of the cottage. Smaller trucks filled with mulch had invaded the estate as well, and everywhere she looked Wylie saw shovels and wheelbarrows in action. She stood to the side of the seeding truck, surprised that Darwin's grandpa would hire a company that used such old school methods. The words *Seed Sower* were sprawled across the tank in bright green. She moved a little closer to get a better look at the man seeding the lawn just as the motor petered into silence. He was tall and dark and familiar looking, although from where Wylie couldn't think. When he walked to the back of the truck and pulled a lever, the hose retreated into a hidden compartment with a whoosh.

"Hi there," the man said to Wylie, walking toward her with his hand outstretched. "You must be Darwin's friend. He told me you were staying here, helping out with the yard work. Name's Ed."

Wylie shook his hand cautiously, realizing why this guy looked so familiar. Ed looked toward the back of the property and spoke into his earpiece. "Hey JoJo, make sure they finish up back there. Don't want any calls about half-done jobs."

"I know you," Ed said, turning back to Wylie. "You're the one with the dog, that night in the rain. Glad to see you made it back okay."

"Yeah, I thought you looked familiar. Thanks for your help that night."

"You're welcome. Looks like you landed on your feet."

Wylie looked around the radiation-shielded estate. The fruit trees were about to burst into pink and white blossoms. Clusters of yellow daffodils had poked through the cold earth, and soon the tulips would follow in a majestic array of color. Red breasted robins flitted to and fro, some with grass and twigs held in their beaks. In the mulberry bush at the corner of the lawn a cardinal sounded his loud metallic click. There was no doubt that this was the most beautiful place Wylie had ever lived. "Oh, right," she said sweetly. "I guess this is a great job . . . for an Uncommitted."

Ed's smile faded. Wylie had no reason to be angry at this guy. Without his help, who knows what might have happened to her that night? Nevertheless, she could not stifle her rising resentment. "And I still have another few months to live here, too, before your new Bill of Rights makes me homeless again. Yeah, I really did land on my feet. Thanks again." She looked into Ed's eyes with more contempt than she knew she could produce.

"Okay, maybe I deserved that," Ed answered calmly. "But we never got to finish our conversation that night. And unfinished things, they don't sit right with me." He handed Wylie a slip of paper he'd retrieved from his pocket. "Check this out when you're ready. They'll be someone there to help you."

Wylie crumpled the paper into a ball and flicked it across the lawn. "It's not that I don't believe you, Ed, but no thanks. We'll figure it out on our own. I gotta go let my dog out now." She ran to the cottage and slammed the door on Ed's good intentions. A little late now for help from the Committed, she thought. Where were they when Delores needed them, or was she too outside their idea of normal to be worth bothering about?

She waited for Ed and his troupe to clear out before she let Monty escape and watched with satisfaction as he peed his way across the newly seeded lawn. "Are you finished, boy?" she asked when he bounded back to her, tongue out and tail wagging. "Yeah, I guess we both are," she told him. "Let's go inside."

Wylie sat on the edge of the bed and stared at the gold-framed Church-State flag on the opposite wall. Darwin had offered to remove it, but Wylie insisted it remain as a reminder that she did not belong in this cozy cottage. Below the flag was a gold plate with the inscription, "First of its kind—2041." She wanted to rip down the ostentatious symbol of everything wrong in her world and smash it to bits, but she couldn't repay Darwin's kindness by trashing his grandfather's place. Instead, she threw a rolled-up ball of socks at the flag. The would-be weapon hit the edge of the frame just hard enough to jar it loose and send it sliding down the wall to the table below. Wylie panicked for a minute. Inspecting the wall, the table, and the frame closely, she breathed a sigh of relief that no damage was done. She turned the frame over and ran her hand along the smooth brown paper backing where she spotted a note scribbled in cursive, the pencil so faded that Wylie could barely read it. Only one word stood out, clearly: "finish." She replaced the fame on the wall and set up the Butterfly one last time.

19

"Someone you know was admitted this morning," Abby read in a text from her mom. "Said he went to school with you. Steve Johnson. Said to tell you hi."

Abby hadn't thought about Steve for a very long time. So much had happened in the ten years since she'd left Great River that the horror of her first position almost seemed like it had happened to someone else. She'd heard Steve had gotten married a few years ago, but not much else about him since then.

"Hold on, you skipped something," Wylie interrupted. "Why have we jumped ten years into the future?"

"The narration proceeds as programmed by the creator," the Butterfly replied in its robotic voice.

This was no digital autobiography left for future generations, Wylie realized. Abby had told a specific story for a specific reason. A question that had been nagging at Wylie for months once again pushed its way to the surface. How did the advanced technology of the holodrive end up at the bottom of a box of old videos in the library archives? It was not left there by accident, she was sure of that. And how hadn't she noticed it sooner? With no answers in sight, her only options were to finish the story or forget the whole thing.

"Continue."

Abby checked her calendar. She had a sermon to prepare and a major assignment due at the end of the week, but she felt compelled to squeeze in a visit to the hospital. When she arrived, she was shocked by what she found. A gaunt, sickly Steve with yellow-tinged skin and dark circles under his eyes was barely recognizable. Two elderly people sat in chairs at the foot of the bed and a younger woman squeezed between tubes and hospital equipment sat at Steve's side, holding his hand and staring at the rise and fall of his chest as if waiting for his shallow breathing to stop at any second. Abby couldn't tell if Steve was sleeping or too weak to focus. The young woman noticed her standing in the doorway and gently released Steve's hand.

"Hi," Abby whispered. "I'm an old friend of Steve's from school. I don't mean to disturb—just wanted to check in. I can leave if he's not up to a visit."

"Oh, well, he's sleeping just now." The woman rose and walked into the hall with Abby, closing the door behind them. She was tall and thin and blond—exactly the type Steve would have chosen, Abby thought, immediately admonishing herself for being so petty.

"I'm Jenny, Steve's wife. Are you Abby?"

"Yes. How did you know?"

"Your mom mentioned you. Thanks for coming by."

"Of course. I'm so sorry to see Steve like this. What happened, if you don't mind me asking?"

Jenny wiped a tear from her eye and any last vestige of resentment Abby harbored toward Steve dissolved.

"It's liver disease," Jenny explained. "He's on the list for a transplant, but he needs a series of transfusions first. The problem is that there's a shortage of blood, or blood that will match his, anyway. The hospital is working on it, but . . . " Jenny's voice cracked. She pressed her hand to her collar and took a gulp of air. "I'm sorry," she squeaked out.

"It's okay," Abby said, gently taking Jenny's arm. "Why don't we sit down for a minute?"

She led Jenny to a small, empty waiting area. Jenny perched at the edge of her chair and dabbed her eyes with a worn tissue.

"Thanks," she said. "I can only stay for a minute, in case he wakes up. He likes to see me next to him."

"Of course. This must be so hard on you."

"On all of us. I did need a break from his parents, though. There's been such an air of desperation around us. I feel like I'm suffocating." She closed her eyes and continued talking as if from a script she'd committed to memory. "Steve needs blood, and with the bad winter and heavy flu season, there's a shortage. We're just praying he can hold on long enough for the hospital to secure the blood type he needs. They're doing everything they can."

Abby nodded sympathetically. When she felt a nudge within, she didn't waver. "Maybe I can help. Would the hospital allow a directed donation?"

Jenny's eyes popped open. "I, I'm not sure."

"Let's find someone to ask. Because if they do, I could donate blood. Maybe that would be enough to hold him over until they find more."

"Are you O negative?" Jenny asked, hope lighting in her eyes.

"Not exactly, but . . . "

"Then it's no good. He needs O negative."

Abby hesitated, not wanting to give too much information. "I think we can work something out. Why don't I find someone to talk to about it while you get back to Steve?"

They parted, Jenny looking doubtful but too exhausted to argue. Abby found the desk nurse and within an hour she was sitting at the hospital's small donation center with a tube in her arm, watching a plastic bag fill with her blood. Abby had tried to talk them into taking more than one unit, but Steve's doctor had refused.

"You realize, don't you, that if for any reason you would need a transfusion, it would be almost impossible to find a match."

"I know," Abby answered. "I just want to help."

"You can give more at a later time and you're helping more than you know. It's not an exaggeration to say you're saving Steve's life. This will hold him over until the O negative arrives. He's lucky to have a friend like you."

Maybe it was the sense of depletion, or maybe the feeling of exposure that came from losing blood. For whatever reason, Abby felt compelled to tell the truth.

"I wouldn't say we're friends, exactly. We knew each other a long time ago in college and then we met up again for a bit after. Acquaintances, maybe, but no, not friends." She didn't consider describing the pain she'd suffered because of Steve and the others at Great River. That was the past, and she'd long ago forgiven them.

"Well, I'm sure Steve and his family will be very thankful. He'll owe you, that's for sure."

"He won't owe me anything. Freely received, freely given. It's all good."

"Stop!" Wylie shouted. Instantly the scene froze but remained visible. "It's all good? It's all good! How can she say that, after what he did to her? It wasn't good, it was horrible! It was evil! And this is karma! She should let him die." Wylie paced back and forth, but did not remove the Butterfly's soft cap. The disorientation of being inside the hospital room and the cottage at the same time made her head spin.

The Butterfly, still paused, waited patiently. "Continue narration?" it asked when Wylie took a breath, but she couldn't stop mid-rant.

"It's because of him, and people like him, that the world is so screwed up. He made those kids sign that statement! He even wanted them to sign it in blood!" That was the beginning of the Reclamation, right there. Wylie was sure of it. "If I could go back there I'd unhook every tube and watch him die, like he deserves," she shouted. "I'd even help him along. Why not? Think of all the lives I'd save."

Wylie continue to pace, her heart pounding and her thoughts racing. As she imagined holding a pillow over Steve's face to smother his last dying, gasping breath, a strange idea began to form in her mind. She knew that somehow, someway, she'd touched the supernatural over the last months. She'd had moments bordering on the miraculous that couldn't be explained or denied. Maybe this was to be one of those moments.

Wylie tried to calm herself. "Butterfly," she asked in a quieted voice, "can you take me back there?"

"Do you wish to enter the narration as a character or to take the perspective of the creator?"

"If I did that, could I change what happened?"

"You may add to the holostory if you enter active narration. However, the ultimate outcome has been programmed by the creator."

"But, would that change things?"

"You could add to the holostory if you enter active narration . . . "

"I know I could add to the story," Wylie interrupted, "but what I want to know is . . . " she hesitated because what she was about to say sounded bizarre even to her own ears. "What I mean is, could I change what really happened, back then? Could I . . . could you take me back in time, back to that day, to change things for real?" Wylie knew it was crazy, but so was water flowing and blood stopping and people dying at the touch of her hand, to say nothing of what had happened on the day of the implosion. Was it any crazier to think the Butterfly might be some kind of time machine, and this was her chance to turn the world right-side-up again? Why else had the holodrive suddenly appeared at the bottom of that box of old videos? Someone had left it there for her. What other explanation could there be? If Steve was one of the constructors of the Reclamation, as Wylie suspected, and he died there, that day, maybe the Reclamation would never happen. Wylie pictured the world around her shifting, phasing into a new—what did the old movies call it? Timeline? Alternate reality? Maybe Steve's death would have a cascading effect that would ultimately result in a different world for Wylie and Del and millions of others. Would she remember the old reality? It didn't seem likely—how could she remember something that had never happened? Wylie hoped the change would be so complete that every shred of this world would be wiped from existence.

The Butterfly whirred for a moment and answered. "This unit is designed to recount a holostory at varying levels of viewer participation or indoctrination. That is its only function."

"Oh. So . . . it's not a time machine?"

"There is no answer to that question within the databanks of this unit. For more information, request unit specifications."

Of course. Wylie laughed at her own stupidity. "Not necessary," she said. Her one last crazy glimmer of hope smoldered to ash like the charred remains of a ChurchState book burning.

"Do you wish to continue?"

"How much longer is it?" Wylie didn't know how much more she could take. She'd spent so many hours living in Abby's story, and for what? Nothing she'd seen had helped. Delores was still gone, and the world was still broken.

"The holostory is almost complete," the Butterfly said. "Only a few minutes in exterior time remain."

The machine was set up, and she was wearing the cap. She might as well see the ending. Then she'd give the whole thing back to Darwin and forget about Abby and her horribly perfect, perfectly horrible world. "Okay, then, finish it."

The doctors, nurses, and technicians who had been fawning over Abby left her to herself for a few minutes while the bag beside her filled with blood. Thankful for the moment of quiet, she closed her eyes and opened the inner doorway to the presence of peace and light. Wordlessly, she entreated for Steve—for healing and for a future that was different from his past. Abby pictured a healthy Steve, smiling, visiting at the nursing home, praying with a brokenhearted teen, distributing baskets of food on Thanksgiving morning. She imagined Steve with his wife, Jenny, playing ball and riding bikes with their kids. "Let this be," she whispered softly.

"I hate this part," Wylie grumbled.

Abby opened her eyes and stared straight at Wylie. "You probably hate this part, my sweet little Wylie," she said with a sad smile. "But I'm hoping with time, you'll understand. The doors will open. Don't be afraid to walk through them."

The scene disappeared and Wylie was left alone.

"Wait," she cried. "What was that? Come back!"

The unit remained silent.

"Butterfly, replay that last scene!" Wylie commanded, but the machine remained lifeless. The vibrant scenes of a now-gone world had disappeared for good. Wylie pulled off the cap and tossed it to the floor. She'd tell Darwin to take the whole thing away tomorrow. Maybe by then she'd be able to convince herself she'd imagined a woman who lived sixty years ago uttering her name.

20

Wylie had hoped to bury her head in the pillow for at least ten hours, but Monty would not allow it. He whimpered in Wylie's ear until she gave in and took him out. Standing in the thick morning fog, Wylie thought again of Abby's last message. She knew what she'd heard. Or did she? Perhaps the time she'd spent in the Butterfly had scrambled her neurons. What if the ChurchState's most effective indoctrination tool had lasting damaging effects? Or, worse yet, what if someone was intentionally messing with her mind? By the time she dragged Monty back to the cottage Wylie was deep into an all-out argument with herself. She sipped at a cup of coffee, watching out the window and trying to let the warmth of the mug in her hands settle her.

Now that the mulching was done it was time to start the spring planting. Darwin would arrive soon, ready to head to the nursery to pick up a truckload of pansies. Should she tell him about Abby's message to her? Wylie hated to keep another secret from Darwin, but spoken words had a way of giving shape to reality and this just could not be real. She'd keep it to herself and hope that the memory of the Butterfly would fade once it was out of her sight.

A few minutes later Darwin pulled up in his grandfather's hydrovan. He'd only be allowed to drive it for another month; once he turned eighteen, his driver's license would relegate him to noncom vehicles only. As for Wylie, she had two weeks left to ride (and live) in luxury. Finding a new place was still on her to-do list, and her attempts to contact Sharmila had failed. Abby was on her own.

Since Darwin had made it clear that Grandpa would not appreciate dog smell in his van, Wylie left Monty behind in the cottage. She ran across the lawn to meet Darwin, but stopped when she spotted a wadded-up piece of paper on the ground—the same piece of paper she'd flicked away in disgust. Was that just yesterday? She wondered if, along with giving her hallucinations, the holostory had messed with her sense of time. Her brief encounter with Ed the Seed Sower seemed like a week ago. Wylie scooped up the crumpled paper and jumped into the van, where one look at Darwin's familiar face sent her plan of secrecy to an early grave. With a shaky voice she told Darwin of the crazy ending to Abby's story. He didn't respond in the way Wylie expected.

"So, you really thought the Butterfly might be a time machine?" he asked, smiling a little.

"That's what you're focusing on? Yeah, okay, I admit it. I'm an idiot. Now what about Abby talking to me? How could that be?"

"I can't say I blame you, with everything that's happened. But Wy, a time machine? Really?"

"Forget the stupid time machine. I'm sorry I told you that part. How could Abby look straight at me and say my name? How is that possible?" Wylie asked, her voice quivering.

"Okay, sorry. But calm down. This time there might be a reasonable explanation." Darwin touched the dash controls to activate autopilot. With another touch he turned the seats inward so that he and Wylie were facing each other, knees to knees. He held Wylie's hands gently to stop them from shaking.

"Listen, just because Abby was young in the holostory doesn't mean she was young when she programmed it. In fact, she couldn't have been. The technology wasn't invented yet."

"I know that. The Butterfly told me the date it was programmed."

"Okay, so, Abby created the program when she was old, which means you could have been alive and she could have known you. What did she call you again?"

"Little Wylie. 'My sweet little Wylie,' she said."

"There you go. You must have been young, a baby, probably, when Abby programmed the story. Stop freaking out."

Wylie took her first real breath of the day.

"What we have here is real-life mystery, and mysteries can be solved. We just have to dig deeper and find out who she was. There's nothing miraculous or supernatural about this."

"You're right," Wylie said, letting herself relax. "Nothing supernatural at all." She unclenched her fists and realized she'd been clutching the crumpled bit of paper.

"What's that?" Darwin asked.

"Just some trash," Wylie said, but she smoothed it open anyway. "Where's Ransom?"

"What?"

"It's an address in someplace called Ransom. The lawn guy gave it to me yesterday."

"You mean Ed?"

"Yeah. He's the guy that helped me that night when we got caught in the storm—the night I drove Mara to the clinic in your car."

"Ed was the guy you told me about?" Darwin's eyebrows rose in surprise.

"Yeah. What's so amazing?"

"It's just that Ed's been working for my grandpa for years, and you just happened to run into him all the way out there on his property. Funny coincidence, I guess."

"He gave me this address in Ransom. I'm not sure why."

Darwin sighed. "I'm guessing you want to check it out." He turned the seats face-forward again. "Tell it to the geo and see what we got."

Wylie recited the full address to the geoscope. She studied the map that appeared on the screen. "Looks like it's a little over an hour from here. What do you think?"

"I think Grandpa's pansies can wait. We can pick them up on the way back."

They drove along quietly for a time. Wylie wanted to talk more, maybe pick Darwin's brain about Abby. Who could she have been? Delores certainly never mentioned her, but then Delores never mentioned anyone from her past—no friends, no family, no one. Although Del had never said it, Wylie had always assumed their family had gone Committed and abandoned her long before Wylie was born. She knew nothing about her father, or if she had grandparents, aunts, uncles, or cousins. Delores had made sure of that. The van entered the Graham tunnel and though it was less than a mile long, Wylie felt that its narrow darkness would never end.

"Does this thing fly?" she asked when they emerged into the hazy morning.

"Of course. But if we register a flight plan we risk being tracked. Do we want to let the highway guard know where we're going?"

"So don't register a plan."

Darwin gave Wylie a long look that said he understood. "I'll pull off the highway and we can take it up out in the country, away from the trackers. But just for a minute."

Sweet, kind Darwin. Always willing to do whatever it took to make her feel better. Maybe it was time to give their relationship the chance it deserved. Wylie was too wired to talk about it now, but she made a mental note to bring up the subject after work. Maybe she'd even cook a real meal for a change and invite Darwin to stay for dinner.

She closed her eyes and didn't open them again until she felt the van lift off. Then she drank in the gray blankness that surrounded her. She longed for the void of the empty sky, but in the overcast she saw Abby hooked up to tubes, giving herself to save someone who didn't deserve it. *Why?* she asked, for a split-second mirroring Abby's habit of inward prayer. Horrified, she turned to Darwin.

"I've had enough. Let's see what's at this address so we can get back to work."

They landed and the geo led them down a country road to an abandoned campground a few miles outside of a small town. They circled around the site, passing dilapidated cabins, rundown dorms, and an abandoned pool filled with broken furniture and trash.

"It doesn't look like anyone's here," Darwin said.

They continued along the perimeter of the campgrounds until they approached the road they'd come in on.

"Well, that was a wasted trip," Wylie said, disappointed and more than a little annoyed. That's what she got for trusting a Committed.

Suddenly, Darwin braked hard to avoid hitting a pair of whitetail deer that lurched out of the patchy undergrowth, their ribs protruding through their molting coats. As Wylie watched them vanish into the woods, she noticed a narrow trail running through the brush.

"What's up there, do you think?" she asked.

"Probably nothing," Darwin answered. "But we've come this far. Might as well find out."

They left the van on the side of the road and walked along the trail single file, with Wylie in the lead. Seeing ahead was no problem, since decades of acid rainfall had left the trees with little to no foliage.

"Hold up," Darwin said when she got too far ahead. Wylie turned and saw he was marking the trunk of a decimated fir tree with his pocket knife. "Just a precaution," he explained. "I'm not sure how far these woods go and I don't want to get lost."

Wylie almost smiled. Leave it to Darwin to think of that. The kid who grew up scrounging in the trash bins of suburban sprawl and digging through junkpiles for auto parts was somehow versed in woodland survival skills.

"We'll probably turn back in a minute anyway," she said. Chances were this trail through the woods would lead to nothing but more woods. She trudged along, looking down and stepping carefully over roots and rocks until, to her surprise, the trail widened. A few minutes later the trees thinned, the trail became a path, and the path became a road, still narrow but wide enough for Wylie and Darwin to walk side by side. When the woods ended altogether, facing them was a stack of deserted railcars perched three rows high on thick cement blocks and covered in grime and graffiti.

"Looks like these were dumped here decades ago, before the Church-State transports were built," Darwin said.

"I guess these are the old tracks," Wylie said, stepping carefully over half-buried strips of steel.

"Yeah, and this must have been a hangout once." Darwin pointed to scattered bottles, cans, and cigarette butts inside a rough circle of logs. He picked up a bottle and read the label. "Expired over twenty years ago. No one's been here for years."

Wylie walked closer until she was only an arm's length away from a train car. "There's something funny about the windows. Why are they so dark? They look different from the empty buildings on campus."

"You're right," Darwin said. "They're boarded up from the inside, even the ones at the very top."

"That's kind of weird. Why take the trouble to board up the windows of cars too high to reach?"

"That's not regular plywood either." Darwin said.

"Doesn't look like it," Wylie answered. "Boost me up."

Darwin squatted low and Wylie slid onto his shoulders in the move they'd perfected in childhood. When he stood again she was high enough to knock on the window board.

"This isn't wood at all. It feels like some kind of drywall." She knocked harder. "Why go through all that trouble for some broken-down railcars?"

"Maybe they were soundproofed," Darwin offered.

"Maybe, and maybe weatherproofed, too." She smoothed her fingers over the rough metal exterior of the car. "It looks like they used some kind of sealant in all these old cracks." She pressed her hand flat against the surface, which was warmer than it should have been on an early spring morning.

"I think someone's in there," Wylie said. "Let me down."

They walked around the entire perimeter of the train car, looking for an entrance. Every door and window was covered with the same dark material.

"I don't see any way in or out," Darwin said.

Wylie sat on a log and looked up at the faded graffiti images of the upper level. Under scrawled black lettering a picture of a solemn face with high cheekbones and deep eyes was still visible. The forehead sprouted a string of railroad spikes jutting out like pins in a pin cushion. The more she looked at the face, the clearer it became and the more it seemed to be looking back at her. She jumped up, suddenly startled.

"Let's get out of here." She pulled Darwin by the arm, anxious to leave this place and get to the van, but she hadn't gotten far when the sound of grating metal from above grabbed her attention. The mouth on the face slid open to reveal a light shining from a narrow doorway.

"Are you coming in?" a woman called and then disappeared inside. A moment later a rope ladder lowered from the open door like a summons.

Wordlessly, Wylie walked toward it.

"I guess we are," Darwin said.

21

Wylie liked to think that nothing could surprise her, but when she climbed through the opening of the railcar, she was met by two unexpected sights. First, the woman waiting at the top of the ladder was Nightingale, the Avian nurse Wylie had met that day in Sharmila's building. Seeing Nightingale brought Wylie back to the time before the implosion, the dividing line of Wylie's personal before and after. During the before she'd been a typical Uncommitted, poor but savvy enough to scrape by under the radar. Now, in the after, she'd gained materially (temporarily, at least), but had lost something essential, some purpose she hadn't understood until it was gone. After Sharmila left, she and Delores had gradually exchanged roles, and all the years of taking care of Del had, at least, given Wylie someone to focus on other than herself. Now, with Delores dead and Sharmila gone, Wylie felt both motherless and childless. Soon she'd be homeless as well.

But thoughts of before and after fled at the second surprise. The room she entered was not the dark, rusted space she'd expected. Instead, she found herself in a well-lit, carpeted office filled with busy people on old-style headsets and computers.

"Welcome, Wylie," Nightingale said. "We've been hoping you would find us."

"What is all this, and how do you know her name?" Darwin asked warily.

Wouldn't you know it, Wylie thought. The one secret from Darwin she'd buried away refused to stay in the ground. She'd never told him about her experience with the Avian, and she didn't especially want him to find out now.

"We have a mutual friend," Nightingale said.

"Ed," said Darwin. "Ed sent us here, didn't he?"

Nightingale nodded. "This is one of the Compendium's underground headquarters."

"The what?" Wylie asked.

"The Compendium is a collection of people working together for a common cause," Nightingale explained.

Darwin spoke with quiet awe. "It's an underground resistance. You're saying there's an underground fighting the ChurchState."

"In a manner of speaking, yes, although there's no physical fighting involved. We're using other means to bring about change."

"I don't understand," Wylie said. "Isn't Ed a Committed, and aren't you Avian?"

Darwin raised an eyebrow and Wylie could have bitten her tongue for giving away her own secret.

"Long story for another time," she said, brushing off Darwin's puzzled expression. "The point is, how are the Committed and Avian working together? Aren't you guys mortal enemies?"

"I'm a nurse first and foremost. I go where I'm needed, no questions asked. As for Ed, he has other motivations." Wylie thought back to Ed's parting comment that night in the woods— something about serving, she recalled.

"That's kind of hard to believe, but okay. Now, what exactly is this place?"

"Yeah," said Darwin, "and how is it possible?"

"Why don't I show you around?" Nightingale led them to the next car and the cars after that, all set up as office spaces filled with the din of people working on computers and talking through headsets. When they reached the end of the row, she stopped. "The rest of this floor is devoted to housing."

"You mean people live here?" asked Wylie.

"Yes, exactly that. More and more Uncommitted are becoming displaced, as you probably know, and recent legislation has added to the problem. Unfortunately, we don't have room for everyone, but we provide temporary housing for families while we work on other options. That's partly what all these folks are doing."

Housing for *families*, of which she had none unless she counted Monty and the house drone she'd disabled. Figures, Wylie thought. Even to the underground, she was an outsider.

"What do you mean by other options?" Darwin asked.

"The Compendium has been busy for several years now renovating deserted properties in secret." Nightingale led them up a metal ladder to the floor above, where they walked through car after car of maintenance equipment and supplies. At the end of the row they climbed a ladder to the upper level and stepped into a cafeteria. Wylie's stomach rumbled and she realized it was lunch time. A line of mostly women, children, and elderly folk waited to be served what smelled like vegetable soup. Among the workers Wylie spotted two college-aged kids wearing red ChurchState polos. She stopped in her tracks and stared.

"I don't understand. Aren't those ChurchState cadets? I could swear they chased me around the campus one time or another."

Before Nightingale could answer, one of the workers noticed Wylie and left her post to walk toward her.

"I'm Prisca," she said, searching Wylie's face. "I think I know you."

"Yeah," Wylie answered, hackles raised. "I'm one of your targets. Sorry you didn't get your bonus points for converting me."

"I'm the one who's sorry," Prisca answered without a second of hesitation. Her dark eyes glistened and Wylie couldn't help but notice the absence of the usual vapid missionary grin. Prisca reached out for a handshake. "I'm so sorry for harassing you. Can you forgive me?"

Did this girl think she could erase years of ChurchState intimidation with a flimsy apology and a handshake? Wylie gave Prisca a cold stare and kept her hands at her sides. When Prisca's tears brimmed over, Wylie rolled her eyes and turned away.

"It's okay," Nightingale said, dismissing Prisca with a nod. "Let's continue. You might have a special interest in our clinic." Wylie ignored her knowing look.

As they made their way through the complex of narrow rooms that seemed to serve multiple purposes, Nightingale was interrupted more than once with questions from frazzled underlings. Wylie didn't get everything that was said, but it was clear that the Compendium's reach went beyond anything she could have imagined. Equally clear was Nightingale's position of authority.

During one of these interludes, Darwin took the opportunity to question Wylie.

"Who is she, and what's with your interest in the clinic? What aren't you telling me?"

"Not now."

"Okay, but you're going to tell me on the way home."

Nightingale led them to an open space where the walls between cars had been removed and where staff in white lab coats attended patients in beds, surrounded by beeping medical equipment.

"How is this possible?" Darwin asked. "The food, the supplies, and now all this medical stuff—it must cost a bundle. Who's paying for it?"

"We have friends in high places," Nightingale said with a closed-lip smile.

"Do you mean Ed?" Wylie asked.

"Ed is one funder among many and sometimes functions as a liaison. But it takes more than money to keep places like this quiet. It takes influence."

"You're saying that higher-ups in the ChurchState know about this place?" Darwin asked, unconvinced.

"A few. And they not only know about it, they make it possible."

Wylie took a closer look at the patients. Most of them were very young or very old, although she got a clear view of a pregnant woman preparing for a sonogram before the staff pulled the curtains closed around her. In a bed at the far end of the room, Wylie once again saw the red polo of a ChurchState cadet.

"What's he doing here?" she asked. "Did he revoke his signing or something?"

"Most Committed have easy access to healthcare in ChurchState medical facilities," answered Nightingale. "But every once in a while, we take in a special case, like Barnabas, that even the ChurchState can't help. To be honest, we had you in mind for this one."

Wylie's heart began to pound. Old memories of Del's warnings rose to the surface—*Your blood is the only valuable thing you own, so protect it. Most importantly, never tell anyone about your blood type.* She'd carried the weight of her mother's words as long as she could remember.

"Say what?" said Darwin.

"He has a liver disease that requires transfusions, but unfortunately, his blood type is extremely rare."

"What does that have to do with Wylie?" Darwin demanded. He stepped between Wylie and Nightingale, but Wylie gently brushed him aside.

"It's okay, Darwin. I can handle myself." Wylie focused on sounding braver than she felt.

"I don't mean to upset anyone," Nightingale said. "But Wylie has donated before."

"To the Avian, yeah," Wylie said. "That's what I was going to tell you, Dar. Remember the Avian in Sharmila's basement? I traded with them— blood for groceries to help Sharmila and those kids. But donate my blood to help a Committed? Never. I'd never give my blood to someone who doesn't deserve it." *I'm not Abby,* Wylie thought. *I'd never be that stupid.*

"Totally your choice," Nightingale said. "I can't say I blame you. But are you sure you don't want to meet Barny before you decide?"

"I'm sure. And I think I've seen enough. Come on, Dar. Let's get out of here."

They left the clinic with Wylie in the lead. Nightingale had remained behind, talking through her headset. "They're on their way down," she said, and Wylie understood they were tracking her movements. She picked up the pace until she was almost running, retracing their steps as best she could through the railcars, trying to remember which way they'd come. She was suddenly gripped by fear she'd be grabbed, strapped to a table, and slowly drained of blood. By the time they reached the ladder to the bottom level she was in such a panicked state that she missed two steps and fell to the ground, scraping her leg against the cold metal and landing on a twisted ankle. The jolt of pain made her panic worse; she doubled over in a swell of nausea. Darwin jumped to her side.

"Are you okay?" he asked.

Wylie struggled to catch her breath. "Just help me up and let's get out of here."

"Wylie, calm down. No one's chasing us."

But Wylie had the inexplicable feeling that she *was* being chased. A drop of sweat fell from her forehead.

"Not yet, or not directly, anyway," she answered. "But someone's been watching me. They must want something." She hobbled forward a few steps and stopped. "I've lost my bearings. Do you remember which way is out?"

"Straight ahead, I think," Darwin said. "We need to find that first car—the one that looked like a lobby."

Wylie limped along, hanging on to Darwin for support. Her scraped leg was bleeding enough to earn the attention of every bystander they passed. Around them people looked up from their work, but no one interfered.

After a few more painful minutes they entered a car free of people but filled with supplies. "This doesn't look familiar," Wylie said. "We must have gone the wrong way."

"You can hardly walk, Wy. Let's stop to rest."

"No. I need to get out of here." She felt overwhelmed by the sense of being chased and the dread of being caught.

"Wylie, come on. Sit down and let's look at that ankle. It's a long walk to the van. Do you plan for me to carry you?"

Wylie hadn't thought of that. She let Darwin lead her to an old metal chair and collapsed into it, not protesting when he rested her leg on a case of water bottles.

"It doesn't look too bad," Darwin said as he touched Wylie's ankle gently. "A little swelling, no bruising. I don't think it's broken."

"Definitely not broken," Wylie replied. "I just need to wrap it so I can walk. Then we can get going."

"What about these cuts?"

"I'll clean them later."

Darwin sighed and took Wylie's hand.

"Do you want to tell me what the heck is going on with you? Why the sudden panic? What are you running from?"

It was a fair question, to which Wylie had no real answer. She pushed his hand away.

If Darwin was hurt, he didn't show it. "Have you taken a minute to digest all this?" he asked, looking around at the stockpiles of provisions that surrounded them. "Have you let it sink in? Wylie, there's a resistance. There are people, lots of people, big, important people, who've formed an underground. There's hope. Finally. I never thought there would be, but there's hope for us, Wy. Aren't you just a little excited about that?"

Wylie couldn't meet Darwin's expectant gaze. She stared over his shoulder blankly, trying to calm down and sort out her feelings. She'd been afraid they'd take her blood, but now a suspicion settled on her that had nothing to do with her blood type. Committed and Avian working with Uncommitted to undo decades of oppression? It was all too hard to believe.

"It's just . . . " She let her voice trail off into silence. What she was thinking was unthinkable.

"What, Wylie? It's just what?"

"It's just that there's Committed here, didn't you see that?" Wylie burst out. "What are they doing here? How can you trust anything they're involved with, after all that's happened? For all we know this is just another subtle indoctrination scheme. Or what if it's something worse, something more dangerous? Round us up, feed us, make us feel safe, then move in for the kill. How easy that would be if we're all in one place, away from public view."

"Come on, Wylie, you're getting carried away."

"Am I? It's happened before—read those history books you love so much. I'll never trust them, not after what they did to Ab . . . Delores, I mean. I'll never forgive them, either."

"Okay," Darwin said, nodding slowly. "I get it. But I don't feel that way. I want to be part of this. I'm coming back here as soon as I can." He searched Wylie's face for understanding, but she refused to meet his eyes.

"I'm going to get some help," Darwin said. "Wait here."

Wylie had no intention of waiting there or anywhere else. She tried to stand, but when she put weight on her ankle, the throbbing forced her down. Reluctantly, she swallowed her determination and let Darwin have his way.

"You win. Get me a bandage and something to lean on, if you can. I'll take care of the rest when I get home." Home. That was funny. Grandpa's little cottage had never been her home, and never would be. But this place, whatever it was, this place wasn't home either. To Wylie's thinking, this place should not exist.

Hoping that Darwin wouldn't be gone more than a few minutes, Wylie tried to distract herself by taking a closer look around. The railcar was lined with supply shelves on three sides, neatly organized and sectioned off by categories. Shelf after shelf of nonperishable foods, bedding, clothing, and cleaning supplies were grouped together in such abundance that Wylie could have been sitting in the middle of a ChurchState supermarket. Darwin was right about one thing—it took money, lots of money, to fund this operation, the kind of money that only higher-ups in the ChurchState controlled. How could that be? *Fascists*, she heard Delores say. Why would fascists fund all this? There was a wrongness here that Wylie couldn't shake away.

At the far end of the railcar was a wall devoted purely to books. Unable to resist, Wylie hopped over, half dragging, half leaning on her chair for support. She could tell by the worn covers that all of the books were used. Wylie touched their spines lightly, almost reverently, the way one might touch an ancient artifact in danger of disintegrating. She let the feel of the books calm her. At first glance none of the titles and authors were familiar, but that was no surprise since the ChurchState censors had completed their purges years before Wylie was born. Fiction, in general, was deemed "unedifying," and only the most didactic texts had survived. Over the years Wylie had managed to rescue a novel from a dumpster here or there or trade for one at the noncom flea market, and, of course, there were some ChurchState-approved novels left in the fiction section of the campus library. But never before had she seen so many disallowed books in one place. They were in no discernible order; mystery, romance, fantasy, biography, and more were mixed together, gleaming at her like jewels in a dragon's lair. So many stories of lives before the Reclamation. A person could hide in this treasure trove forever, lost in the dreams of a thousand worlds all better than her own. A small sign taped to the middle shelf read, "Please borrow, share, or return as you wish." In spite of her rant to Darwin, Wylie realized that whatever this place was, it was not an indoctrination center. No ChurchState official would allow these books to survive, let alone be read and shared by the malleable masses. She breathed in the scent of the bound pages and let her inner alarm go quiet.

Wylie scanned the rows of books, not quite sure what she was looking for. She thought of the stories she'd devoured over the years, finishing hastily before Delores made her get rid of the contraband that could lose them what little they had. Now and then she'd jumped into a story with both feet only to realize she'd landed in the middle of a series with no way of reading the beginning or ending. One in particular had stayed with her—the story of the orphaned boy wizard whose name she couldn't remember. She'd always wondered how that story ended. Many a day she'd longed to get lost in that world again where the powerless gained power, good and evil were clear, and everyone found a place to belong. Leaning on her chair for support, she combed through the books row by row, now on a hunt for a vaguely remembered cover. After several minutes, her eye was drawn to a series of thick hardbacks on the second shelf from the top, just out of her reach. She squinted to read the titles and realized, there they were, the books she'd been thinking about. As if by magic they'd appeared, sitting under a row of pre-Reclamation Bibles, which Wylie recognized by the absence of the flag on the binding. Normally she would have hopped up on the chair to reach the books, but her throbbing ankle vetoed that plan. Instead, holding onto the chair for balance, she grabbed a book from a lower shelf, thinking to use it to pull the last book of the series toward her.

Just as Wylie almost reached her target, a siren shrieked and the rail-car went dark. She lost her balance and fell to the floor, still gripping the book she'd pulled from the shelf. What now? Was this a power outage, or was something more ominous happening? The alarm continued, laughing at her—that's what she got for letting her guard down. She sat up and waited for her eyes to adjust to the dark, afraid to move and afraid to stay put. After a moment the door at the end of the car cracked open to reveal a silhouette holding a flashlight.

"Darwin?" she asked, blinking hard.

"Wylie, it's me. We need to get you out of here."

Wylie recognized the voice immediately. "Sharmila? What are you doing here?"

Although it was too dark to see clearly, as Sharmila approached, Wylie noticed something different about her. Sharmila's hair, which was usually pulled back in a long, tight braid, hung down in dark waves past her shoulders.

"There'll be time for questions later," Sharmila said. "Right now we have to go."

Together they moved through the dark cars, rushing past people running in every direction. It seemed everyone had a flashlight except Wylie. Three cars down they met up with Nightingale, standing above an opening in the floor.

"This way," she said, signaling them to hurry.

"Wait," Wylie said, pulling away from Sharmila. "What's going on? Where's Darwin?" She wasn't moving another inch until she had some answers.

"This is just a precaution," Nightingale explained. "Our cameras spotted someone snooping around the area. It may be nothing, but we don't take chances."

"I thought you said you have friends in high place," Wylie said.

"We do, but even they can't help if the broadcasts find out about this place. Now, let's go. If they do find us out, you don't want to be here."

Protecting her bad ankle as best she could, Wylie stumbled down the ladder into a narrow, dimly lit tunnel where Darwin was waiting with a wheelchair.

"Follow the tunnel as far as it goes, and you'll find yourself about a half-mile from your van. Sharmila will go with you."

As Nightingale disappeared back up the stairs, Sharmila helped Wylie into the wheelchair. Then she knelt down, pulled a mini jet-injector from her pocket, and gave Wylie a shot for the pain. Her hair hung over the side of her face as she worked. When she was done, she wrapped Wylie's ankle and bandaged her cuts, just as she'd done so many times before.

"I hope you have a chance to read that," Sharmila said. "We're not out of the woods yet."

Wylie realized she was still clutching the book she'd grabbed from the shelf.

"You still haven't told me why you're here," Wylie said as she rode through the bumpy, damp tunnel.

"It's because of you, Why-Why-Wylie," Sharmila answered, and Wylie could hear the smile in her voice. She'd missed that voice so much. "After the arrangement you made with the Avian, Nightingale started to check in on the kids, and she never stopped. When we got evicted, she found me squatting in another apartment and brought me here. I'd lost track of Mara and the kids by then."

"Are there other Avian here?" Wylie still couldn't get over the idea of reclusive Avian, arrogant Committed, and destitute Uncommitted all in one place, working toward a common goal.

"A few. But mostly they help behind the scenes. When it comes to appropriating resources and moving them without detection, they're the experts. They have no great love for non-Avian, but they'd do anything to bring down the ChurchState. There's an old saying: 'the enemy of my enemy is my friend.'"

"And what about the Committed I saw?" Wylie asked. "If they're so bent on helping, why haven't they revoked their signing? How can anyone connected to the ChurchState be trusted?"

"These Committed are different," Sharmila replied. "They think of themselves as pre-Reclamation believers. It's hard for us to understand what that looks like, since the ChurchState is all we've ever known."

But it wasn't hard for Wylie to understand at all. She knew what pre-Reclamation belief looked like, because Abby had shown her. Unfortunately, Steve had shown her, too.

They made their way through the passage, Sharmila lighting the path ahead and Darwin pushing the wheelchair. Through the darkness, Wylie could just make out the cement walls that surrounded them. Every now and then they passed a vent that pushed air into the tunnel. Impressive, she had to admit, but she wanted nothing to do with any of it. The further away from the Compendium she got, the better. She couldn't shake the feeling that someone was following her. Uneasiness growing with every step, she glanced over her shoulder, but there was only ominous darkness behind them.

Darwin, meanwhile, could barely contain his excitement. He pumped Sharmila with questions with a hopeful lilt in his voice. *How long had this been going on? How many other centers were there? Did the Compendium have political influence?* Wylie tried to tune them out, peering ahead for the opening into daylight.

"How much longer?" she interrupted.

"Almost there," Sharmila said. "Are you okay?" She shone the flashlight on Wylie's ankle.

"Fine. Just want to get back on my feet and out of here."

Sharmila and Darwin took the hint and continued in silence. A bit of guilt crept up on Wylie; she was sorry to put a damper on Darwin's excitement, but he needed to come back to reality. As Delores always said, when something seems too good to be true, it most likely is.

Finally, the upward slope and the change in the air told Wylie they were nearing the end of the tunnel. Darwin grunted with effort as he pushed the wheelchair the final few yards toward four slimy cement steps.

Wylie stood on one foot and glanced at the cover of the book she was still holding. "Shine the light here for a second," she asked Sharmila. *Beloved*, Wylie read, and allowed herself a tiny smile. She had no idea what the book was about, but the title was fitting for the day she found Sharmila again. Maybe she could convince Sharmila to come with them. She tucked the book into the waistband of her jeans. In the back of her mind she pictured herself escaping into the dream of its story that night, Monty snuggled up next to her and Sharmila fiddling around in the kitchen. Leaning on Sharmila, she put a little weight on her bad ankle.

PART III: THE CHASE   149

"I think I can make it," she said. She half walked, half hopped up the stairs, where a locked iron grate covered an opening just large enough for an adult to squeeze through. Sharmila unlocked the padlock and pushed herself through. Without too much trouble, Wylie followed, relying on Sharmila to pull her to her feet on the other side. Darwin squeezed through last and closed the grate behind them. The sun was high by now, blurred behind the smog.

"I'll run ahead to see if I can get the van any closer," he said, and took off down the trail.

"It was wonderful to see you, Wylie," Sharmila said. "I'm glad you're safe."

"You're going back?" Wylie asked, disappointment in her voice.

"I live here, Wy," Sharmila said kindly. "I'm part of the Compendium now. I have nowhere else to go."

Wylie nodded. "It's just—it's been so long. I was hoping, somehow, we could be together. Find a place, maybe, after I turn eighteen."

Sharmila hugged Wylie close. "I miss you, too, Wylie. But things are changing, and they're going to get worse before they get better. There's a good chance we'll lose our citizenship with the next Appointee vote, and if that happens, who knows what's next? This is important work, Wylie. We're in a fight we have to win. Join us. Promise me you'll think about it."

Wylie wiped her eyes with her dirty hands. She didn't want to fight. She just wanted a home with Sharmila. She knew she was being selfish and unreasonable, but she felt orphaned yet again.

"Your hair is different," she said, hoping to divert attention from her tears. Sharmila turned away abruptly, but not before Wylie noticed something on her cheek hiding under her thick, dark waves.

"Sharmila, what's that? What happened?"

"Nothing. It's nothing for you to be concerned about."

"Of course I'm concerned. Let me see." She brushed back Sharmila's hair and uncovered a bright red 666 marring Sharmila's beautiful brown complexion.

"Oh, Sharmila," Wylie gasped, staring at the angry raised scar. "What did they do to you?"

Sharmila's shoulders slumped. She shook her head, struggling to compose herself and flinching from the salty sting of tears that rolled over her damaged skin.

"Crying is not good," she said, her voice shaking. "It irritates the wound. No tears, okay?"

"Right, no tears," Wylie answered, steeling herself for Sharmila' sake.

"When they passed the Uncommitted Designation bill, we knew something was coming, but I never imagined this. I'd hoped to avoid it, but they took me just days before Nightingale found me."

"But they said tattoo, not branding," Wylie groaned. The broadcasts hadn't been specific, but she'd pictured the "designation" would be a small symbol tattooed on the hand or wrist. How stupid, how naïve she'd been, hiding out in the pool cottage, warm, fed, and safe, while Sharmila and who knows how many others were rounded up like cattle and permanently disfigured. She promised herself then and there that she'd never underestimate the cruelty of the ChurchState again.

"Local jurisdictions have added their own spin on the law," Sharmila answered. "Our district decided to use tattoos on those who come voluntarily. For those who are caught—well, you see." She smoothed her hair and pulled it over her face to cover the scar. "They call it the 'walk-in, call-in policy.' This way, they get the Uncommitted to do the work of rounding us up for them. Pretty smart, you have to admit."

"What do they mean—the numbers?" Wylie asked.

"They said it was 'the mark of the beast.' Who knows where they got that from—some cryptic biblical prophecy, I'm sure."

Wylie thought of the Bible passages she's heard Dr. Michaels talk about during his long-ago classes. She thought of Abby standing in front of those church kids, reading from the Bible as she spoke of love and forgiveness. How could that be the same book the ChurchState was using to justify this new horror?

They stumbled through the emaciated woods, Wylie grateful that the walk took too much effort for conversation. Soon they saw Darwin coming toward them.

"Don't tell him," Sharmila said. "I'm not ready for more sympathy yet, and you two have enough to worry about. Promise?"

Wylie nodded. "Promise."

With Darwin's help they reached the van quickly. Wylie took the book from her waistband and handed it to Sharmila. "Better put this back," she said. There was no room for dreams in her world, even from a book.

22

They drove home in thick silence. Wylie tilted her seat back and closed her eyes, overwhelmed with the jumble of the day's emotions. Hope, fear, suspicion, sorrow, anger, and despair, topped off with the horror of Sharmila's disfigurement, and all within the four hours since she'd left the cottage that morning. It was all too much. She just wanted to hide away some place and never be heard from again.

Eventually, Wylie tried to put Sharmila out of her head and glanced in Darwin's direction. Although he hadn't said a word, from head to toe he exuded hope in equal measure to her despondency.

"Do you even know you're smiling?" Wylie asked.

"Am I?" Darwin tried to shift his face muscles into neutral, with little success. "But Wy, come on, you have to be just a little excited," he said. "Something incredible just happened, for God's sake."

"Don't use that term," Wylie answered.

"Huh?"

"God. Don't use that term."

"What are you talking about? It's just an expression."

Wylie didn't answer.

"I think that Butterfly messed with your head," Darwin said finally.

Wylie frowned, stewing in the knowledge she'd promised not to share. Again, she tried to stop picturing Sharmila's face. If only she could go back to a time when all she'd had to worry about was daily sustenance. "Life was simpler, before," she said.

"Before what?"

"Before I started watching the tapes. Before the—whatever you call it. Miracles." She almost spit the word out. Some miracles. Miracles were supposed to help, weren't they? Miracles were supposed to make things better; even she knew that. Yet here she was, worse off than ever, and now she could add confusion to her emotional thesaurus. Before the tapes, she could keep religion within the exclusive realm of the ChurchState. Religion was corrupt because the ChurchState was corrupt, no further discussion required. The Bible was an ancient, arcane book that brought her nothing but destitution. But now she was somehow part of it. She'd lived something so implausible she hardly believed it herself, yet she couldn't deny her own experience. And now, equally far-fetched was the sudden appearance of Committed in the form of decent human beings, ready and willing to help her. Where had they been all this time?

"It's like I'm being followed," Wylie said. "No matter where I go, something crazy follows me." But it wasn't just the unexplainable events that troubled her. She thought of how the atmosphere around her had changed with each unfathomable, post-tape episode. In those moments she'd sensed something almost tangible. Was it the same something that Abby was somehow connected to? What if there was something real, something true trying to push its way in on her? Not the ChurchState's dogma—that was obviously more about power than truth. But what if there really was some being, some presence, some will that existed outside of her notions of reality? And what if that being was following her, as if it wanted something she wasn't willing or able to give? The thought scared her more than any ChurchState intimidations ever had. She'd never be able to run far and fast enough.

"Speaking of being followed," Darwin said, "look who's behind us."

Coming up fast were three slick highway trooper cyclecars, one directly behind them and two in the lane to the left. Their sirens were quiet, for now.

"Are they here for us?" Wylie asked.

"Not sure, but let's find out." Darwin picked up speed and the three-wheeled cyclecars kept pace. He slowed and moved into the noncom lane to see if they'd pass, but the troopers stayed with him, mirroring the van's movements.

"I think it's safe to say they're here for us," Darwin said.

"Can we outrun them?" Wylie knew the suggestion was ludicrous, but she was gripped with an uncontrollable urge to flee. As if tempting her, the cyclecars backed off a bit. "Let's fly," she said, adrenaline pumping so hard she felt she could almost take off on her own.

"Are you insane? Have you ever seen those things move? They'd be on us in a heartbeat. Do you want to give them an excuse to shoot us down?"

"They'd do that?"

"If we give them a reason," Darwin said. "Besides, this is Grandpa's van, and I'm allowed to drive it until my birthday next month. We have nothing to worry about."

Darwin pulled to the shoulder and stopped. The troopers surrounded the van, engines idling as if ready for a chase. The only female among them approached. "Documents," she said to Darwin, who handed her his Uncommitted ID, noncom driver's license, and the van registration. She scanned them and glared at Darwin suspiciously.

"Exit the van slowly," she ordered.

"What's the trouble?" Darwin asked in his most humble Uncommitted voice. "Everything should be in order. I have permission to drive my grandfather's van."

"Exit the van, both of you," she said again, placing her hand on her weapon. Wylie and Darwin obeyed.

"Be careful," Wylie said under her breath. She limped around the van to stand with Darwin. The other troopers approached in a practiced flanking maneuver.

"Let's see some identification from you," the trooper said to Wylie. She looked down at Wylie's bandaged ankle, but said nothing to acknowledge it. By accident, Wylie touched the trooper's gloved hand as she gave over her ID. Perhaps because she sensed danger, the touch sparked memories of previous touches, touches that had resulted in the inexplicable. But there was no flash of energy or change of atmosphere. The trooper passed Wylie's ID through her scanner. She jabbed at the screen, then showed it to the others.

"Does it make sense to you that two Uncommitted kids have access to this man's van?"

"He's my grandfather," Darwin said again.

"So you say. And does your grandfather know that his vehicle was tracked making an unauthorized flight this morning?"

Wylie realized with a sinking feeling that this was all her fault. She'd insisted Darwin take the van up, and that short flight had put them on the highway troopers' radar. If they were lucky, they'd get away with a ticket. But if she wound up in the hands of the Comcops, she'd need more than luck to get her through.

"Does this Uncommitted's story sound reasonable to you?" the trooper asked the others, pointing again to the screen.

"I can't say it does," said the one on her right. "Doesn't make sense that a man of his stature would have anything to do with Uncommitted, no less be related to one."

"'Train up a child in the way he should go and when he is old he shall not depart from it,'" said the other in a sing-song voice. "There's no way a Founder would allow one of his own to slip away."

"I'm telling you, it's true. Call him and you'll see," Darwin said.

"I'll do that, and you will turn around and place your hands on the van."

Wylie bristled at the show of power that she and Darwin had done nothing to deserve. She wanted to protest, but she knew better, being well-versed in how to minimize risk when interacting with ChurchState-sanctioned authorities. That was a talk all Uncommitted had with their kids, and even Delores had not neglected it. *Train up a child*—they got that right, anyway. Del had trained her well.

"Don't worry," Darwin whispered. "My grandpa will work this out."

"Why did they call him a 'Founder'?" Wylie asked. They dared not look at each other as they spoke.

"Because, unfortunately, he was one of the founders of the Church-State, way back when."

"Oh. I knew he was a big shot, but I didn't know how big."

"Enough talking, you two," said the trooper closest to Wylie.

"Sure, no problem," said Darwin. Wylie rolled her eyes on the inside.

A few minutes passed as the female trooper continued her phone conversation. Wylie's ankle was beginning to throb again. Whatever Sharmila had given her must be wearing off. How much longer was this going to take?

When the female trooper finally returned, her face was even harder than before.

"You're free to go," she said to Darwin begrudgingly. "But there are some questions regarding your friend here. It seems she's an unsupervised minor with no custodian on record."

"What?" Darwin's voice rose. "She's an employee of my grandfather. That puts her under his supervision, doesn't it?"

"We have no official documentation of that. We're turning her over to the ChurchState police for processing. If you resist, they'll have to take you in, too."

Stop talking about me as if I'm not here, Wylie wanted to shout. But shock and fear had stolen her voice and she kept her mouth shut. The two male troopers took her arms and led her to the Comcop transport van that had landed behind them.

"You can't do this!" Darwin shouted.

"This is your last warning," sneered the female. "Mind your place, Uncommitted. I don't care who your grandpa is." When she placed her hand on the taser that hung from her belt, Wylie found her voice.

"Darwin, stop," she said as calmly as she could manage. "I'll be fine. They won't be able to hold me long. Besides, you have to take care of Monty. He needs to go out and be fed." She didn't resist as the Comcops guided her into the back seat of their vehicle.

"Don't worry, Wylie. We're going to get you out of this," she heard Darwin say, but she kept her head down because she couldn't bear his look of helplessness. The transport took off and within a minute they were in the air. *Well*, she heard Delores say, *you wanted to fly. Be careful what you wish for.*

* * *

Most of the time Wylie spent being "processed" consisted of sitting in an empty room about the size of the closet back at the cottage. She'd thought they'd take her to the nearest ChurchState police station, but instead they'd flown on for quite some time. She had no idea what direction they were going or even if they'd left the state.

"Is it legal for you to take me across state lines?" she'd asked after an hour of flight.

The Comcop on her right laughed. "There's only one state, the Church-State," he said. "And you are an illegal alien in it."

Wylie had never been called that before. She'd been an outcast, yes, but never before had she been made to feel that her very existence was illegal. It seemed the change that Sharmila feared was happening on the ground.

They'd finally landed and drove down a deserted road to a broad compound protected by a series of fences. They were allowed entrance immediately and Wylie was bustled into a cement building, past a main desk, and through a corridor that led to rows of holding cells filled with desperate-looking people. She thought she'd be placed in one, but she'd been isolated in the tiny cell instead.

"Can't put you in with the others since you're a minor," a Comcop spit out without looking her in the eye. Wylie knew better; one of the cells she'd passed contained a group of teenagers who looked younger than she was. But she was no ordinary criminal. She was Uncommitted, and the ChurchState couldn't allow her to garner sympathy from Committed, even those accused of lawbreaking.

So Wylie waited in the closet-sized room with nothing to do but worry. A narrow bench on the back wall allowed her just enough room to sit sideways and elevate her ankle. She kept her other leg anchored on the cement floor and leaned back on the cinderblock wall in a position that might have been almost comfortable for a few minutes, but not for the hours that stretched before her. When they'd walked past the front desk she'd seen a clock. It was 3:00 p.m. already. She wished she'd eaten breakfast. *Always eat when you can*, Delores used to say. *You never know when you might get another chance.* Her mother had warned her of so many things, as if she'd been trying to keep

Wylie from this place, this here, this now, but in spite of all Del's warnings, here she was. She thought again about the unknown *something* that had led her here through a series of events that included her mother's death, the same something she'd sensed following her. She didn't understand how it could lead and follow at the same time, but that was the feeling she had. Suddenly, Wylie sensed the something in her tiny prison, seeping in and filling the room with an indescribable presence like vapor through the ventilation system. Startled, she looked around the cell, but, of course, she was alone. No, she thought. No more. She'd had enough.

"Get out," she said through gritted teeth, and the presence evaporated. A little gray mouse in the corner stopped in its tracks at Wylie's command and skittered through a crack in the wall. "Not you," she said more gently, but the mouse had disappeared, leaving Wylie completely and totally alone.

Wylie never did find out why she was left in the small holding cell for eight hours. Maybe it was an oversight, or maybe it was an attempt to break her. She had one visitor during that time—a female Comcop who'd walked her to the bathroom and allowed her to stop at the water fountain on the way back. No one spoke to her or even looked in her direction as she passed. Eventually, she stopped wishing she'd eaten breakfast. Wylie knew how to be hungry. She'd learned years ago it was best not to focus on the lightheaded-ness or the hollow churning in her stomach. If she ignored them long enough they'd subside, at least for a while. What Wylie had never learned was how to be bored. There'd always been plenty to keep her busy: her work and Del's, taking care of Monty, scrounging for supplies, exploring the noncom areas or the deserted campus with Darwin, and reading whatever she could get her hands on. She'd spent hours writing in her journal, and even her mundane schoolwork was preferable to doing nothing. An inkling of fear began to take shape in her mind. What if this was to be her fate? What if they left her alone in this room, or one like it, forever, with nothing to do but think until she thought herself into a place of madness? Wylie couldn't imagine anything worse. Once she might have hoped that the ChurchState couldn't be so cruel, but after what had happened to Sharmila, she knew they could and they would. She took a deep breath and tried to push away the fear, but fear wasn't as malleable as hunger; she could banish the thought, but not the emotion. She closed her eyes and tried to empty herself of any thoughts or feelings at all. After a few minutes weariness set in, so she sat on the floor and rested her head on the bench, hoping to doze.

The Comcop found her in that position an hour later. "These Uncommitted can sleep anywhere, can't they?" she said, her insipid laughter startling Wylie out of that place between waking and sleep. "Let's go, unless you want to stay here till next shift."

Wylie jumped to her feet, wincing in pain, but the Comcop offered no support. The hours she'd spent alone had done their work; Wylie followed without a sound, afraid to be sent back to the cell at the whim of the Comcop if she stirred up trouble. She hoped to be taken to an administrator who had heard from Darwin's grandfather. Instead, she was led through a back door to another transport vehicle.

"Where are we going?" she asked, willing her voice not to shake.

"You're being handed over to the Appointees. They'll figure out what to do with you."

The Appointees. Why would the highest echelon of ChurchState law enforcement get involved with an insignificant Uncommitted like her? What could this mean? The transport took off and reached full speed just as Wylie fainted from hunger.

23

" Wylie, wake up," said a familiar voice above her. "Come on. Wake up and
eat something."

Wylie opened her eyes slowly and allowed a woman to help her to a
sitting position. Her head was pounding.

"Water," she said. "I need a drink."

"I know. Here."

She drank greedily from the plastic cup the woman held to her lips.

"Slow down—little sips. That's it. Now eat."

Wylie took a few bites of sandwich filled with a mystery meat spread
that even Delores couldn't stomach. Nothing had ever tasted so good. Once
she felt strong enough to focus, she took in her surroundings. She'd been
lying on a plastic mat and covered with a thin, mylar blanket. She blinked
and tried to count the rows of mats just like hers, but her head was too fuzzy
for an accurate count. At the foot of each mat was a plastic crate containing
a few essentials—a towel, soap, a plastic comb. People were lying or sitting
up on their mats, dressed in the same orange coveralls that she, herself, was
wearing. Someone had changed her clothes; that fact made her feel more
violated than anything else she'd experienced. Her face must have shown it
because the person sitting next to her, still holding her cup, was telling her
to calm down. Wylie took a closer look and recognized Mara, the woman
who'd lived with Sharmila. Her children hovered nearby, watching silently.
The oldest swayed gently, holding a baby in his arms.

"It's you," she said. "What happened? What is this place?"

"Welcome to Camp Noncom—that's what we call it, anyway. You're
at an Uncommitted relocation camp run by the Appointees. Don't you remember arriving?"

Wylie rubbed her forehead and rested her head in her hands. The fog
of the last several hours was starting to lift. She remembered the transport,
then blank. Then being half-dragged through a wire fence into a cement

compound, then blank again. Then Mara's calm, no-nonsense voice talking to her while she helped her into the coveralls.

"What . . . what did they do with my clothes?" Wylie asked. Nothing she'd been wearing had value; she hadn't even been the first to own the jeans and sweatshirt she'd thrown on to pick up Grandpa's plants at the nursery— how long ago now? She'd lost track of time.

"They don't let us keep personal belongings here. Sorry."

Wylie couldn't answer. They'd taken her clothes. What else would they take?

"As for where we are," Mara continued, "we're not exactly sure, but somewhere in the southwest, probably the old Arizona. They've been redistricting and renaming like crazy out here, so no one's exactly sure. And the guards aren't all that forthcoming with information."

Wylie nodded and took a closer look at Mara's kids.

"You remember Sam, Shawn, and Sadie, and this is Sarah, the baby you almost delivered," Mara said. Wylie did remember them, although the kids were taller and thinner than she remembered—not quite gaunt, but almost. The baby must be about six months old by now. Wylie took the cup from Mara and washed down what was left of her sandwich.

"Can I have more water?"

"Sadie, can you fetch some?" Mara asked and the little girl in the group went running. She returned a minute later with a cup full of lukewarm water.

"Plenty of water," Mara said. "Food, not so much."

Wylie nodded. That explained the kids' longing glances at her pasty sandwich. "Not surprised," she said. "More surprised they gave me anything to eat at all."

Mara's middle child spoke up. "Actually, they didn't. Mom saved her dinner for you. She knew you'd need it once you woke up."

"That's enough, Shawn," Mara said. "It's bedtime, all of you. Put the baby down with you. I'll come and get her later." The kids obeyed and Wylie was left with Mara.

"Is that true?" she asked.

Mara nodded reluctantly.

"You shouldn't have. I've been eating well for many months and you've been here—how long?"

"Just over a month. After we got evicted from Sharmila's place we lived in an abandoned shed for a while until the Comcops picked us up one day behind the supermarket." Mara didn't need to explain what they'd been doing in that particular location. Wylie knew all too well. But Mara had been lucky—she must have been picked up before the "designation" had begun.

"Have you heard from Sharmila?" Mara asked. "It's our fault she's homeless. I hope she's okay."

"She is." Mostly, Wylie thought. She didn't have the heart to tell Mara the whole truth. "I was with her yesterday." In hushed tones, Wylie described her meetup with the Compendium. Although she trusted Mara, she was careful not to mention the location of their base.

"We heard there was a resistance, but I had no idea it was so established." Mara smiled for the first time. "Good for Sharmila. I'm glad she's safe. We owe her a lot. And we owe you, too. I won't forget what you did for me the day Sarah was born."

The dim overhead lights blinked twice and then went out completely. "Get some rest. I'll show you around in the morning." Mara said. "And one more thing—don't mention the Compendium to anyone else. You realize this knowledge puts you in danger, right?"

"Of course," Wylie answered. The ChurchState would stop at nothing to root out any threats to its power. Just one more secret to add to her growing list.

True to her word, the next morning Mara showed Wylie around the compound. She noted several cement buildings adjacent to the dorm she'd slept in. One housed the laundry facilities and kitchen, another was a garage for staff vehicles, and the rest were for storage. Aside from some of the minors, all camp occupants were female. Wylie wondered if there was an identical male facility somewhere nearby.

They walked, Mara's kids trailing behind, through a dusty dirt courtyard to the kitchen building. There was no cafeteria—detainees ate in the courtyard or on their mats in the dorm. The entire compound was surrounded by a tall, tightly woven metal fence.

"I guess we're not going anywhere on our own," Wylie said. She wasn't surprised, but seeing the fence made her status as a prisoner real.

"Nope," Mara responded. "That fence is electric. The word 'camp' is purely a euphemism."

Wylie squinted through the gloomy morning sky and noted a maze of old brick buildings several hundred yards away.

"What's back there?" she asked.

"Abandoned buildings, mostly. I'll show you after breakfast," Mara answered.

Breakfast consisted of a white substance in a paper bowl that reminded Wylie of the plaster she'd once mixed to repair a hole in the wall. She ate it without complaining, and every bit of it, too, since she'd been told to expect only two meals a day—the gloopy mix in the morning and the meat paste sandwiches after sundown, which the guards carefully rationed, one per person. On good days, packaged snacks were distributed mid-afternoon.

"But don't expect too many good days," Mara had warned. Wylie thought of all the times Darwin had tried to force-feed her a steaming hot breakfast.

Mara's kids finished quickly and ran off to play as Mara sat on a broken bench and held the baby to her breast. "Their resilience fills my heart and breaks it at the same time," she said, her eyes locked on Sarah. "These kids deserve better. It's my fault they're here, for refusing to sign their wretched Statement. But I couldn't. Not after what they did to my father."

Wylie waited for Mara to continue.

"He was mowed down by one of their finest. This was back when protest rallies were still legal. The guy drove right into the crowd—knocked them over like bowling pins. I can't forget that. We tried to make it for a while, but my husband finally signed. He left last year. Couldn't take the pressure, I guess. I didn't even know I was pregnant yet. And then, well, you know the rest."

"But how can they keep you here?" Wylie asked. "You're not a minor like me, and you haven't committed any crime."

Mara laughed. "You know the ChurchState operates with impunity, and I doubt the outside world even knows this place exists."

Wylie had to admit that in all her travels as Uncommitted she'd never once heard of relocation camps. They were either new or a very well-kept secret. The fear that she'd been keeping at bay rose from her gut and got stuck in her throat. Here they were, all in one place, out of public view. Perfect opportunity to begin "designating."

"Does anyone ever leave?" she asked.

"Sure, people come and go all the time. I've asked around and no one seems to stay over a year. But where do they go? Are they released, or do they end up somewhere worse? I think we're all here on borrowed time, my family most of all. When Sam turns twelve next month we'll be separated and I have no idea where they'll take him. I have to figure out a way to get us out of here by then."

Another birthday that signaled danger. For some kids, birthdays meant cake and parties and presents. Not in my world, thought Wylie. In my world, birthdays brought you that much closer to impossible decisions with drastic consequences.

Wylie made a quick decision.

"Mara, I need to tell you something. There's another reason you need to get your family out of here."

Mara looked over her shoulder at her kids playing in the courtyard. "Listening ears," she said. "Come on, let's go for a walk." She unlatched Sarah and zipped up her coveralls.

"I'll be back in a few minutes," she called to Sam. "Stay right here and watch the others,"

Two older women and a group of children sat on the ground nearby, scraping pictures into the hard dirt with sticks. "We'll keep an eye on them," one said.

"Thanks, Flo," said Mara with a nod.

"Florence and Cleo are artists," she explained to Wylie as they walked. "Brought here because they defied the ChurchState censorship. There are others like them here—artists, teachers, journalists—all here because they refused to be silent."

Wylie nodded. They'd looked almost peaceful, sitting there with no idea of what might be coming down the pike. Trying to keep her voice steady, Wylie told Mara what had happened to Sharmila.

A look of horror swept across Mara. "You think that's coming here?"

"I don't know. But it seems likely, doesn't it? There's no one in authority here to object, not that anyone would."

"What about the kids? Surely they wouldn't brand children!"

"I wouldn't put anything past the ChurchState, but as of now the law applies to people over thirty," Wylie answered. "But think what it would do to them to see their mother branded."

Mara took a deep breath. "Or something worse."

"Like what?" Wylie asked with a sick feeling in her gut. She knew that Mara was skirting around a topic she'd been trying to avoid.

"I'm sorry, Wylie," Mara said. "I'm not trying to scare you any more than you're already scared. But I keep asking myself, what are we doing here, lounging around on the ChurchState's dollar? Why haven't they put us to work? Our existence is costing the ChurchState money, much more than if they'd just left us alone. And I've never known them to give anything without getting something back, have you?"

"Not to Uncommitted, no."

"Not to anyone. So, if we're no use to them, and we don't stay here long, what's the point of this place? Why go to so much trouble for a group of Uncommitted? Are they keeping us here temporarily while they tie up the loose ends?"

Wylie swallowed hard. Her ankle, which had felt better after a full night's rest, began to ache again. "What do you mean?"

"Just this—maybe we're kept here until they find a way to fake our deaths. Once they've accomplished that, they're free to get rid of us. No one will ask any questions. Have you noticed an uptake of Uncommitted 'accidents' in the broadcast reports lately?"

Wylie thought back. She didn't watch the broadcasts often because they reminded her of Delores. But she did remember hearing about an entire Uncommitted family who died in a car crash a few weeks ago. The announcer had said the driver was drunk, and the kids weren't wearing seatbelts, but Wylie had known enough to doubt the veracity of that story. From what she'd seen in the last few days, she knew Mara could be right. Maybe the "accident" wasn't an accident at all.

They approached the rows of abandoned buildings, some roofless and many with dark, wound-like gaps where windows had once been. The ground around them sprouted crumbling brick, rusty nails, and broken glass like a sawtooth garden. Wylie limped through an alley between buildings, trying to avoid sharp objects and wondering why Mara had taken her to this deserted part of the compound. When they reached the structure at the furthest end, Mara stopped.

"There's someone I want you to meet," she said. "This is where she lives."

"Someone lives here? Alone? How can that be?" Wylie couldn't imagine why someone would be allowed to live this far from the populated part of camp.

"I think the guards are a little afraid of her. Besides, they won't come back here. They think the area is radiated. This used to be a hospital facility, and rumor has it the former residents never properly disposed of the waste. So they figure, if an Uncommitted wants to live in a toxic dump, why should they care? They don't send food back here, so we help out where we can."

Mara shifted Sarah on her hip and showed Wylie a napkin full of dry crackers she'd stowed in her pocket. When they entered through the decaying wooden doorway, Wylie could see how this building had once been part of a hospital complex. The hallway was lined with rooms that had once housed patients. The wood floor was warped, but the ceiling had recently been repaired. Clearly, someone had gone through some trouble to maintain a living space for whoever it was that lived here.

"These are all empty," Mara said as they passed a row of deserted rooms. When they reached the middle of the hall she stopped at a door with a picture of a butterfly carved in the rotting wood.

"Here's the one," she said, knocking gently.

"Come in," said a thin voice.

Wylie followed Mara into a surprising oasis of color. The walls to the adjacent rooms were gone, creating a large, open space, and everywhere were green potted plants topped with round clusters of pink, white, and orange flowers. She blinked and realized that a woman was sitting in the midst of the plants, wearing a flowered shirt and studying her own arm. Her frosty white hair fell to her shoulders and her skin was wrinkled like the rings of a fallen oak.

"I never thought I'd be able to raise them here," the woman said. "But the wet-bulb temperature is rising, even here in what used to be desert." She looked up at Wylie and smiled. "You've brought a guest, I see."

"Yes. Wylie, I'd like you to meet Mother Gale."

When the old woman stood, a butterfly flew from her arm and landed delicately on a nearby flower. That was when Wylie noticed them—butterflies fluttered from flower to flower in bursts of vibrant color.

"Please, come in," said Mother Gale. She motioned toward a sofa covered with a pink and purple floral patterned sheet. "I'm happy to meet you, Wylie, although I'm sorry you were taken here."

"Wylie arrived last night," Mara said, handing Mother Gale the crackers. "We're hoping her stay at Camp Noncom is temporary."

Mother Gale nodded. "As we hope for all. If there's anything I can do, let me know."

What could this frail woman possibly do for me? Wylie wondered. From the looks of her, she should have been asking for help, not offering to give it. What was she doing here, all alone?

"I don't understand. What is this place?" Wylie asked. She looked into Mother Gale's cloudy brown eyes. "How are you—why do they let you live here?"

"It is a bit of a miracle, isn't it?" Mother Gale answered. "If you believe in that sort of thing. The guards' superstitions work in our favor. I leave them alone, and they leave me alone."

"But, the flowers, the supplies. How did you get them in here?"

"Oh, I have my ways. I guess you could say I have friends in high places."

Was she talking about the Compendium? But that didn't make sense. "Then," Wylie said, "I don't mean to be rude, but why are you still here? Why don't your friends get you out?" Prison life could not be good for a woman that age, butterflies or not.

Mother Gale smiled. "Lots of *whys*, huh? Fitting for a Wylie. I expected no less. To answer your question, I'll be leaving soon enough. For now, this is where I'm supposed to be."

Wylie frowned. *Supposed to be?* What kind of answer was that? None of this was supposed to be. Maybe this Mother Gale wasn't quite all there. Wylie squirmed and looked toward the door, trying to think of an excuse to leave.

"Tell me about yourself," Mother Gale said.

Before Wylie could answer she heard a timid knock.

"It seems we have more visitors," said Mother Gale.

The door sprang open with the force of a tsunami, and in blew Mara's kids and the pack they'd been playing with earlier.

"I told you a hundred times, wait for someone to say 'Come in,'" Mara scolded.

The children flew into Mother Gale's open arms. Gathered close to her like baby chicks, their joy was palpable. Wylie felt a little sad.

"Can we have a story?" Sadie begged.

Mother Gale looked to Mara, who looked to Wylie. "Do you mind?"

Wylie did mind, though she couldn't say why. There was something unsettling about Mother Gale, something that made her want to leave and never return. She shrugged weakly.

"All right then, you'd better sit down," Mother Gale said to the children. "This is a story from the part of the Bible called the Gospels. They teach us about the things that Jesus did and said before he went back to heaven to live with his Father."

Oh no, Wylie groaned inwardly. She might have known.

Mother Gale continued, "One day, a long, long time ago, a large crowd of people gathered near Jesus to hear him teach."

"How many people?" Sam asked.

"More than five thousand."

"Is that more people than live here?" whispered a little girl who was sitting on her big sister's lap.

"Hush, Aggie," her sister hissed.

Mother Gale smiled. "Yes, way, way more people than live here. Anyway, when Jesus saw how many people there were, he asked his friend Philip, 'Where should we buy the bread to feed them all?'"

"Were they allowed in the ChurchState supermarket?" Aggie asked, her face filled with longing.

"Remember, this happened a very, very long time ago, in a place very far away from here," Mother Gale said. "There was no ChurchState then, and there were no supermarkets. There were towns and villages and markets that were mostly outside. Jesus knew that they'd never be able to buy enough food to feed all those people, but he wanted to see what his friends would say.

"Sure enough, one of them, named Philip, complained. 'We'll never have enough money to buy food for all these people!' he said.

"Andrew, another friend of Jesus, piped in. 'Here's a little boy with five loaves of bread and two small fish, but that won't be enough.'"

"What could Jesus do? He loved the people, and he didn't want them to be hungry. So Jesus took the bread and the fish, and told all the people to sit down. Then he said a 'thank you' prayer and began to give out the food. And guess what—the food didn't run out! The more food they gave out, the more food there was. Everybody got as much to eat as they wanted, and there was even some left over!"

The children stared, wide eyed and speechless. Only Sam spoke up.

"How can that be? That's not possible."

"You're right," said Mother Gale, "it's not possible. But Jesus can do the impossible, because he's God's son."

"I don't like fish, but can Jesus give me some bread?" asked Aggie. "I'm hungry." This time her sister didn't shush her.

All eyes were on Mother Gale, Wylie's most of all. How would the old woman get out of this? Nothing could make the ChurchState guards change their ways, Wylie felt sure of that. She hoped this deluded old woman wouldn't offer these kids false hope. Best if they learned to accept their fate young, like she had.

"Yes," answered Mother Gale without a second's hesitation. "Jesus loves you so much, and he doesn't want you to be hungry. Let's pray and ask him to help us."

Mother Gale bowed her head and the children followed, eyes squeezed tight. Their expressions of hope were too much for Wylie; this was her chance to escape. She stepped around the kids carefully and glanced back to see Mother Gale smiling up at her.

24

W ylie spent the afternoon alone, wandering through the camp and ruminating about what she'd heard in Mother Gale's quarters. She surveyed the electric fencing that kept her body imprisoned, all the while thinking about the talk of God and miracles that somehow had followed her here, trapping her in a different way. Why couldn't she be free of all that once and for all?

Near the camp's entrance was a small administration building where the guards spent most of their time. The expected afternoon snack had not been delivered, and Wylie's stomach was shouting to be fed. She got close enough to see through the window that several guards were sitting around a table eating burgers and fries. Wylie's stomach notched up a decibel. She walked around to the front of the building and tapped on the double glass door. When no one came, she tapped louder. Still, no one answered. Wylie returned to the back of the building and noticed she'd gathered an audience. The group of women and children watching her every move didn't offer support but didn't tell her to stop, either. Mara stood off to the side, balancing Sarah on her hip and comforting a whimpering Sadie at her side. Emboldened by the little girl's tears and by her own hunger, Wylie knocked loudly on the window. The guards sitting around the table looked up at her, laughed, and kept eating, but Wylie noticed a young, skinny guard with a buzz cut, the only male in the group, sitting in the corner, away from the others. He tossed his half-eaten burger in the trash (Wylie couldn't help wondering when the trash went out) and motioned for Wylie to come to the front of the building. His uniform was crisp and new, and he couldn't have been more than a year or two older than Wylie. The others ignored him when he left the room.

"Hi," Wylie said as if there were nothing at all unusual about her interruption of his lunch, "I'm Wylie. Sorry to bother you, but I'm new here, and I was just wondering when the afternoon meal would be served." Sadie's cries got louder and a few of the other kids joined in. "The kids are getting kind of hungry," she added.

The young guard stepped outside and closed the door behind him. He shifted his weight awkwardly, looking from Wylie to the crowd and back again.

"You're saying they haven't eaten all day?" he asked.

His voice had a higher tone than Wylie had expected and suddenly she wasn't sure if she'd gotten the guard's gender right. The name inscribed above his uniform pocket said, "Zella Gershom," which sounded female. Wylie hesitated, not wanting to blow her chance at more food for everyone by offending the only person who had taken an interest.

As if he were reading her thoughts, the guard said, "Call me Zed. I'm new here, too." He looked almost as lost as Wylie felt.

"Oh—hi, Zed. Yeah, like I said, they're supposed to give us something to eat in the afternoon. Everybody's pretty hungry."

Zed glanced back at the administration building.

"I bet those burgers were really good," Wylie said.

Zed slumped and shoved his hands in his pockets. "Look, I don't know if there's anything I can do, but I'll try. They're putting me on kitchen duty. Maybe I can get the evening meal served earlier. Would that help?"

Wylie was so surprised she almost couldn't answer. She'd expected re-buff, rebuke, and maybe retribution. This bit of empathy threw her off balance and put another small chip in her assessment of the ChurchState monolith.

"Thanks," she stuttered. Their eyes met briefly before Zed turned and headed for the kitchen. The crowd dispersed, and only Mara waited to walk back to the dorm with Wylie.

"That was weird," Wylie said.

"I'm not sure you realize how weird it was," Mara said. "The guards don't speak to us. They usually don't even make eye contact."

"He's definitely not like any Committed I've met before. He seemed sad and out of place. Maybe he'll get us some food."

"That would be a miracle," Mara said. "How's the ankle?"

Wylie realized she'd almost been walking normally. "Better, I guess."

When they reached the dorm they were surprised to see Zed waiting for them with a box of packaged crackers.

"This should hold them over," he said. "Dinner coming soon."

He handed the box to Mara and rushed away. She distributed the crackers quickly, and within a few minutes, crunching replaced the usual din of conversation. Wylie retreated to her mat, hoping to think through what had just happened, but Shawn, Mara's middle child, sat down next to her, and his siblings followed. They'd secured a pack of brand new playing cards and they needed a fourth player.

"Play Thessa's Edict with us," Shawn begged. "Please?"

"Where did you get those cards?" Mara asked. "They don't belong to us."

"Zed gave them to us," Sam answered. "When he brought the crackers." He proceeded to deal Wylie in, not giving her a chance to refuse. They played for a while without keeping score, since Wylie had just learned the game and Sam didn't think it was fair to point out her deficiencies. Then, as promised, the meat paste sandwiches arrived.

"Maybe we should save these for later," Mara said. "If we eat them now it'll be a long stretch until breakfast." Everyone around her, including Wylie, ignored Mara's advice and ripped into the sandwiches. With a sigh, Mara gave in and opened hers, too. Wylie noticed she saved half and placed it in her pocket.

"For Mother Gale?" she asked. Mara nodded. "I'll slip back there later if you keep an eye on the kids."

Wylie tore a quarter of her sandwich off and handed it to Mara.

"You don't have to do that," Mara said, but Wylie shrugged and kept chewing.

Late in the day, when she'd played every card game known to humankind and some she was sure even Monty knew, Wylie was surprised to see three women enter the dorm with more trays of sandwiches. They wore orange jumpsuits not unlike her own, except for the words *Department of Corrections* stamped across the back. Some had a large letter *T* embroidered in scarlet across their chests.

"This is new," Mara said. She approached the woman closest to her and had a quiet conversation. Once the women left she explained what she'd learned.

"Meet the new kitchen night shift," said Mara. "It seems the relocation center is taking advantage of free labor from a nearby women's prison."

"What does the *T* stand for?" Wylie asked.

"They're convicted terminators—they joined the ChurchState and then reneged. That's why they're in prison. Anyway, someone left them an order to hand out dinner."

"'Someone' being the new kid?" asked Martha, Aggie's mom.

"Seems that way," Mara answered. "I don't know how long it will be until they figure out the mistake, but for now we can expect three meals a day plus the afternoon snack."

"Is it a miracle, like the story Mother Gale told us?" Sadie asked, mouth full of sandwich.

"Miracles aren't real," Mara answered. "But it's an awfully strange coincidence."

Wylie took her sandwich and walked out to the courtyard, alone. Strange coincidence indeed.

25

Time at the camp passed at the pace of a dawdling snail. By the third day Wylie had met all of the detainees and had heard most of their stories. Most, like Mara and her kids, were homeless Uncommitted picked up by the Comcops while scavenging in Committed neighborhoods, although some had signed the Statement but were later censored for holding "unauthorized" opinions. A few naïve souls had gone to their local ChurchState municipalities for help when they'd been evicted from their homes, and had promptly been turned over to the Appointees and transported to the relocation center. None had been convicted of a crime other than the unofficial crime of failing to live within the ChurchState's restrictive boundaries.

Wylie was not surprised that the guards ignored them. Like all Committed, they'd been taught from childhood not to associate with Uncommitted except as potential converts, and apparently these folks had not been assigned the role of missionary. Only Zed stopped in now and then, and although he was quiet, his eyes sought Wylie out, and he didn't leave until he'd acknowledged her with a nod. Wylie heard nothing from Darwin. So far, Grandpa's connections had not been sufficient to gain her freedom. She bided her time and tried not to panic.

One evening, a week into her stay at Camp Noncom, Wylie was overcome with a feeling of loss, not for a specific place, but for Monty. She knew Darwin would take care of him, and she wasn't lonely, exactly. In fact, she was very rarely alone, with all of them cramped into one big room all night and a good part of the day. But she missed her dog's big head and broad chest and the way he nearly knocked her down when he saw her after five minutes of being apart. She knew dogs couldn't smile, not really, but Monty's pant had always looked like a smile to her. Feeling too sad to play with the kids, Wylie extracted herself from Sadie's grip and slipped out into the night air. She walked past the garage to the fence, where she was surprised to see a guard walking a dog on a leash. As she got closer she saw it was Zed.

"Wait up," Wylie called. Zed and the dog, a light-haired poodle mix, both looked happy to see her. Wylie let the dog sniff her hand.

"Who's this?" she asked.

"Meet Garbo."

"She yours?"

"Yeah."

When Wylie squatted to scratch the dog behind her ear, Garbo jumped and knocked her over.

"Garbo, stop," Zed said. He reached down to help Wylie up.

Wylie laughed. As she brushed herself off she caught the aroma of something rich and nutty. Chocolate. It seemed like years since she'd tasted any.

"Want some?" Zed asked, offering her half of his chocolate bar.

"Thanks." Wylie bit down and let the flavor warm her insides. "I'm surprised you're still here. Isn't your shift over?"

"Yeah, but . . . " Zed looked away. "I guess you might as well know. I live here now."

"Oh. I thought the guards all left after shift."

"They do. But my parents thought it would be better if I stay here, out of view, so to speak."

Wylie didn't know what to say to that.

"Want to take a walk?" Zed asked.

"Sure. You won't get in trouble?"

"Nah. They have to tolerate my presence, but no one pays any attention to me."

They strolled around the camp's perimeter, stopping to let Garbo sniff around where she wanted.

"What about you?" Zed asked.

"What about me?"

"Do you have someone at home worrying about you? Your parents, maybe?"

"Nope. No parents, anyway. I do have sort of a surrogate mom, I guess." Would Sharmila know what had happened to her? Wylie hoped not. "She's safe, for now, no thanks to your ChurchState friends." Wylie heard the bite in her tone and stopped herself from going further. What was the point in taking it out on this poor kid who, from the look of it, was no friend of the ChurchState.

"Sorry," she said. "Didn't mean to snap at you like that."

"It's okay. I guess you have a pretty good reason to be mad. I shouldn't have pried."

They meandered further in silence, until Wyle spotted a tractor sitting behind one of the storage sheds.

"Mind if I have a seat?" she asked, climbing up before Zed could answer. "I used to do this all the time at home. Back when I had a home. I'd hide out in the shed, just sitting up on the tractor for hours, until Darwin came looking for me."

"Who's Darwin? Is he your brother?"

"Sort of like a brother. Or like a best friend." Darwin with his kind face and caring heart. Darwin who was the smartest, truest person she knew. Maybe she'd been missing Monty so much tonight to avoid thinking about how much she missed Darwin. For the first time she let herself imagine how it would feel to open herself up to Darwin in the way he wanted her to, and it didn't feel so strange or wrong. It felt maybe a little right.

"Or more than a friend," she said. "Maybe. I don't know. If I ever get home, I guess I'll have to figure it out."

"You probably miss him a lot," Zed said, and when Wylie saw the look in his eyes she realized how lucky she was to have someone to miss. Suddenly, thinking about Darwin caused an ache in her throat. She worried she'd lose it right then and there if she didn't get up and move. She hadn't given in to tears since she'd been at the camp and she didn't plan to start now. Behind that door was a flood that couldn't be contained.

"I'd better get back," Wyle said as she jumped off the tractor.

"Yeah. Okay, bye then. I guess I'll see you tomorrow."

"I'll be here."

Zed and Garbo walked off and Wylie returned to the dorm just before lights out, feeling sad, but a little less lonely than she had an hour ago.

"Looks like you made a friend," Mara said from the mat next to her. "Good for you. It can't hurt to have someone in authority on our side."

"I don't think he has much authority," Wylie answered. "He seems like kind of an outcast."

"For obvious reasons. His kind of difference doesn't sit well with the ChurchState. You know that better than anyone."

Wylie nodded in the dark. "I think his parents are big shots."

"They probably sent him here to protect him," Mara said.

"And themselves," Wylie answered.

"True. Committed who climb the ChurchState ladder know how to insulate themselves from accusation. It wouldn't do to have what's considered an aberration right in their own household. Poor kid."

The next night Wylie slipped outside again and, sure enough, there were Zed and Garbo, waiting for her. Their evening strolls soon became a habit, and one night, a week or so later (Wylie was beginning to lose track of time), as she approached their usual meeting spot, she saw Zed sitting on a bench in the courtyard, his back to her. He was talking to a young girl through a holocast. She was maybe twelve years old or so and wearing a frilly pink party dress. She looked over her shoulder nervously as she spoke.

"Hi Zella," she whispered, "It's my birthday party, and I snuck into Mom's study to use her holocaster. She's too busy taking care of her big shot friends to notice I'm gone. I just wanted to say I miss you. When are you coming home? Mom says all you need to do is give up on—well, you know what—and you can come home any time." The holo figure looked pleadingly at Zed. "Can't you just be who you used to be? Maybe if you grow your hair again, and start acting like a girl sometimes, at least when they're around, everything can go back to normal."

Zed hesitated, looking for the right words. "It doesn't work that way, Rachel."

"But you can pretend you're a boy when we're alone, like you used to."

Zed shook his head. "I know it's hard for you to understand. When I was home with Mom and Dad, I was pretending. Everywhere I went, I was pretending. As bad as this place is, at least I'm not pretending anymore."

"Please, Zella?" Rachel begged. "Can't you at least try?" She stopped and listened for a moment. "Someone's outside the door. I gotta go. Promise me you'll think about it, okay?"

"There's nothing to think about," Zed answered, but his words hung in the air when the holo figure blinked out. "And it's Zed," he added quietly, rubbing his sleeve across his eyes. Wylie considered sneaking back to the dorm, but Garbo saw her and barked a greeting. Zed shoved the holoplayer into his pocket and stood.

"Sorry, am I interrupting?" Wylie asked.

Zed cleared his throat. "Not interrupting. Today's my sister's birthday, but I guess you heard."

"You were very patient with her," Wylie said. "That must be hard."

"Yeah, but I don't think she'll ever understand. It's not her fault."

As they wandered through the quiet grounds, every step took Wylie deeper into this unexpected friendship. Funny how two people from such different backgrounds could have so much in common. Take their moms, for instance. Although they were polar opposites—Delores, who took little interest in the mundane details of everyday living and Zed's overbearing, driven mom who'd tried, unsuccessfully, to shape and control every aspect of his life—both had failed spectacularly in their maternal roles. And when Zed described feeling like an outcast, well, of course Wylie could relate to that. But although she didn't say it, she sensed the pain of Zed's isolation went deeper than her own. It's not a contest, she told herself; still, Wylie realized for the first time that even among the Committed, some people lived in prisons more profound than the physical constrictions of this camp.

They repeated the pattern of walking and talking every night until Wylie came to look forward to their times together so much that the long, hot, empty days became almost bearable. Another week went by, but not as slowly as the one before. Much to everyone's surprise, the extra daily meal continued. One night, Mara stopped Wylie on her way out of the dorm and handed her a sandwich and a pack of crackers.

"With Sarah teething and all, I haven't gotten a chance to visit Mother Gale today. Do you think you can stop by and give her this?"

Although many of the others visited Mother Gale regularly, Wylie had not been there since the day after she'd arrived. Why should she feel so uneasy about seeing the old woman again? With no good reason to refuse, she took the food and left to meet up with Zed. When they reached the strange living space at the back of camp, Zed was astonished to hear that an old woman lived there, alone.

"How are they allowing this?" he asked.

"If by 'they' you mean the guards, I've been wondering the same thing. I thought maybe you'd know."

"I've never heard anyone mention her. It's as if she doesn't exist, back here. Or like she has some kind of magic protective shield around her."

Wylie frowned. "Someone's protecting her, that's for sure, but I don't think there's anything magical about it. She has friends in high places—she said so herself."

"You're saying the Appointees know about her? That's hard to believe."

"I'm not sure what I'm saying." Wylie knocked on the Mother Gale's door. "Anyway, let's give her the food and get out of here."

"Whatever you say."

Mother Gale opened the door wide and invited them in as if they were long awaited guests. "Welcome, Zed," she said. "Mara told me about you. Welcome, Wylie. Please, come in."

Before Wylie had a chance to refuse, Garbo pulled Zed through the door. He turned to Wylie with a shrug and entered the room, immediately mesmerized. Wylie had only been there in the daytime, and even in her reluctance she had to admit the space looked enchanting in the dark of evening. Strings of light twinkled from the ceiling like fireflies and candlelight flickered invitingly. Zed let Garbo off her leash and sat with Mother Gale on the sofa. So much for "let's give her the food and get out of here," Wylie thought. With a deep, exasperated sigh, she perched uncomfortably next to Zed, feeling like a spectator and ready to bolt at the first opportunity.

"Tell me about yourself, Zed. You've had a hard time of it, haven't you?" There was no small talk, no warming up to a sensitive subject. Mother Gale spoke as if she'd known Zed for years. Wylie squirmed, but instead of pulling back or avoiding her potent gaze, Zed leaned in.

"Yeah. I guess I never really fit in, no matter how hard I tried. School was the worst," he said. "The spotlight of being an Appointee kid made everything so much harder."

"What?" Wylie interrupted. Had she heard right? "Say that again?"

"I was afraid to tell you before—my mom is an Appointee. That's how I got this posting." Zed looked away sheepishly.

Wylie couldn't hide her shock. She tasted disgust like bile. Zed, an Appointee kid? The Appointees were largely responsible for the passage of every major piece of legislation that had made life impossible for Uncommitted. Because of the Appointees, she'd grown up scrounging in trash and looking over her shoulder at every turn. Because of the Appointees, Delores was dead and Sharmila was branded. They were the political power, the teeth of the Reclamation. Her anger was rising, but for Zed's sake, Wylie tried to stifle her feelings and control the loathing on her face. It's not his fault, she told herself. Zed didn't choose his parents any more than she chose Delores. And at least she'd grown up with the ability to keep her enemies at a distance. She'd had the sanctuary of home; untended and bleak as it was, ultimately, she'd been safe there. What would it be like to grow up where home is enemy territory and the enemy is your mom? Zed had enough people judging him—Wylie didn't want to be added to that list. She unclenched her teeth and tried to meet Zed's eyes. She needed to show him that she didn't blame him for his mother's actions. This new knowledge would not stand in the way of their friendship.

But Wylie realized she'd worried for nothing; her reaction didn't matter at all because neither Zed nor Mother Gale were paying the least bit of attention to her. They were locked in to each other's gaze, and for the next hour Wylie listened in awkward silence while Zed told this strange woman he'd only just met the story of his life. From early childhood he'd been forced into a mold he couldn't bear of dresses, parties, and gender initiation ceremonies. Wylie tried to picture Zed in a dress, but she couldn't fully conjure the image. When Zed resisted, he was cajoled. When he rebelled, he was punished with suspension and isolation at school and separated from his sister at home.

"In case I might corrupt her. They took away the one person who really loved me," Zed explained, eyes glistening. "My parents were always mad, or hurt, or disappointed, from when I was a little kid. They thought it was something I could control, like I could will myself to be what I was supposed to be if I just tried hard enough. They never understood that this isn't something I asked for or wanted. Who would want this? I used to lay in bed every night, praying for a miracle. But every morning I woke up to the same old me. That's when I knew that miracles aren't real. After that, I stopped believing."

The irony of the situation didn't escape Wylie. Zed grew up Committed, but didn't believe in miracles. She grew up Uncommitted, yet she'd come to believe that something existed beyond herself, although she wasn't sure exactly what. With all that happened, what choice did she have? Whether the something was good or evil, worthy of trust or deserving of fear and flight, Wylie had not yet decided.

Mother Gale shifted her compassionate gaze from Zed to Wylie.

"Miracles come in all shapes and sizes," she said. "Sometimes they're big and unexplainable, like the miracles in the Bible. But other times they're more like natural events with unexpected results."

Like the extra food rations, Wylie thought.

"The fact that we're here, together in this place, for example," Mother Gale continued. "Think of how we've come from such different places, from entirely different lives, yet here we are. There must be some purpose in that, don't you think?"

Mother Gale focused on Zed again. "Of course, the greatest miracle of all is God's love for us," she said. "Know that God loves you Zed, just as you are. You're not a mistake, although you've been made to feel like one. God knows you. He understands your questions, your doubts, and your pain. He feels it with you."

Wylie tried to turn away, but a butterfly fluttered past her and landed on Mother Gale's shoulder, and Wylie couldn't take her eyes off the outline of its wings in the flickering candlelight. How silly, she thought. It's just an insect. Yet with it came a vague sensation of a presence—the presence that seemed to turn up when least expected.

Zed's broken voice rasped through the surrounding twilight. "I grew up in the faith. I've heard about God all my life. I tried to believe. No one forced me to sign the Statement. I did it on my own, thinking maybe it would change me somehow. But it didn't work, and in the end it turned out God wasn't interested in someone like me."

Mother Gale smiled. "And now you're learning that God is interested in you, very, very much. And it's not the end, not for either one of you. You, Zed, have grown up not in faith but in a deviant, corrupted form of religion. And you, Wylie, have grown up in no faith at all. But even no faith is better than corrupted faith; perhaps that's why Wylie believes and you don't, Zed. Isn't that so, Wylie?"

The question startled Wylie. Her, a believer? She hated the ChurchState almost as much as Delores had. But Mother Gale's question had nothing to do with the ChurchState—Wylie knew that.

"He's been pursuing you, Wylie," Mother Gale said, "like a hound on a hunt." The memory of Monty chasing that mouse back at the college library flashed in Wylie's mind. "You've felt it, haven't you?"

"I, I don't know," she stammered, but again, Wylie did know. She sensed a gentle coaxing to tell Mother Gale about all the times she'd had that exact feeling, like someone or something was following her. But she stopped her words and looked away.

"I can never forgive them," she said instead.

"No worries," Mother Gale said gently, and Wylie saw through the darkness the kindness in the old woman's cloudy eyes. "But someone once told me something very wise: choosing not to forgive is like drinking poison and expecting the other person to die. I know they've failed you, Wylie, in every conceivable way. But don't let your hurt and anger stand in the way of something waiting for you just over the ridge. If you do that, they've really won." As a sudden burst of rain clattered against the decaying roof, an intangible quickening stirred the atmosphere, surrounding them like a warm cocoon. No one spoke or even moved. Wylie closed her eyes and listened, losing track of time until, finally, the rain subsided. When she opened her eyes she realized she'd been crying. Zed, too, was wiping away tears.

"You two better head back," Mother Gale said. "But there's something I need to tell you first. Do you know the story from the Gospel where Jesus calms the storm?"

Wylie shook her head, but Zed spoke up, his voice clearer than it had been before. "I remember that one. The boat is being swamped by wind and waves, and all the while Jesus is sleeping in the back, right? And when the disciples wake him up, Jesus rebukes them for not having faith. My teachers used to tell that story if they thought our faith was weak. Don't be like the disciples, they'd say. Soldiers need to be strong."

Mother Gale sighed. "Predictably, your teachers missed the most important point. Jesus was always with them, even when he was asleep. He never abandoned them to the raging winds, and he won't abandon you, either. He woke and calmed the storm. Wylie, people are coming who mean you harm. Before they come, a storm will arrive that will change everything. Stay together, no matter what, and hold on tight. You're going to need each other."

Wylie had a million questions, but Zed asked the one that hadn't come to her mind.

"What about you? Will you be okay back here by yourself?"

"I seem to travel with the storms. The night I arrived a tremendous gale rose from the east and almost took the fence down. Did you know that's why they call me Mother Gale? My real name is Abigail, but everyone has always called me Abby."

"Abby? You're Abby?" Wylie stammered, but a deafening roar of thunder drowned out her words. Garbo, who'd been sniffing around at the other side of the room, let out a panicked yelp and leapt at the door, scratching to escape.

"This is only the beginning," Mother Gale said. "Tomorrow the real storm will come. You won't see me again, but you must remember what I said."

PART IV
The Storm

26

They rushed back to the dorm through the electrified air, but as Mother Gale predicted, the rain held off. In the morning, the sky remained dark, and a suffocating blanket of humidity pressed down on them. Garbo, anticipating the coming tempest, refused to budge from the small room she shared with Zed.

Although it wasn't her turn, Wylie volunteered for bathroom cleaning duty. She needed time alone and if scrubbing toilets was the only way to get it, that was fine with her. The name Abby swirled around in her head as she tried to make sense of last night's conversation. Could Mother Gale really be Abby, her Abby from the Butterfly? It was hard to tell how old Mother Gale was, but if she was close to ninety, the math made it possible. What seemed less possible was that they both ended up here, in this time and place. How could that be a coincidence? Over the months she'd tried to quell the idea that she was part of a larger plan, but now it surfaced once again. But whose plan, and why her? *Why, why, Wylie,* she heard Delores say.

That afternoon when he delivered the snacks, Zed motioned for Wylie to meet him outside. They paced around the deserted courtyard, the wind whipping through Wylie's hair and intermittent hailstones hitting her face like bullets.

"The shelter in place order is coming," Zed explained. "Most of the staff are gone and the rest are leaving within the hour, trying to beat the storm. I just heard the highways are expected to flood."

Wylie squinted through the pellets. The camp consisted of low buildings on flat terrain. "They're leaving us here? What if the camp floods? We'll have nowhere to go."

"And there's something else. This morning, when the office emptied out, I took a look through the computer files to see if there are any scheduled visits. You know, because of what she said about people coming to hurt you."

Wylie didn't need to ask who *she* was.

"I couldn't find anything specifically about you, and nobody important is coming, not the Comcops or the Appointees," Zed continued, looking relieved. "They *are* sending medical teams, though, to do workups and take care of the kids—give flu shots, vaccines, stuff like that. That's good news, right? That can't be what Mother Gale was talking about."

Two lightning strikes hit the ground in a V shape just beyond the gates.

"You'd better get back inside," Zed said.

Wylie didn't move. Her brain was a runaway train rushing to an inevitable conclusion. Again, she heard Del's voice—*Be smart. Since when does the ChurchState give a hoot in hell about Uncommitted kids?*

"What is it?" Zed asked, ducking at the sound of thunder as if a bomb had dropped nearby.

"I find the sudden altruism of the ChurchState a little hard to swallow, that's all."

"What do you mean?"

"Why would they care about Uncommitted kids all of a sudden? Why spend money on vaccinations all the way out here, away from the general population?"

Zed hesitated. "They're not all bad. Maybe one of the Appointees is trying to change things."

"One of them being your mom, you mean?"

Zed nodded half-heartedly.

"When was the last time you even spoke to her?"

"Months, it was months ago," Zed admitted. "She won't take my calls anymore."

Wylie's heart wanted to break for this kind, sad person whose mother had turned her back on him. With all of Del's dysfunction, Wylie had learned not to doubt her love. *She's not really angry at you*, Sharmila always said. But there was no time for memories now, or for sympathy, for that matter.

"Look," she said, "I know you've been through a lot, and it's horrible, the way they've treated you. But whether you're a true believer or not, you grew up with all the benefits of the ChurchState and under the protection of your Appointee mom. You've never been without food, or medicine, or a nice place to live. You'll never understand what it feels like to wonder where your next meal is coming from, or if you'll have a place to live tomorrow. Deep down, you learned to trust the ChurchState."

Zed's face turned pink, but Wylie kept going. "Even now, look at us. We both had a rough deal, okay, but who's the guard and who's the prisoner?"

Zed studied the gravel as if he were counting the pebbles.

"I'm not trying to make you feel bad," Wylie said. "But you gotta understand, they are not to be trusted, not when it comes to Uncommitted.

They are not coming here to take care of a bunch of Uncommitted kids they stuck in a detention center."

"What, then?"

"It's more likely a medical team will come to take, not to give. Isn't there a blood shortage among the Committed?"

Zed nodded again. "It's all over the broadcasts."

"I'll bet my life that's why they're coming. They'll test for disease first, then they'll take blood from those who are clean. And once they test me, they won't stop at a pint. They'll take me."

"What? Why?"

"My blood type is rare, which makes me a special kind of universal donor. Once they find out, they'll never let me go. And one more thing—I take it you've heard about the latest ChurchState horror, the 'Designation Clause'?"

Zed nodded grimly. "The tattooing. I didn't think that started yet."

"It started, only they're not tattooing. They're branding."

"What?"

"You heard me. Sharmila was branded right on the face. Although I don't know if they'd bother branding people they plan to get rid of, anyway. I guess that's some consolation."

Zed looked as if the final brick of his shaky house had crumbled. "I, I guess I was too caught up in my own issues to see what was happening around me. I'm sorry."

Lightning crackled, and the hail came down in great, unbroken sheets. "Come on," Wylie said, dragging Zed by the arm. "We've got to get inside."

They ran to the empty storage building where Zed opened the door with his pass card. The room was dark except for an emergency light flickering in the corner.

"So she was right," Zed said, "Someone is coming to hurt you. We have to find a way to get you out of here."

"We all need to get out. If this place floods, no one will be safe. We have to find a way to get through the fences. Do you know how to turn the power off?"

"The fences are connected to the power station separately. If the power goes out, the fences stay on."

"What if the power station goes out?"

"Then everything goes out. But it doesn't matter because all the vehicles are gone. Even if we got past the fences, we'd be swept away in a flood in the middle of nowhere."

The emergency light flickered as if it were mocking them. Zed swept the room with his flashlight and focused on the shelves in the back. They were filled with boxes of the packaged food the guards had distributed so stingily, along with bread, protein tins, and peanut butter. A lonely bushel of apples sat in the corner.

"Look at all this food, just sitting here. I've never seen them give out apples," Wylie said.

"They save those for themselves."

"Of course they do. Well, come on. If we're going to drown, we might as well do it on a full stomach. Grab that box of flashlights, too."

With no guards standing in the way, they dragged as much as they could to the dorm where Mara organized the food distribution. They'd just settled in on their mats when the storm came full force. Sitting there, warm and safe for the moment, Wylie's love of storms resurfaced. She watched Zed play with Sarah while Sadie tried to feed Garbo some of the meat paste she was eating directly from the tin. Garbo sniffed and politely refused.

"I guess even Committed's dogs eat better than that," Mara mumbled through bites. Zed looked away, embarrassed.

"Relax," Mara said. "It's not your fault. I know that. And we appreciate your help. Right, Sadie?"

Sadie threw herself at Zed and nearly knocked him over. Steadying himself with his free arm, he managed to keep hold of Sarah while Sadie hung on his neck.

"Whoa, slow down," scolded Mara. "Let Zed breathe!"

"Is this a hurricane?" Sadie asked. "Sam says they used to name hurricanes with real people names. I wish they'd name a hurricane after me."

"You don't need a hurricane named after you," Mara replied. "You are a hurricane. Come back here and finish eating."

Sadie complied with a disappointed pout. "I still think it would be cool to name them. Why did they stop?"

Zed answered, "We studied this. It went against the sanctity of life doctrines. Bestowing a name is a blessing, and only living things should be named."

Mara and Wylie exchanged a doubtful look.

"Yeah, that was their story," Wylie said. "More likely, as time went on there were too many hurricanes to name."

"And why give attention to the destruction you caused by your anti-science policies?" Mara added.

"Oh," Zed said quietly. "I never thought of it that way."

"Listen, friend," Mara said more kindly, "if you're going to feel guilty every time we criticize the ChurchState, this friendship will never work. You're not to blame, okay?"

"Okay," Zed said, lighting up as if this were the first time someone had called him friend. Wylie realized it probably was.

The howling outside grew louder, but the cinderblock walls of the dormitory held strong against the gale-force wind and pounding sheets of rain.

"For once, I'm glad this building has no windows," Mara said. "Anyone still hungry?"

When they had eaten their full, Zed kept the kids entertained with a never-ending stream of card tricks. Try as she might, Wylie could not discern their secrets.

"How did you get so good at this?" she asked.

"Lots of time alone in my room to practice."

Since she'd arrived at the center, Wylie had played with the kids as a favor to Mara or to keep herself from going crazy with boredom. But Zed was different. His eyes were bright and his smile was genuine as he performed trick after trick, laughing with as much delight as the children that surrounded him. Wylie realized that the only time Zed looked truly relaxed was when the kids were around.

The absence of guards and the presence of food had made the atmosphere in the large open space almost festive, but the louder the storm grew, the more anxious Mara became.

"I'm not worried about the building collapsing," she whispered to Wylie, "but how high is the water outside? We have to be near flood stage. I'm going to take a look."

"No," Wylie said. "You stay here with the kids. I'll go."

Just as Wylie and Zed (who'd followed her) reached the door, the lights flickered and died.

"Power's out," Zed said. "No surprise there. We're on lockdown now." One by one, flashlights lit the room like beacons.

Zed pressed his keycard to the lock and when he and Wylie opened the door a crack, water rushed in around their feet. Zed quickly shut the door, but not before Wylie saw the devastation the storm had wreaked already. The cement structures still stood, but the less sturdy sheds were now piles of rubble. The fences, too, were down, not that it mattered since there was nowhere to go. Debris whirled and crashed to the ground in the deafening wind. While they'd been eating and playing games inside, much of the world outside had been ripped from its foundations.

"The water is rising," Wylie announced, trying to keep her voice calm.

Mara pointed her flashlight to the bottom of the steel door. "It's seeping in. We need something absorbent to shove under the door."

The women sprang into action, grabbing T-shirts, towels, and whatever they could find to slow the water's entry. Mara pulled Wylie and Zed aside.

"Listen, I've been through enough storms to know that a couple of rolled up towels aren't going to keep out the flood if the water really rises. We need a plan."

"It's still safer in here than it is out there," Wylie said.

"For now. But no building can resist the force of a flood for long. Water always wins. It'll find its way in, that's for sure. Is there any way out of here? Are there any weather shield vehicles hiding away somewhere?" asked Mara.

Zed shook his head. "Nothing. The staff took everything when they evacuated."

"We've got to find a way to higher ground."

"Can we get higher in this building?" Wylie asked. "Is there any space up in the ceiling where we could wait for the storm to pass?"

"There's nothing," Zed answered. "Only an access ladder that leads to the roof. But that's the last place we'd want to be in a storm like this."

"It may be just that," Mara said. "Our last place. At least there's the chance of rescue, slight though it may be. It's better than drowning in a big cement box. I wish Mother Gale were here. She'd know what to do."

"Mother Gale! I can't believe I forgot about her!" Zed exclaimed. "She can't be safe in that old building, all alone. Half of the roof was gone already." He started for the door. "I'm going to bring her here."

Wylie grabbed Zed's arm. "It's too late. You'll never make it there and back. Besides, she knew what would happen, remember? She told us we wouldn't see her again."

"I have to try!"

"No, you don't," Mara said calmly. "You may have forgotten about her, but we didn't. We've known her a lot longer than you have."

Technically, that's not true, at least not in my case, Wylie thought. But her connection with the woman who raised butterflies and made the intangible real was a story for another day.

"She knew what was coming and she made us promise not to put ourselves at risk for her," said Mara. "That includes you, Zed."

"And she told us to stay together, remember?" Wylie said.

Zed nodded, tears rolling down his cheeks. "I just can't bear to think of her facing the storm alone. She's just an old woman."

"She's much more than that," Mara said.

"And I don't think she's ever alone," added Wylie and looked away, embarrassed that she'd said it out loud.

One of the women at the door called out to Mara. "It's no use. It's seeping through." An inch or so of water was gathering at their feet.

"Maybe we can stack the mats and put the kids on top," Wylie suggested, "to keep them dry."

Under Mara's direction the women created a platform of wooden benches, chairs, and mats at the far end of the room and lifted the youngest children and Garbo to the top. In a sudden burst of joy the kids began to jump up and down.

"It's a trampoline in the dark!" Sadie exclaimed. "Watch this!" She bounced the flashlight beam up and down from ceiling to floor, laughing with delight. Garbo yipped and pranced on her hind legs among the jumping kids.

Every mother in the place shouted in unison, "Stop!"

"Sit down before you fall," Mara commanded. The kids, bubbles burst, flopped down on the plastic mats with a whoosh, knocking Garbo over. Confused and more than a little disappointed, she settled on Sadie's lap. Wylie and Zed couldn't help but laugh.

"Shh, listen," one of the women said. "What's that noise?"

"It's rushing water," answered another. "But where is it coming from?"

"And what is that smell?"

The unmistakable stink of sewer backup was emanating from the bathroom. When Wylie and Zed went to investigate, they found two inches of muck covering the floor with much more on the way.

"The drains are backing up," Zed said, shutting the door on the stream of dirty water flowing toward them. Outside, the rain intensified as the rising water seeped through the building's foundation.

"Don't worry, Mama, I can swim. You taught me last year, remember?" said Aggie.

"Not in this," Martha answered. She turned to Mara, her brow wrinkled with worry. "We've got to get them out of here. This water is toxic. None of us should be standing in it."

Helping to boost and stabilize each other, the adults joined the kids atop the shaky, makeshift platforms as the foul water seeped its way into the room.

"It's not slowing down anytime soon," Wylie said. "Martha's right. We have to get out of here."

"Maybe we can make it to the administration building," Zed suggested.

"We need something that's not connected to the sewer line," Mara said. "What about one of the storage buildings?"

"I'm not sure any are still standing, but we can check," Wylie said. She and Zed stepped down carefully. Wylie held her breath and tried not to look at what floated around her ankles. They waded back to the door through the filthy water.

"Ready?" Zed asked. He unlocked the door and slowly pulled it toward him. In a split second the force of the rising flood flung the door wide open, knocking Zed and Wylie to the ground. Half covered in sandy muck, Wylie regained her balance and pulled Zed up by the arm. Cleo and two other women rushed over to help and together they tried, unsuccessfully, to close the door.

"It's no use," Wylie shouted. "We'd never make it through this with the kids."

They slogged to the other side of the dorm as the groundwater rose and rain pelted through the doorway.

"Where's that access ladder?" Martha asked.

"You can't be serious," said Wylie.

"I used to work in the sewage industry, and I know this part of the country. The treatment plants out here closed years ago. This is stagnant sewage. Do you understand what that means? It holds every kind of bacteria, virus, and parasite you can think of and then some. You and I might be able to recover if we get sick, but without medication these kids will be in deep trouble."

"She's right," Mara said, speaking to the group. "It's your choice, but I'm taking my chances up top. We can tie ourselves together with blankets and hope for a rescue. Zed, will you let the ladder down?"

There has to be a better way, Wylie thought. We need a way out. She closed her eyes and for the first time in her life did what Abby had done so many times in the Butterfly. Wylie prayed. *If you're real, this is the time to prove it. Show us a way out. These kids don't deserve to die like this.* But the feeling of presence that had invaded Wylie so many times before was nowhere to be found. She opened her eyes and saw a decaying, naked hatchling float by in the rising waters. So much for prayer, she thought. They needed to get the kids out of there, and up was the only way out.

The women moved quickly, tying blankets together and looping them around each other as best they could until they formed a kind of human chain with the youngest interspersed between older kids and adults. Florence and several others stood to the side and watched. "You're crazy to go up there," she said. "We're staying." Without a word, Cleo untied herself and stood next to Flo.

"Okay," Mara said. "The ladder is there if you change your minds." She took Sarah from Sam's arms and looked around desperately. "I need to secure her to myself. Are there any blankets left?"

Zed took off his heavy uniform jacket. "Use this." Mara held her baby close as Zed and Wylie used the jacket to bind mother and child.

"What about Garbo?" Wylie asked.

"I'll just have to hold her," Zed answered, tucking her inside his shirt. "She'll be all right."

Together they carried the kids through the putrid water to the access ladder where slowly and steadily they climbed. Mara went first and Zed last, with a train of terrified souls in between. Every few seconds a child tripped and had to be steadied by the adult who was following. As she climbed, Wylie could hear the wind whipping, but nothing had prepared her for the mayhem she found when she pushed herself through the small opening to the roof. The force of the wind took her breath away and would have lifted her off her feet if she hadn't been tied to the others. Rain and hail assailed her, and wind gusts howled in a deafening cacophony. She knew they wouldn't be able to withstand this onslaught for long.

Huddled together in the middle of the roof, the adults used their bodies to shield the children from the gale-force winds. Wylie saw a panicked Garbo yipping and scratching at Zed, trying to escape the confines of his grasp. The little dog clawed her way up Zed's chest and neck until she finally broke free and jumped out to the rooftop. Soaking wet and terrified, poor Garbo ran in circles, looking for somewhere to hide. Sadie, who was tied between her two brothers, lunged after her, pulling all of them to the ground.

"Garbo, here!" Sadie called. "Come to me!" She jumped up and yanked at the blanket that tied her to Shawn, and, trying to get her to stop, Shawn yanked back in a sibling tug of war that might have been entertaining in less dire circumstances.

"Sadie!" Mara yelled desperately, but it was too late. The knot connecting Shawn and Sadie gave way and with a few twirls Sadie was free. She ran to Garbo and held out her arms, coming dangerously close to the building's edge, but oblivious to her peril. When Garbo spotted Sadie, she stopped in her tracks a few yards from where Wylie stood. If I can just get a little closer, Wylie thought, I can scoop them both up. But she was too tightly bound in mylar to move freely. Without thinking of the consequences, she untied the knot closest to her and freed herself from the blanket restraint.

"What are you doing?" Martha shrieked. "Don't break the chain!"

"I can get to them!" Wylie shouted into the wind. She handed the loose end of the blanket to Martha and pushed her way toward Sadie and Garbo, vaguely aware of Mara's terrified screams in the background. Zed, in the meantime, had also untied himself and was fighting his way through the storm from the opposite direction. If Sadie and Garbo stayed put, Wylie would reach them first, but she was glad to know Zed was on his way.

"Sadie! Garbo!" Wylie called into the wall of wind. A few more steps was all she needed. Garbo remained still, and between heartbeats Wylie dared to think all would be well. But just as she reached out to grab Sadie, a bolt of lightning struck near the corner of the roof and a booming thunder clap sent Garbo scurrying toward the edge. Sadie followed, screaming at the top of her lungs for Garbo to come. They ran past Zed, but although he lunged for them, they were just out of his reach. In two desperate leaps Zed caught up to Sadie and grabbed her by her shirt, but Garbo was still an arm's length away. He fell to his knees, gathering Sadie into one arm and stretching the other toward Garbo. Another deafening clap of thunder shook the building under their feet. Garbo yelped and jumped away. Wylie made it to Zed's side, but it was too late. In an instant, Garbo was gone.

"No!" Zed shrieked, bowing his head and raising his fist to the sky. Mara, who'd finally managed to free herself and hand Sarah off to Martha, lifted the sobbing Sadie out of Zed's arm and moved her to safety.

"No, no, no!" Zed repeated over and over. Wylie crouched beside him and threw her arm across his shoulders, but Zed jumped to his feet and stepped toward the edge of the roof.

"I hate them!" Zed screamed into the storm. "They take everything! I have nothing, nothing left."

Even through the tumult of wind and rain, Wylie could hear Zed's despair. She looked back at the others, huddled around the opening in the roof to help those who had stayed behind through. She and Zed were alone at the edge of the building, perilously close to following Garbo into the darkness.

"I hate them!" Zed howled again, this time the words coming from a deeper place. "I can't do this anymore," he said more quietly, and Wylie shuddered at the suddenly resolute tone of his voice. He stepped toward the ledge and leaned into the wind. Wylie reached out toward her friend and shouted the only word that would come.

"Stop!"

At once, Wylie was surrounded by a light more brilliant than the sun but softer and almost solid in some unfathomable way. "Stop," she said again, taking Zed's hand and drawing him away from the dark edge into the light and the presence that had alluded her until now. "Hating doesn't help," Wylie heard herself say. "It won't hurt them. It will only hurt you. You're too good for hate. There's gotta be a better way."

They stood there together, holding on and needing each other, just as Mother Gale had predicted.

When the light faded, the presence remained, not overwhelming her as it had before, but settling gently in the inexplicable part of herself that made her Wylie. She wasn't sure how long she'd remained in that place when she heard Zed's whisper.

"Wylie, open your eyes. It stopped. The storm stopped."

The sky remained dark, but the wind and rain had ceased.

"It must be the eye," Mara said, still clutching Sadie. "Don't let go. It isn't over yet."

Wylie looked off in the distance and knew that Mara was wrong. The storm might not be over, but their ordeal surely was. Two pinpricks of light grew larger in the night sky. Soon more lights followed, steadily moving toward them.

"Mommy, what's that?" Aggie asked. "Are those angels in the sky?"

"They're flight craft of some kind," Martha answered.

"Weather shields," Wylie said, "the big ones—a different kind of angels. And they're coming for us."

Darwin had finally found her.

The first craft hovered over Wylie and Zed before landing a few yards away. Wylie peered into the vehicle and saw Darwin in the pilot's seat, his face a mixture of worry and relief. Next to him was an elderly man talking into a headset. The door slid open, and Wylie and Zed climbed in just as the host of weather shields began their descent. Darwin stretched over the back of his seat and captured Wylie in a tearful hug.

"We thought we'd lost you," he said. "We couldn't see through the storm, but just as we were about to give up, it calmed and there you were."

"Take her up, Darwin," said the old man in the passenger's seat. Whether from emotion or age, his voice shook.

"Gotcha, Grandpa." Darwin worked the controls, and they lifted into the air.

A flicker of recognition flashed in Wylie but faded at the sound of Zed's heartbroken voice next to her.

"Goodbye, Garbo," he said softly as they lifted into the air.

27

As Wylie sat in Ed's barn, she pondered the ambiguous nature of humans. She remembered meeting Ed in the woods on that stormy night a hundred years ago, dreading something awful. Now here she was, sitting among rows of other people in his makeshift chapel. Ed, a Committed. Ed, the landscape guy. Ed, a leader in the Compendium. The world wasn't as clear-cut as she'd once believed.

Mara, too, was present, along with most of the women and children from Camp Noncom. The memorial service was better attended than Wylie had expected, given the secrecy of the event. Although Abby's body had not been found, there could be no doubt that she was gone. With Darwin on one side and Zed on the other, Wylie's thoughts shifted from Ed to Abby/Mother Gale, pondering her strange connection to this woman she'd known as both young and old. There was a force at work, a link between them that Wylie had yet to fully discover. So many questions remained unanswered. How had Wylie come to find the holodrive that last morning at the library, the day that Delores died? She could swear it hadn't been there before. How did Abby know her, and why did she speak to Wylie directly at the end of the holostory? And how had they both ended up in the same detention center, out in the middle of nowhere?

Zed reached down to scratch behind Monty's ear, never taking his eyes off the plain wooden cross hanging at the front of the barn. Funny how the dog had instantly attached to Zed, as if he'd sensed the empty space in Zed that Garbo had left behind. Wylie might have been bothered by the bond, but she wasn't the jealous type. She knew that Monty was capable of more than enough unconditional canine love for both of them.

Ed took his place under the cross, looking awkward in a formal black suit and tie.

"Welcome, everyone," he began. "We're here today to honor a beloved friend and leader, Abigail Winters, known by many of you as Mother Gale."

Wylie sat up with a jolt. "Winters?" she interrupted. "Did you say Abigail Winters?"

Ed nodded solemnly.

"But, that's my name."

"I know, sweetheart," Ed said gently, "all will be explained."

He addressed the group again. "I'd like to introduce someone who doesn't often step out of the shadows, but who has been our benefactor for many, many years. Quietly, behind the scenes, he's supported us with funds and influence. Without him the Compendium would not exist." Ed turned his attention to the first row. "We give our thanks to Mr. Steve Johnson, one of Abby's oldest and dearest friends."

After the storm, Wylie had been too numb to put two and two together. Now understanding dawned. Darwin's grandpa was Steve Johnson. Abby's Steve. The Steve who had ruined Abby's life all those years ago. The Steve that Wylie hated for Abby's sake. She'd wanted to go back in time and make him pay for what he'd done to Abby, to Cora, to Jane, and to Becca. But this was also the Steve who had protected Darwin and, more recently, her, from the worst of ChurchState tyranny. Not only were people ambiguous, Wylie realized, they possessed the ability to change. That same ignorant, pompous person, the arrogant, uncaring Steve, had years later housed and fed a homeless Uncommitted girl and had rescued her and the others from a raging storm at considerable personal risk and expense. When Steve/Grandpa stood, leaning on a cadet for support, Wylie knew that the young, hateful Steve was long gone. Her words to Zed came back to her. Here was proof that hate didn't work. Steve had been changed by something far more powerful than hate.

"Thank you, Ed," Steve said, voice quivering. He looked past the crowd as he spoke. "There was a time, long ago, when I loved the spotlight. I've learned a lot since those days, mostly due to my friendship with the person we're here to honor, Abby Winters. Abby taught me what I was too thick-headed to learn through all the sermons I heard and Bible classes I attended when I was young. Back then, I thought God was anger and judgment, but Abby showed me a God who is love. She showed me that even judgment is part of the great, deep, never-ending love God has for each of us. I had some notion of earning God's love through a self-righteous goodness, but Abby showed me that God doesn't love us because we're good; he loves us because he's good. Back then, I thought I was at war with the world, and God was my military commander. Abby showed me a God who is my Father. Oh, I was at war, all right, but I came to understand that my greatest battle was with my own arrogance. Lost in that arrogance, I thought I had all the answers. Abby showed me I was asking the wrong questions."

Steve cleared his throat and coughed, pressing his palm to his chest. He coughed and coughed until he doubled over, gasping and trying to gain control. Ed jumped up with a glass of water and whispered something to him, but Steve took a sip and waved Ed away, determined to continue.

"Many years ago I hurt Abby badly," he said, wheezing and struggling for breath. "When I think back to what we did to her . . . well, I was a different person then, an angry, vile person. Abby could have hated me. Should have, really. But she didn't. Instead, she forgave. And then, for no reason other than the love of the One who lived in and through her, she saved my life. That was the beginning for me, my real beginning in Christ. Before that, I was consumed with a view of Christianity that was . . . well, I don't know what it was. I thought I could fight the enemy with the enemy's tools: anger, fear, cruelty, scorn, derision. But Abby showed me we can't. We can't wield the tools of the enemy—they'll wind up wielding us, and ultimately they'll take over and destroy us. Jesus showed us a better way. He said, 'By this all will know that you are my disciples, if you love one another.' I learned through Abby that the kindness of the Lord leads to repentance, and the joy of the Lord is our strength. Kindness, joy, love, mercy, forgiveness, redemption. Those are his tools, the tools that Abby showed me, not by her words, but by her example. I know Abby did the same for you, or you wouldn't be here today, remembering and honoring her life." He stopped for a minute, wiped at his eyes, and took another sip of water. Ed sat at the edge of his seat, ready to jump to Steve's aid. Darwin, too, was on alert; he stood and moved to the aisle, watching his grandfather with concern. The old man ignored them both.

"Unfortunately, I learned all this too late to stop the catastrophe I'd helped set in motion. After the Reclamation, things happened so fast there was nothing I could do to stop it, and if you want to see the results of using the enemy's methods, you need look no further than our present system of government. But I don't have to tell you that. Most of you have lived it." Steve looked into the faces of the crowd with tears in his eyes. "All I can say is I'm sorry. I'm so very, very sorry." He paused and took a moment to compose himself.

"Anyway, after the Reclamation, Abby and I chose different paths, but always, we worked together toward the same goal, to share the gospel—the real gospel, not the nationalistic, pious rubbish the ChurchState peddles. I chose to work from within, while Abby stayed on the outside, slowly, steadily building the Compendium. It cost her everything, but Abby never gave up. Not when we drove her from her first position, not when the Reclamation turned our world upside down, not when she was falsely accused by her husband, and her own child was taken from her.

"Abby tried for years to find her daughter. When she finally tracked her down, it was too late. Direct contact was impossible—by then she was deep underground and on the run. She tried to reach out through me, but her daughter wouldn't return my calls. Can't say I blamed her.

"Although her daughter was lost to her, Abby wanted her grand-daughter to know her and, maybe, catch a glimpse of a different life. We'd removed every trace of Abby's identity from the state-a-base years before, so she recorded her story and I made sure her granddaughter found it. The last time I saw Abby, she knew her time on this earth was short, just like I know mine is now. She made me promise to watch over her granddaughter, the girl she only met at the very end of her life."

Steve lifted his chin and looked directly at Wylie, tears flowing down his wrinkled cheeks. "Your grandmother loved you Wylie, and it broke her heart that she couldn't do more to help you. But I tried to keep my promise to her. And when I'm gone, my grandson will keep it for me."

At that, Steve gave in to a fit of uncontrollable coughing. He hacked and wheezed until Ed and Darwin led him from the barn. Wylie and the others sat in awkward silence for a moment, not ready to leave, but not sure what to do. A few women nudged Mara, who stood and walked to the front.

"I think some of us would like to say a few words to remember and honor Mother Gale."

Wylie's head was pulsing with all she'd heard; she needed to get out before it exploded. She slipped past Zed, stepped carefully over Monty, and out of habit waited for him to follow. The dog sat up and tilted his head as if to ask, "Which one of you needs me more?"

"Stay," Wylie said. Monty rested his head on Zed's lap.

Outside, Wylie found Darwin sitting on an old wooden bench with his head in his hands. She sat next to him and leaned on his shoulder.

"How's Grandpa?"

"Not so good. They're taking him to the hospital. I wanted to go, but he insisted I stay. Wanted to make sure you were okay." He looked into Wylie's eyes. "So how are you handling all this?"

"Did you know?"

"About Grandpa being a double agent, you mean? No. Not until you got arrested, and I went to him for help."

"Did you know he was the Steve from the tapes?"

"Not a clue. I never did see his face and I guess his voice changed over all those years."

"And Abby? Did you know about Abby?"

"Of course not. Don't you think I would have told you? Come on, Wy, you know me better than that. We've never had any secrets. At least not on my end."

"Okay. Yeah. Sorry." They sat together and stared through the haze at the blurry sunset.

"There is something you need to know, though," Darwin said. "I haven't exactly been keeping it a secret, I just haven't had a chance to tell you. You're not going to be happy."

Wylie gave an incredulous snort. "Since when is 'happy' in our repertoire?" But she knew she had the power to make Darwin happy. Maybe this was the time to tell him that she'd decided to give them a chance. "I have something to tell you, too. You first."

Darwin took a deep breath. "I signed, Wylie. I signed the Statement of Commitment."

A block of ice slid over Wylie's heart. Darwin had been more than a brother to her for as long as she could remember, and through all those years he'd cursed the ChurchState and swore he would never sign. And now, just when she was starting to think there could be something more between them, this. She sat motionless, too frozen to react.

"I had to, Wy," Darwin said, mistaking her stillness for anger. "It was the only way. Grandpa doesn't have long, and they need someone on the inside. He's leaving everything to me, so when he goes . . . " Darwin's voice cracked, " . . . when he goes, I'll be in control of his money, and Wylie, he has a lot of it. Enough to continue the work and to take care of you. You'll never go hungry again. I can keep you safe. Don't be mad, okay?"

Wylie sighed and took Darwin's hand.

"I'm not mad."

"No? But we said we'd never sign."

"That was before, when we were two hungry kids with no hope, struggling to survive. Everything is different now. Like you said, there's a resistance. We can fight."

"Then you'll sign, too?" Darwin's eyes filled with hope. "Stay with me, Wy. We can work together. I need you."

Wylie stood, letting go of Darwin's hand. The idea of happily ever after flickered and died like a spent match.

"Never. I'll never sign."

A bunch of kids bounded out of the barn just as an old car rattled to the edge of the field. Almost before it came to a full stop, a woman burst from the passenger's side, ran to Wylie, and grabbed her into a ferocious hug.

Wylie should have known Sharmila would come.

"We heard what happened," Sharmila said. "I was so worried. Thank God you're safe."

There, in the arms of the only real mother she'd ever known, Wylie exhaled and let herself thaw a tiny bit at a time. It hurt, like when she'd come in from the cold with her fingers close to frostbitten and Sharmila would rub the life back into them. Oh God, it hurt. As the ice melted, the tears began—tears for Delores and Abby and the family that might have been. Tears for Zed, and Garbo, and the little dead hatchling that floated past her in the flood. And tears for Darwin, her Darwin, the Darwin she'd lost that day.

"It's okay," Sharmila whispered again and again. "Everything is okay now."

Although she knew it wasn't, Wylie let herself be comforted.

"What are you doing here?" she asked when she was able to compose herself.

"We came for you, of course, and for Zed," Sharmila answered. "He's joining the Compendium. The others are welcome, too."

Wylie realized that Nightingale was there, talking quietly with Zed and Mara.

"Will you come with us this time?" Sharmila asked. "We could use your help."

Wylie looked back at Darwin. Leaving him would be excruciating, but at least he'd spared her from that decision. There was no place for her in the world he had chosen, undercover or not. Maybe it would lead to nowhere, but she needed to explore the path that Abby had shown her without the obstacle of the ChurchState in her way. She smiled sadly. Whatever might have developed between them didn't matter now. In that moment Wylie resolved never to tell Darwin how awful their timing had been.

Then Darwin was at her side, whispering goodbye.

"We can still work together, like Abby and Steve," he said. "Me from inside the ChurchState, you with the Compendium. They'll never know what hit them."

"Maybe," Wylie answered. "But I sort of hope they do."

She felt Darwin's eyes follow her as she walked through the freshly-mowed field to the waiting car, Sharmila on one side, Zed and Monty on the other, and Mara and her kids trailing behind with Nightingale.

"It's gonna be a tight squeeze," Wylie said, smiling.

"We'll make it work. Hey, are you sure you're okay?" Sharmila asked. "I haven't heard a single *why* from you yet today."

"There is no why," she answered. "There's only who."

Epilogue

K endra needed a few minutes alone in her office before the event. She
had a headache already, and it was going to be a very long day. For
once, all was quiet; her entourage was elsewhere, taking care of business.
She'd memorized her speech, but she worried it lacked the pizazz befitting
the occasion. Maybe if she focused on something else for a while, inspira-
tion would come. She poured herself a glass of water and, looking for a dis-
traction, picked up a small box from the pile of gifts sent from well-wishers.
Probably another congratulations holo, she thought. Well, why not? Hoping
a little positivity would give her the boost she needed, she sank into the sofa,
put her feet up, and placed the holobud in her ear.

A young man with brown skin and dark, curly hair the same as her
own appeared before her.

"Pause," Kendra said. She looked from the holo figure to a photo on the
wall and back again. "Grandpa?"

Immediately the holo resumed.

"Hello, Kendra. Yes, it's me. I arranged to have this little greeting
delivered should this day ever arrive. I imagine I've been gone for quite
some time."

"Almost twenty years." Kendra felt a catch in her throat. Memories
of the elderly man who'd been her playmate and teacher during childhood
and her mentor through the hard years that followed (and there'd been
plenty) filled her with a mix of emotions: joy at the sight of him, sadness
at the loss, guilt at how little she'd thought of him lately, and, most of all,
disappointment that he wasn't real.

"You look so young," she said.

"And you probably look a good deal older. I can't actually see you, of
course."

Kendra laughed. "Yes, quite a bit older. I'm a grandmother myself now."

The young man nodded. "I'm sure you're wondering the purpose of my visit. You probably realize this is more than just a casual greeting."

Of course she did. Her grandfather was many things, but casual wasn't one of them.

"Are you about to tell me how to update my stock portfolio? Or who you recommend as the next Chair of the Board?"

"Nothing like that. I thought I'd share one last bit of wisdom with you before I recede to the inner reaches of your memories. You'll remember the saying, 'Life can only be understood backwards, but it must be lived forwards.'"

Kendra smiled. Even from the grave, Grandpa was quoting Kierkegaard. "Yes, I remember. It's on your tombstone, Grandpa."

"Hmm, well, all right then." The young man cleared his throat. "I know that you've always been a doer, Kendra, always ready to move ahead and grab life by the horns; it's how you arrived at this place on this day. But I'd like to help you slow down, just for a minute, and take some time to reflect backwards before you move forward. May I introduce you to a few friends?"

When Kendra nodded, two figures appeared on either side of her grandfather, both as young as he was. The girl studied Kendra pensively, while the other young man greeted her with a warm smile.

"Kendra, meet Wylie. And this is Zed, who you might remember."

"Of course. Actually, Zed is still with us. I spoke to him only last week."

"Somehow, that doesn't surprise me," Wylie said. "He always did live the clean life. Not like us two reprobates." Wylie and Darwin laughed while Zed rolled his eyes.

"So," said Kendra in awe, "the trinity appears. This is an honor."

Zed squirmed and looked up as if he expected to be struck by lightning. "Don't call us that."

"Loosen up, Zed," said Wylie. "It's only an expression. She's not comparing us to the real thing."

Zed's frown remained.

"Sorry," Kendra said. "But what you three accomplished was amazing. Miraculous, even."

"I can't argue with that," Wylie said.

"And we *were* like the Trinity, in a way—in a good way." Darwin touched Zed's shoulder. "I mean, in the way that we're reflections of God's essence—made in his image, right?" He looked around for support. "Right, Wy?"

Wylie shrugged. "If you say so. I'll leave the theology to you two. But God's essence I know about. I felt it too often to deny."

"There was something special about your connection to God," Zed said. "I witnessed it many times."

"That's my point," Darwin said, pacing to the window and back. "Like the second person of the Trinity, people saw God through you, Wylie."

"You're not comparing me to Jesus, I hope. Give it a rest, Dar."

But Darwin was in rev-up mode and couldn't stop now. Kendra had seen her grandfather swept away by the passion of his own words before, but never with his two best friends at his side. He and Zed had kept their distance so as not to arouse suspicion. Although there had been many surreptitious communications, Kendra had never before seen them together. And Wylie— she studied the image of this ordinary looking girl with a mixture of curiosity and awe. So this was the Wylie she'd never had the chance to meet. This was the Wylie who'd died before Kendra was born and whose sacrifice had saved many lives, ultimately fueling a movement. Grandpa had a point.

"And Zed," Darwin continued, "your work within the restored church quickened the memory of what was lost."

"Not lost," Zed replied. "Just temporarily forgotten, buried under layers of fear and neglect."

"And you helped them remember. You nurtured the Second Reclamation, teaching and supporting, helping the church to reclaim its biblical roots until, finally, the *Ameri* in *AmeriChristianity* fell by the wayside for all but a few diehards. You helped resurrect the spirit of what the church was meant to be."

"I suppose that makes you the father, Dar," Wylie said. "Should we start calling you Dad?"

"I hate to admit it," Zed mused, "but it does sort of work."

"Oh no, you too?" Wylie groaned.

"If you think about it, all things come from the Father, and the material thing, the funds that helped right the wrongs of the past, did come from Darwin. His money helped the Compendium become a political power. Without that, nothing would have changed."

"Thanks, Z," Darwin said. "I knew you'd see it my way."

"Are we done now?" Wylie asked. "I thought the point of this was to inspire Kendra on her big day, not to bicker like a bunch of kids."

"True," Darwin said, growing serious. He walked toward Kendra and placed his holographic hand on her head. Although she could not actually feel his touch, she closed her eyes and waited.

"Receive this blessing, granddaughter: Go forward in peace and power, but look to what came before as you do. Keep one eye on the past to ensure its errors will not be repeated. And always remember the sacrifices that brought you to this day." Darwin glanced at Wylie. "Remember and restore."

"Remember and restore," Wylie and Zed said together.

"I will, Grandpa," Kendra said, wiping away a tear. "I promise."

As the images faded, a gentle knock sounded at the door.

"Come in."

Kendra's assistant stood in the doorway. "Do you need any help with your speech?" she asked.

Kendra removed the holobud and stood. "No," she said resolutely, "I think I got all the help I needed."

"Okay, then," said the assistant. "Time to go, Madame President."